I0590348

THE BROKEN QUEEN

THE ROYALS OF RAKE FORGE
BOOK TWO

ASHLEY MUÑOZ

The Broken Queen Copyright © 2025
by Ashley Muñoz & ZetaLife LLC
ISBN: 979-8-9926052-6-6
ISBN:9798269719115

ALL RIGHTS RESERVED

No part of this book whether in electronic form or physical book form, may be reproduced, copied, sold or distributed. That includes electronic, mechanical, photocopying, recording, or any other form of information sharing, storage or retrieval system without the clear, lawful permission of the author.

This book is a work of total and complete fiction. **No AI tools, programs or apps were used in any part of creating this work.** The story was thought up from the authors curious and thoughtful brain.

Any names, places, characters, businesses, events, brands, media, situations or incidents are all made up. Anything resemblances to a real, similar, or duplicated persons or situations is purely coincidental.

The author acknowledges that while it was not her intent to use trademarked products, it is possible that a few slipped through. The publication or use of these trademarks is not authorized, associated with, or sponsored by the trademark owners.

NO AI TRAINING: Without in any way limiting Ashley Munoz (the author) and (and Zetalife LLC) exclusive rights under copyright, any use of this publication to "train" generative artificial intelligence (AI) technologies to generate text is expressly prohibited. Ashley Munoz reserves all rights to license uses of this work for generative AI training and development of machine learning language models.

Cover Design: Neptune Designs
Content Editor: Memos in the Margins
Editor: Rebecca Fairest Reviews
Proofread: Logophile Editing Services

 Formatted with Vellum

To those who have broken for someone or something, may your cracks and all the places you shattered be where you find hope.
For hope finds a way to grow in the most narrow of spaces.

Spotify Playlist
Pinterest Board

CONTENT WARNING

This book is intended to be read after book one, The Lost Kings.

Intended for mature audiences of 18 and over.

Graphic Violence and Death.

Funeral/Burial Scene

Grief

Depression

Sexually Explicit Scenes that include MFM (while the males do not touch in any way, it's essential to understand they're both present.)

FAMILY TREE

MALLORY & DECKER
JAMES
⌄
CARTER MARIE

TAYLOR & JUAN
HERNANDEZ
⌄
ALEXANDRIA (ALEX)
GIOVANNI (GIO)
KINGSTON (KING)

RYLIE & KYLE JAMES
⌄
PRESLEY

SCOTTY JAMES: UNCLE TO
⌄
DECKER & KYLE

MALLORY & TAYLOR ARE STEPSISTERS

THE
BROKEN
QUEEN

ASHLEY MUÑOZ

PROLOGUE

Unknown: Greetings, Mr. James. I'm delighted to inform you that I recently learned of your interest in creating an alliance.

Scotty: ... how did you get this number?

Unknown: What a waste of a question. Let's discuss the alliance.

Scotty: The alliance is already set. I was told you'd have no reason to get involved.

Unknown: I'd like to ensure the terms are still suited to both our interests.

Scotty: I was under the impression they already were...did something change?

Unknown: I think you know they have.

Scotty: I need to be clear…. she's not to be harmed.

Unknown: You'll marry her off knowing all that you do, and you're concerned I'll be the one to harm her?

Scotty: Adesso seems genuine in his feelings.

Unknown: I couldn't care less about his feelings for her. It's his loyalty to me that I need solidified. Perhaps we can find a way to encourage that loyalty.

Scotty: I don't like repeating myself, but she's not to be harmed.

Unknown: I'd like our new queen whole, so I agree that she'll remain unharmed. However, you of all people should know how easily it is to break someone without ever laying a finger on them.

I'll be in touch.

CHAPTER 1
KINGSTON

The stillness got to me.

Not only in the air, but the walls, the grounds...the haunting feeling that someone who once took up so much space was now absent.

At first, the quiet seemed to suffocate me. So much so that I had to stay busy and surround myself with people. El Peligro offered a distraction in the form of indulging in taking what should have belonged to us from a certain motorcycle club. My brother helped keep the ghosts at bay, the regrets that lingered in my chest, cutting my soul up into the most insignificant pieces. Together, we were able to push past the memories and the realization that Presley was lying in bed at night with another man.

I didn't think about if she'd tried on a wedding dress or not.

The anger inside of me was too intense to consider if she was scared at night, or if she too had shed tears over the loss of our friendship and the love we could have had. My father trained me to utilize weapons, especially knives, but he'd never warned me that the one I had to worry about the most was the blade I had within my own heart. The one capable of cutting and murdering hope that was within reach. If he'd warned me to be conscious of the possibility of ruining my entire life, I would have fucking sat down and listened.

His silence only added to how quiet my life was now. The stillness that now felt like it was haunting me. Over time, the rage that somehow bonded my brother and me had simmered to hurt, and now just pain. Quiet hurt that breeds resentment.

My arms burned as I swung the sledgehammer into the wall, but at least the burn reminded me I was alive. The loud burst of wood battled the quiet and the dust, as splinters disrupted the air.

"Dad was looking for you." My brother entered the room quietly, but the fact that he'd spoken to me had my head lifting briskly.

Tossing the sledgehammer down, I turned toward him and hated that I could see the lack of sleep highlighted in his sunken eyes and the bags underneath them. I knew what kept him up at night because it was what ran through my mind as well. *Regret, and even further down, the determination to fix everything.*

"Where is he?" I asked, trying to adjust to hearing Gio's voice again. He'd been sulking so much lately, we'd gone nearly a full month since we last spoke. Seeing him now felt like a physical blow, like looking in the mirror but seeing the version of myself I wish I were. He had the same inky black hair as I did, the same warm brown skin, if not a tiny shade lighter, thanks to our mom.

Gio's blue eyes looked grayer today as they found the floor where the rest of the debris was tossed into a pile. "You got pretty far."

Glancing around the old farmhouse, I nodded. "Keeps me busy."

He didn't respond, and I didn't remark on how he used to help me out here until he just decided to sink into the cavity in his chest and not talk to anyone, including me.

"Where's Dad?" I repeated, wishing I could ask how my twin brother was doing. I already knew he wouldn't tell me, and if he did, he'd somehow reveal all the things I'd been worrying about. That I'd broken him when I chose to punish Presley. I ruined the only shot we'd ever had at having her together, and now she was about to marry someone else.

Gio finally cleared his throat and took off down the front steps. "He's in your garden."

The garden I hadn't touched in months.

The one I couldn't even stand to look at now that Presley wasn't here. I'd once asked her to tend to it for a year and a half, not realizing how painful that would have been without me here. I didn't blame her for allowing it to die. I didn't deserve that happiness. I had a feeling Gio felt the same about tracking stars and solar systems.

Without her, what was the point?

Walking down the steps, I tipped my head back and watched as the sky turned white with little strips of gray. Snow wouldn't fall, but the boards I'd been pulling out would be stiff and cold. Didn't matter, I'd still pull and yank until they all came free. I'd worked through the humid, hot summer months and toiled during the brisk autumn. Winter was no different, even as we edged closer to spring.

Our stride through the frozen field was long; our conversation subdued. I thought back through the past year and how insignificant it felt, yet so much time had passed. It took us six months to infiltrate the motorcycle club and discover our father's sister, who had somehow gotten tangled up with them. October, we'd rushed back home and found Presley here, helping our aunt after our property had been breached.

The shock of seeing her left both my brother and me practically speechless. Gio couldn't help but try to go to her, but he was shut down just as I was. We had tried to get her attention all throughout dinner, even as our eyes lingered on her bare finger, curious where her engagement ring was. The next morning, she was gone.

It had been nearly four months since then and a total of nine since we'd fucked her, and acted as if we couldn't have cared less that she'd chosen to give us her virginity. Nine months since that day when we watched Adrian whisk her away, out of our lives, and suddenly, the insatiable need to push down the rage burst from my brother and I in the form of destruction.

Frenzied hearts often did reckless things, and once ours lacked the tether to the only person who ever made our worlds make sense, we indeed became *reckless*.

She blocked our numbers and hadn't reached out. Her parents and Scotty traveled to see her often. Scotty remained there regularly, but not a single person ever told us how she was doing. Not if she'd married Adrian yet... We would ask, but we had removed the possibility of knowing anything when we declared war against the family.

The peace was tentative, so we never dared bring her up, knowing her existence was a trigger.

Gio's boots crunched some dead branches behind me, and it made me want to ask him where he'd been sleeping. Neither one of us lived in the manor anymore, and if we were around, we spent time on the farm. I had moved into the barn so I could spend every waking hour on the farmhouse, but I had no idea where Gio had been.

"You talk to Dad recently?" I tossed the question over my shoulder, and when my brother's gaze met mine, pain twisted around my heart. He wasn't doing well. I could sense it; it made me nervous because of how dark things got for him when we were in Mexico. There were places his mind would go that were too vast and deep for me to understand.

"I go over for dinner every now and then."

Irritation burned under my skin as we drew closer to the manor. Red brick four stories tall loomed ahead, the roof was black, and from here I could make out the iron railing that led from our side of the house to Presley's.

"Ever consider inviting me?" I joked, but my brother would be able to pick up on the seriousness of my tone. Gio had abandoned me, and while I had mostly understood it all these months, it hurt.

My twin's head remained dipped, his eyes on the ground. He ignored me, and I decided to ignore him too as we neared our part of the manor and my small garden came into view. Our dad stood amongst the weeds and frozen soil, wearing his chino pants and a black turtleneck, brown loafers on his feet.

I greeted my father with a nod.

He turned, narrowing that assessing gaze on me. Sometimes the guilt over how badly we'd fucked up dug inside me so deep that I worried I'd never recover. Our father was disappointed in us, but it went deeper than that. We'd taken the dangerous thing he'd inherited and had successfully used for good and broken it. Twisted it once more and made it bend to our demands, and now we were its leaders.

Reluctantly and begrudgingly.

"Kingston, thank you for coming up here."

Gio stepped next to me but kept a wide berth. I felt like I was stuck in a bad dream. One where my brother hated my guts, and my father couldn't stand the sight of me. Except this was real.

"What's going on?" I flicked my eyes over the garden. Nothing had grown here in so long it was difficult to even make out that it was once a thriving plot. Flashes of small fingers digging into dark soil and a dimpled smile ran through my mind, going back in time to when Presley would help me grow things.

Dad stepped closer. "Your mother and I are considering leaving. We think it might be time for our family to start over."

My chest ached, heavy and blunt. The worry felt like a rock.

"Where would you go?"

My gaze slid to my twin. Thankfully he looked just as taken aback by the news as I was.

Dad kept our gaze. "Chicago, maybe Texas. We aren't sure yet."

"Alex is going with you?" Gio asked.

Dad's eyes flicked between the two of us before he let out a small scoff. "I was hoping to take all of you."

Gio and I both shook our heads at the same time. "We aren't leaving."

He knew we couldn't. The ink over our hearts demanded we stay; required us to lead. We didn't have the twenty years Dad did in managing the beast that was El Peligro. It had only gotten worse with the new ties to the cartel that our uncle had developed over the past few months. It was stronger now than ever, and more dangerous.

I desperately wanted to ask Dad how he led it back when he did, but I never would. Not when he'd worked so hard to subdue it, only to have us fuck it all up.

"Hand things over to the man who helped stage the coup for the gang to leave my leadership in the first place. Henry, right? Step away while you still can. The link to the cartel is dangerous, and not something to take lightly. You boys need a clean cut."

Shame hollowed out my chest as I considered how he'd view Henry. He had been loyal to my father once, but he'd been the one whispering in our ears to return the gang to the initial vision our grandfather once had for it. Instead of confirming anything about Henry, I asked, "How do you know about the cartel link?"

Dad's jaw hardened. "Because it runs in my fucking blood, Kingston. Those men were loyal to me for twenty years. They may have wanted to return to the initial vision, but it didn't change who they consider the true leader."

Fuck, that hurt. He was right, but it was humiliating. El Peligro wasn't something my brother or I loved. We abused it, and in turn, the men felt it.

Gio spoke, shaking me from my thoughts. "Even if we wanted to go, we can't. They'd hunt us down. You know this."

Dad's jaw worked back and forth as if he were biting back a thousand different words.

"If you hand things over to family, they won't. Henry is a blood relation to my uncle, they'll follow him."

Our dad glanced between us. I knew he understood what our hesitation was about.

If there was still a chance that Presley needed us, and while we knew she hated us, if we could ever use what connection we had to the gang to protect her, then we would.

Our silence answered for us, and we had to watch as fresh hurt worked through our father's gaze, cutting us down to the bone.

"She isn't coming back. While we haven't been in communication with Kyle or heard how she's doing...I know Presley. She will do whatever it takes to keep *her* family safe, and whatever you did made it to where we are no longer a part of it."

Cold numbing truth slid through my veins at his harsh reprimand. We had ruined everything. *I* had ruined everything. Gio would have never gone this far if it weren't for me.

"What about your friendship with Kyle? Haven't you both been through enough not to leave him like this? Markos is going to kill them."

Dad didn't even wince or flinch as he dismissed the idea. "Kyle has always worried about his family. It's time I do the same."

Shock was the first thing I felt. Ever since we could remember, Kyle and my father seemed more like brothers. Even more so than Kyle did with his own brother, Decker. Dad and Kyle were cut from the same cloth, the same fear and obsessions of keeping what they cherished safe...and yet.

"Dad, you can't do this," Gio argued, shaking his head. He pushed his dark hair back, revealing a new tattoo snaking along his forearm. Something about punishment and penance.

Our father gave us one glance before turning toward the patio doors. "I didn't do it, Son. You two did. We warned you not to ruin the family."

He didn't understand, no one was fucking trying to understand. "Adrian is going to kill her. You don't believe us, but we know our intel is solid."

Dad paused with his hand on the doorknob for a fraction of a second before turning. "And yet he hasn't in nine months." His eyes burned as he glared at us both, his voice rising.

"She's been in Italy, living happily for nine months."

I winced, lowering my head. Hearing it was too painful because it was what went through my head every night when I closed my eyes, what I heard every morning. What I thought of every time I considered tracking her down.

"She's been engaged for *nine months,* and nothing bad has happened to her. She's happy."

"Stop," Gio warned, his voice cracking.

Our dad's eyes blazed as he took a step closer. "She's rich, being completely spoiled and not covered in bruises. She's not fighting anymore. Isn't that what you always wanted?"

My brother was shaking, and I felt that same quivering wherever it was my blackened soul lingered. Of course, we always wanted her happy and safe, and fucking whole. We wanted her to find joy in this life, but fuck, did it have to be without us?

"He's not who he says he is. Markos is—"

"Dead," Dad snapped, and I froze. Gio's eyes slid over, meeting mine.

I whispered because my voice didn't seem to want to work. "How do you know that?"

"Because Markos once wanted to marry your mother. Their marriage had been arranged since her birth, and when she turned nineteen, she was to become his bride. It was the entire reason I picked up the colors of El Peligro and stamped my chest with that fucking black heart. Years later, Markos tried his hand at ruining us again through Riley, but Kyle nearly castrated him for it. We've never stopped tracking him, and when you mentioned his name, I made it my mission to find him. I would have killed him myself except he was already dead when I arrived."

"Even if he's dead, that doesn't change anything," Gio said, finally stepping closer so we were nearly side by side.

Dad scoffed and then gave us one last shake of his head. "It changes everything."

With that, he entered the house and kept us standing out in the cold, staring at a dead garden that now represented this family.

CHAPTER 2
GIO

Being angry with my brother wasn't a new sensation for me. I'd spent plenty of time being frustrated with him over stupid shit that didn't really matter. Even the times I was angry at him over Presley, things were never that serious. We'd always be in the same room at night, and I'd see his stupid face the following morning, and my anger would just leave when he smirked and tossed a pillow at my face.

I would tell myself not to blame him, and then I'd remember how he fucked all this up for us and I'd draw up the courage to distance myself from him. Kingston always had some demon rifling around in his head, providing him enough pride to cut the distance between him and whoever it was he actually cared about. I'd give him the benefit of the doubt, knowing he didn't mean it.

But this time things were different.

"You going to just ignore me again?" Kingston's voice echoed behind me as I walked away from him.

I was too angry to talk. My jaw was tight, my fists curled, and my chest felt like it might explode any second.

"Great. Yeah, that's just fucking great, Gio. I lose Pres, you, and now we're losing Alex and our parents."

My mouth parted the slightest bit, wanting to argue with him. He knew exactly what to say to bait me, but I'd gotten better at ignoring him.

"Gio, please. Fuck." My brother's voice cracked.

I spun around, coming to a stop just close enough to throw my fist out. It landed with a crunch as it connected with his nose. He wasn't expecting it, so he went down immediately.

Standing over him, I glared down. "Why are you acting surprised that you're alone?"

He spat out the blood pooling in his mouth and groaned. "You blame me for all of this?"

"Why shouldn't I?"

Getting to his knees, he had mud smeared all over his arms and shirt. I kicked his ribs so he rolled onto his back. He caught my foot and yanked hard until I was on the ground next to him.

"I never forced you to do shit, Gio. Don't put all this on me."

"You wanted to fuck her that night and then leave her. You wanted to take sides against her." My voice echoed right back as I rolled to punch him again. He dodged and caught my hand, then twisted.

"Gio. Stop," he rasped.

I hit him in the gut with my free fist. Then I got enough leverage to get my feet up, and I kicked him in the leg.

He groaned in pain, twisting to the side, while I clamored to my feet. "She always wanted you more than me. Did you fucking know that?" Tears burned the backs of my eyes, but I held them in just like I had done since she walked out of our lives.

"You took her fucking first kiss. Her first orgasm. You touched her first. She wanted *you*. There was no having her without you, and you fucked it all up. I would have never lost her if she were mine. If you weren't involved, she would be here with me right now. She would be safe and loved and spoiled *by me*!"

Kingston coughed, rolling to his side once more.

I kept going. "Having her was never good enough for you. You always wanted to hurt her, downplaying what we felt and what he shared. You were scared that if you were open with her and she shot you down, then you'd be embarrassed. We should have told her when she was sixteen that we loved her. We should have never left her for that year and a half, but that was your choice too, wasn't it?"

I kicked him again. "I hate you."

Tears streamed down his face, mixing with blood and dirt, and something inside me cracked, making my own fall.

My chest heaved as sobs worked through me, shattering my vision and bruising my heart. I dropped to the ground, landing on my ass hard enough that my teeth slammed together, then I swiped at my face and reached for my brother.

"I didn't mean that."

He croaked in reply, "You should."

But I didn't. "You're a good brother, Kingston. You've always watched out for me. Always made sure I was okay."

His eyes remained on the sky as more tears tracked down his cheeks. It was silent between us until he let out a shuddering breath.

"I know I messed it all up, but it did hurt. It hurt that she was taken from us when we left, and that it felt so impossible to save her from this fate Scotty and Kyle forced her into. It hurt that she didn't trust us enough to give it up. Even without our love, she always had our friendship, and she should have trusted us. She pushed us out, Gio, and when I found out how long she'd waited to contact us... something in me just snapped."

He was still mad about all of it; meanwhile, I just didn't care anymore. Presley was my soulmate, and none of this shit was worth losing her.

"Well then, let her go, King. Release her and go live your life, start over, and let El Peligro go. Go find that happiness that she seemed to find. Start over."

His head tilted, those amber eyes muted and dark as if the light had gone out in them.

"What would you do?"

I met his stare and gritted my teeth. "I'd stay. I'd rather be a wraith here, haunting all she's ever known so the second she walks back into this world, every inch of it is covered in my prints. She won't be able to escape me, and if she wishes to stay away, then she'll have to face me to cut this rope she's tied around our souls."

Kingston let out a shuddery breath. "What if she marries him?"

I shook my head. "Don't give a fuck. The things he will give her won't ever hold up to what we have. You can't trade diamonds for stardust, can't erase a childhood like ours, where our hearts grew together in the same garden. We have time, and Adrian won't ever win against that."

Kingston finally sat up and wiped some of the blood from his nose with the bottom of his shirt before letting out a sigh. "So, what do we do?"

"We?" I quirked a brow at him. "Thought you were leaving."

His face lowered, and I already knew what was going through his head. He was in love with Presley, and everything I had just said was mirrored in his own heart; he was just too fucking stubborn.

"I'll help you get her back. It's the least I can do..."

"And then?" I repeated, trying to force him to say exactly what it was he planned to do, so I could call him out on his shit.

His black hair shifted as the wind blew. "I'll walk away. She's yours, Gio. I promise you that."

It was wrong, and if I knew Presley at all, I knew she'd never go for that.

Regardless, I accepted my brother's hand when he lifted it for me to take.

CHAPTER 3
PRESLEY

The breeze carried hints of citrus and salt as it tugged my hair loose and wrinkled the long curtains on either side of the balcony. I stared out at the vast sea, watching the white capped waves, wondering what it must be like to be created and undone so quickly.

The sky was bright and beautiful, and yet somewhere in my heart, a storm hadn't stopped raging. An anger roiled deep within my core, mixing with hurt and regret.

Regret that I had given so much to the twins, so easily. Regret that this new role was still difficult for me to accept, because after everything, I still cared, which meant they still had a hold of my fickle heart.

Pushing down my emotions, I turned away from the balcony and made my way down the steps back toward the suite that I now lived in.

"Morning, *Bellissima*." Adrian's smile extended across his handsome face as he stretched, allowing the sheet to slip down to his tapered waist. I wore a silk robe, covering the matching night slip Adrian had gifted me.

"Morning." I returned his smile, and before either of us could speak, a soft knock sounded at the door, and an elderly woman walked in with a serving tray. She spoke in a rush of Italian, which Adrian replied to as he brought his phone up and began swiping through notifications.

Good morning, sir.

Your men are driving me crazy. Fire Leon, he's a menace in the kitchen.

I smiled as I listened and resisted the urge to laugh. I hadn't learned her name yet because Adrian's staff continued to rotate with new faces nearly every day. I smiled at her, but she only spoke to Adrian as she set the tray down that held two coffees, two plates of breakfast, and a myriad of other small dishes and silverware.

Once she was gone and the door clicked shut once more, I made my way toward the steaming mug and tried to push down the simmering annoyance that had been more frequent lately. I didn't like how difficult it was to memorize his staff or his schedule. Everything was constantly fluctuating.

"What happened to Gloria?" I poured creamer into my cup and listened as Adrian shifted in the bed behind me.

His sigh wasn't aimed at me, but whatever he found on his phone. "She's likely with Leon in the kitchen. They swap duties from time to time. I leave them to decide all that."

I made a mental note of that information and took the silver cover off my plate of food. Adrian had a small table set up near the balcony entrance in his bedroom suite, which was where I tugged the cushioned chair out and sat to have my breakfast. I glanced up at the view of the cliffs and the waves beneath them while the buttered bread melted on my tongue.

My memory replayed the first time I dined at the table, back when I had come with Adrian after leaving North Carolina for the last time. After stupidly returning home to see if there was any part of me that could reconcile with what had happened. What I found instead was a bonfire of broken pieces the twins had left behind. Not just of what happened with us, but they'd effectively ruined the family by terrorizing a faction of crime in New York that their aunt was involved in. I didn't even recognize them when I had returned, and saw them again. Their recklessness was too much for me to process back then, so I swiftly returned to Italy without looking back. That was four months ago, and when I walked back into the house, Adrian had expected me to head to my old room, but I had stormed toward his instead. That first morning, he sat with me while I cleaned my gun, and he read a book. It was oddly the most peaceful morning I could remember having in years.

While Adrian was perfectly fine with not pushing any physical boundaries of mine, we did share the same bed every night. I hadn't decided on having sex with him yet, but we kissed plenty, and there were other things to keep him occupied, like fucking me with his fingers and tongue as often as he wanted.

While there were things I was still skeptical of and doing my own work to uncover, Adrian did manage to steal a small piece of my heart. It was his alone, not shared with anyone else, and that tiny piece was the only part of me that seemed to be thriving here in Italy. The rest was all fake smiles, pretend kisses, and an elaborate act.

The twins had broken me, but there was a chance their intel wasn't completely wrong, and because of that small possibility, my guard was up with Adrian and the two men who guarded him the closest. Renzo and Benni. They were constantly armed and always in Adrian's business. Which meant they were always in mine.

A warm kiss landed on my neck as I added jam to the toast. My robe slid to the side, revealing bare skin, and Adrian took the opportunity to move his mouth across it, marking me in his own way. Sometimes it felt like we were both playing a game, one we knew the rules to, and that it might end in both of us getting hurt or worse. Yet, each day, we grabbed the dice and continued to roll.

I moved my neck to the side to give him better access and set the toast down as his lips made their way to my ear in a raspy plea.

"You know how I take my coffee, Presley."

My core clenched at his words, already knowing what he wanted from me. This dance we'd done for months, and while I struggled with how much of myself to give away to him, I told myself none of my reasons had to do with the twins.

They'd discarded me as easily as an old napkin.

It was simply because I had reservations about how convinced they'd been about Adrian's involvement with the Mariano family that I had hesitated in fucking him these past nine months.

I didn't hesitate, however, in playing this daily game with Adrian, which is why I spread my thighs and pulled the tie of my robe, so I revealed my aching body to him.

Taking a bite of my toast, I waited for him to realize I hadn't worn any underwear with my nightgown. His hands began pushing the material up my legs, and then a deep groan emanated from him as he yanked my hips, so my ass lingered on the edge of the seat. He muttered a few words in Italian before his head lowered, and his wet tongue slid through my slit.

So fucking perfect.

Mine. Entirely mine.

I took another bite of toast as I stared down at his chestnut hair, and the way his groans increased the deeper into my pussy he licked.

Some mornings, I'd grab my toast and walk over to the bed, where I'd straddle his face while I finished my meal and then came against his tongue. He'd make jokes about how he liked his coffee with the side of cream. The cream being my orgasm on his tongue.

Finished with my toast, I ran my fingers through his hair and began riding his face. Enjoying the sensations of his tongue gliding through my cunt, I ground against his fingers as they slid inside me, adding extra pressure where I needed it most.

The waves echoed through the room from the open balcony, the air was lightly humid with a hint of salt, and I didn't even try to cover my moans as I tipped my head back and rocked my hips against his face. Wetness dripped down my crack, likely soaking the chair, and the sounds he created only made that knot in my core coil so that I made filthy requests for him to fuck me harder with his mouth.

His hand came up to my thigh, where he gripped it hard while spreading me wider. His face lifted the slightest bit, and then his teeth gently clamped around my clit where he sucked it into his mouth so hard that I came with a cry. Fingers tethered to his hair, my legs were practically clenching his face as they shook, and he continued to moan into my center, lapping up every single drop of my release.

With a heaving chest, I watched as Adrian moved from between my legs. He gave me a sexy smirk, his lips gleaming before grabbing the second cup of coffee and sipping it.

Once he set it back down, he let out a heavy sigh. "Perfect."

A laugh bubbled up from my chest, and I realized I had come to like this tradition we had. I loved coming on his tongue every morning, and I loved that he always drank his coffee directly after. I loved that he never pressured me for more, even though he deserved it. He was always so selfless when it came to touching me, kissing me and having me in whatever capacity I would give and he never asked for anything in return.

He never made me feel anything other than desired. He was patient with me, adoring. Kind. So unlike *them*.

The realization of how much I trusted Adrian blossomed in a very broken part of my heart, which is what had me moving to the floor, on my knees in front of him. Our chests heaved as we stared at each other.

A dark brow flicked up as he sipped from his mug as if he were challenging me. His pajama pants were tented, so I crawled between his legs and tugged them down, revealing his slick length.

"Presley," Adrian warned, but I gripped his base and leaned forward to take him into my mouth, swirling my tongue over the tip of him.

"Oh shit." The dishes clanked as if he jumped and jostled the tray.

It only made me take him deeper, while working my fist around the thick base of him. His moans and gasps had me moving faster, gripping him firmly while lifting and swirling my tongue over him.

My eyes found his narrowed ones as I spit over the head of his cock and then used my fist to stroke him. He mumbled quiet Italian before gripping the back of my head and forcing me to remain where I was.

I've waited so long for you to want me like this.

I want you to choke on me. I want you to always want this.

He groaned deep while holding me there, and then began lifting his hips in slow, purposeful movements. I opened wide while his slick length slid in and out of my mouth, and he fucked me how he wanted to. His breathing was shallow, his strokes deep and fast until he froze and hot liquid began coating my throat. I tightened my grip on him and swallowed it all down.

"Fuck, you're incredible."

I hated that I missed the way the twins spoke. How filthy and degrading their words were, until that is, I realized they'd meant it all.

I sat back on my heels and watched as Adrian caught his breath and stared at me as if he'd just realized something. His eyes were bright, mouth parted, and right as he was about to say something, there was a knock at the bedroom door.

Adrian didn't respond, but he didn't have to. Seconds later, the door opened, and Renzo walked inside. Adrian cursed while pulling his cotton pajama pants back over his semi-hard cock, and I gaped at his right-hand man while pulling my robe closed. Renzo glanced between where I knelt on the floor and his boss reclined on the chair, then clenched his jaw.

"The fuck?" Adrian snapped.

Renzo had similar features to Adrian, but his eyes were brown, and his hair was darker. He was also bigger and blunter in places that Adrian was tapered and defined. Renzo glared at me, and I smirked back while swiping at the corner of my mouth before gently licking the tip of my thumb.

Renzo didn't seem phased in the slightest. "Sorry, but there's something you need to see."

They didn't bother speaking Italian around me anymore. I wasn't sure if they caught on that I understood it, or if Scotty had somehow revealed that little tidbit, but they almost never spoke it in front of me unless it was useless chit-chat.

Adrian let out a heavy sigh before getting to his feet. "Is this about the names I sent you last night?"

Renzo tilted his head, as if he weren't sure why his boss was speaking so freely in front of me. "No. It's about a complication that requires your attention. Privately."

Adrian's eyes narrowed before taking my hand and helping me to my feet. He pressed a gentle kiss to my mouth and then stroked down the side of my face. "I'll be back soon. Don't get dressed."

I crossed my arms watching them walk away, but before Renzo completely exited, I couldn't help myself. I yelled at his back.

"Don't forget, Renzo. I'm about to become his wife; you might need to get comfortable speaking around me. I won't always be so willing to let him go off with you."

Renzo froze mid-step and glanced over his shoulder. Adrian's brows rose as he glanced between us. He spoke something I couldn't hear, but Renzo's smirk turned deadly as he faced me once more.

"Don't forget, *Presley*, you may be marrying into the Addesso family, but you will never actually be an Addesso. Adrian would be wise to remember that."

The men exited, shutting the door behind them and effectively freezing me in place.

No man in any crime family would speak of their boss that way, especially when he was within earshot. Not unless, of course, they were blood related and had a powerful role within the family.

Gio's conversation came back to mind.

"Adrian has two brothers who travel with him, acting like security, but

they're some of the most dangerous men in North America. Benni and Renzo Addesso are aware of every move Adrian makes, and they don't make any decisions that aren't unilateral. So the choice to place a hit on your father was made by Benni, but all three brothers agreed to it."

It seemed as though I might have finally tugged at a thread in the Addesso family that might become their undoing.

CHAPTER 4

KINGSTON

My brother had finally started speaking to me again regularly.

Even if it took him beating my ass, and me giving up Presley, it was worth it. Gio was my best friend, and while I did love Presley, I knew she would be happy with Gio, but I would never survive without him. He was essential in every way, so I had to do whatever it took to ensure he got Presley back.

"Why exactly are you pulling Henry and the men into this meeting?" my brother asked while we skirted the side of the house where Henry lived. He maintained a residence off the books in town. It was a shitty setup he shared with a few of his men, but for the time being, it worked for him.

I checked how many cars were out front, made sure I didn't see any police cars or anything out of the ordinary, and then explained myself. "I just have a gut feeling that Dad was lying about Markos being dead."

Gio's light eyes searched the street before glancing in my direction. "Why would Dad lie about that?"

We scaled the wooden porch steps. "To keep us out of it.

Knowing Dad, he doesn't want us to pull El Peligro back into something. I can't prove it, but I need to know for sure if he's alive."

If Markos wasn't dead, then we'd need to begin pulling layers back on all the various members who made up the Addesso family. Nine months; Presley should have been married by now, although she had come back home those few months ago, and I had never learned why.

The white door opened, revealing a member of El Peligro, holding an assault rifle. He greeted us with a nod before moving to the side. My brother and I entered, passing through the living room, around a few members who were counting product they'd just made a deal for. Henry knew the details, but as long as the money was coming in, we didn't care to look too closely at all of it. The less we knew, the better.

Henry had lighter skin than either my brother or I, but his eyes were dark brown, just like his hair. He had on a boxy white T-shirt that did nothing to cover up the myriad of tattoos that covered his hands, arms, and neck. His dark hair was pulled back into a small bun at the base of his neck, and his mouth spread into a smile as he saw us.

"Heyyyyy. Boss one and boss two!" He held his hand out for Gio to grasp and clap him on the back. My brother just watched his outstretched hand until Henry lowered it.

"Right. I assume you're here for a reason."

I pulled out a map and let it plop on his kitchen table, over a few plates and cups. "You'd assume correctly."

"Shit, boss. Let me grab my fucking chicken nuggets first." Henry complained while digging for his plate underneath the map. We caught him up on our concerns while he ate, and once he finished, we stood around his table.

"This is his home?" Gio asked, pointing at a point on the map.

I nodded while using a red marker to circle it. "Yeah, we're headed back to New York."

A few other men joined us in the room, but I had no clue who they were. Henry ran recruiting and vetting all the members and we trusted him to know who should be in the room and who shouldn't. We allowed this, mostly because we just didn't give enough of a shit, but also because Henry did.

One of the men set a tablet in front of us which had pictures of the inside of the mansion we were looking into.

I glanced at the images of the various rooms on the screen in front of me. "Where are the weak spots along the perimeter?"

If Markos were dead, then his estate should be easy to breach.

"The posterior portion of the house, however..." Henry used the marker to draw a line around the front part of the property. "That's also fairly obvious...so it's possible that it's a diversion tactic. We would be safer taking a page out of your old man's book and just go through the front doors."

I caught Gio's expression before looking over at Henry. Dad gave us a little bit of a background on how he knew Markos, but I didn't realize he'd actually gone to war with him. It was never a good look to reveal that you didn't know as much as your men, so I'd keep the fact that I had no idea what he was talking about to myself.

"We'll have two parties set up—use both entrances. Make sure the men are armed and wearing vests."

Henry barked out a few commands to the men, and they dispersed, leaving Gio standing near me with his hands clenched at his sides.

He spoke quietly, "Dad never told us any of this shit."

I shook my head, unsure of what to say in response. There were a lot of our parents' lives they hadn't shared, and while I typically would be angry, I was too hurt over the idea of my parents leaving. Dad had mentioned that we didn't know what we'd gotten ourselves into by reviving El Peligro, and I was inclined to believe him. Better to just leave him to his secrets and allow him to have peace.

This was our problem now.

Gio sighed while pulling his phone out. He'd started doing that more than he used to and I wondered if it had anything to do with Presley and hoping she'd reach out. I knew she wouldn't.

We'd broken her, and I was the one who held the hammer, smashing away at all the goodness and love that was once inside her. If she waited a year to reach out the first time, there was no way she'd consider responding now.

"Should we stop and see tía?" Gio asked, looking a little nervous by the way he rubbed his neck. We were still trying to make up for the shitstorm we'd brewed all those months ago that put her and her two sons at risk. She and her boyfriend, Archer, were more than gracious about forgiving us, but it took effort to make relationships work, and I knew we had both agreed to try and make one work with her and our two cousins.

"We should see if she's in town, might be nice to see her and the boys," I replied and added, because I knew he'd be nervous about it, "I'll text her."

His nod of appreciation was slight before he was back to business.

"Do you want to go in through the front together or are we splitting up?"

Henry was more than capable of handling things without us. "Let's go in through the front, together."

My brother fell into step next to me as we exited the house. I tried to relax, feeling the peace of having him nearby again calmed me. It had been lonely these past three months, all alone in my thoughts. I hated being inside my head, full of regrets and stupid dreams that would never come true.

We drove back to the farmhouse in our armored car in comfortable silence. Having my brother with me again had me thinking of our old Camaro that was parked and covered, inside the barn. I didn't know why I had bothered to keep it, but I wasn't ready to let it go yet.

"Where do you sleep?" Gio asked as he exited the SUV.

I tilted my head toward the barn. "I renovated it a bit, so it's more like a room…"

Gio's blue eyes flashed with something like curiosity as he glanced at the refurbished structure behind me. The barn was the first thing I'd poured my time into. There were fresh boards all along the exterior, and a new roof was added just last month. The inside was newer too, but I kept most of the original setup so when Presley moved back, she'd be able to put her animals inside.

"How about you?" I asked, still curious as to where he'd been.

"I was in one of the outlier buildings, we'd used it as an outpost over by where we store military grade weapons, and the helicopter. But I just moved back in with Mom and Dad after I heard they were wanting to leave."

Guilt tugged at some broken place inside of me for being here instead of there with him, but while we were making progress, I knew it was too soon to be under the same roof again.

"How about the house…there's visibly less holes than the last time I saw it." My brother turned toward the two-story farmhouse, inspecting it as if he were going to go inside. He might have found me in there the other day, but he hadn't gone through and looked at all the changes. He probably didn't even know I had finally ripped out all the old wood on the top floor. We'd been trying to get to the top floor forever.

"It's coming along." Was all I said because he still seemed erratic, as if one wrong word and he'd dash away and go no contact with me again.

Gio stepped closer, twirling a familiar-looking hair tie around his finger. "How many rooms will it have?"

The gravel crunched as I slowly stepped closer until I was a few feet behind him. "Four, and an office."

"That'll be good. She'd like that…" Gio mused, trailing off.

I stared at the side of his head, seeing that his hair had grown out and his skin looked paler than usual. "Would you?"

His head snapped over as if I'd just struck him. "What?"

"Would you want the four bedrooms and the office? Our whole plan here is to get you two back together...is this what you envisioned?"

The way he glared at me made something dark and uncomfortable shift in my chest. As if someone had come and shoved the stone over my heart and realized it was infested with insects and decay.

"So what, you'll build us our dream house and then walk away?" he asked skeptically.

Glancing back at the house, I tilted my head to take in the height. I wanted fresh shutters on the outside of the windows and to build out the porch. I wanted her to be able to sit on it one day, holding a baby that had my brother's eyes, while she watched rain fall on a world that was so different than the one we'd come from.

I shrugged, indifferently. "Gives me something to do, but I can stop if you'd prefer."

My twin waited, watching me intently while the muscle in his jaw feathered. There was a shit ton he wasn't saying. "Saves me a ton of work. Knock yourself out."

With one last glance at the house, he turned toward the path that connected the farmhouse to the manor without looking back.

CHAPTER 5
GIO

Our Aunt Wren lived at the end of a cul-de-sac just about an hour outside of New York City. The second we parked our car, her five-year-old son, Cruz, and her boyfriend's little brother, Kane, burst from the front door with happy smiles. Two five-year-old boys acted like my brother and I were the coolest people in the whole entire world.

"Gio, Kingston!"

I caught Cruz in my arms, and my brother caught Kane.

"Are you guys getting any better at that video game we got you?" I asked while my five-year-old cousin began pushing against my eye sockets.

"Can you still see when I do this?"

Kane did the same thing to Kingston, which made him laugh.

Our aunt appeared seconds later, her smile was bright as she greeted us. "Hi, boys."

"Hey, tía." I said with a smile.

My father's little sister looked just like him: the same brown skin, with warm amber eyes, but where my father was hard and blunt, she was soft and beautiful. Her hair was long and thick, and she was

29

considerably more petite than my father, which was only amplified when her boyfriend, Archer, came up behind her.

"Hey, guys."

I gave him a warm smile, although I still felt mildly awkward, considering only a few months ago, we had tried killing one another. "Hey."

Archer was the president of a motorcycle club from New York, so while he looked like a Viking with his longer hair, tied in a bun, and his shocking blue eyes, he also gave off the vibe that he'd murder you bare-handed if he felt so inclined.

"What brings you boys by?" Wren asked while we made our way into the two-story house.

"Just some business in the city, thought maybe we'd see you guys first," Kingston answered while letting Kane out of his arms.

"Well then, stay for dinner!" our aunt gushed while moving to sit on the armrest of the couch. Archer sat down next to her and quickly pulled her hand into his.

"Sure, we'd love to," I answered while Kingston nodded.

This was so fucking awkward, but if we didn't start trying to put things back together, then we'd never get past what we did. We nearly cost Archer his life, took some of his men's lives, and endangered her kids. We owed them a fucking lot.

Besides, we were going to have to get used to eating humble pie if Presley ever let us back into her life.

"Well, I'm going to get it started. You guys relax and play some video games with the boys, I'm sure they'd love that." Wren stood from the couch and ruffled King's hair on her way into the kitchen.

Archer sat forward, leveling his blue-eyed gaze on us. "You need any backup for your *business* in the city?"

Kingston shook his head while I answered, "We have our men coming in."

Archer nodded in understanding. "Well, if you ever need us. For anything at all, you call me. We're family now."

Something warm and bright moved into my sternum, taking me

back to a time when I used to feel that sense of family every day when I'd wake up in the manor. Carter, Alex, and Presley were all there, and of course King. It was a feeling I hadn't had in a very long time.

"Thank you," I said honestly.

The moment was heavy between us for a few seconds before two five-year-old boys ran back into the room, holding game controllers. "Okay, this time, we're going to win."

Kingston laughed while he helped Cruz sit next to him, and Kane took up the spot near me.

"Let's play teams! Brothers against brothers." Kane yelled excitedly.

Kingston glanced over at me tentatively, as if he were nervous that I'd reject him. "You'll never win against me and Gio."

I smiled back and took my controller, and regardless of how pissed I was at my brother, I agreed.

"Never. It's me and King against the world."

HENRY GAVE us a small salute as he drove past our team of fifteen and continued toward the back. Kingston drove while I rode shotgun; no one else traveled in the same vehicle as us. Dawn had barely broken upon the world, and we were already nearing the residence of Markos Mariano.

We decided to stay the night with our aunt, and enjoyed a fun filled evening with our cousins. However, Archer's men came around, and while we were all working to get past what we'd done, it was still somewhat dangerous to be on his turf. The smallest misunderstanding could end up with a bullet in either my or my brother's head. We left at first light, and now, we just wanted to get this over with and get home.

"Gates are closed and locked." Kingston observed as he began increasing his speed.

"Do we have the capacity to break through that?" I glanced over at him before checking the closed iron gates looming before us. Behind it were acres of manicured lawns and cobblestone, leading to a mansion that rivaled the one we grew up in.

Kingston pushed his foot to the floor. "We're about to find out."

"King, don't be fucking stupid. I'm not in the mood to have my nose busted by an airbag."

There was a grille guard on the SUV, but it wasn't as strong as an armored truck would be.

My brother didn't seem phased in the slightest as we neared the iron gate, and right as we were about to hit them, I cursed and closed my eyes.

"Holy shiiiiiitttttt," I yelled, pushing back into the seat with a wince.

King sped into the entrance, forcing the gates to burst apart. Our car rushed through them and over the tidy lawns, even hitting a few lawn figures. A fleet of SUVs followed behind us, matching our speed and spreading throughout the courtyard.

Kingston slammed to a stop right in front of the stairs that led up to the house, and within seconds, we were out of the car, with our assault rifles up. We wore tactical vests and gear, with thick-soled boots and cargo pants that allowed us to tuck away blades and grenades. King tossed one up near the front door, and we ducked behind a stone wall while the explosion went off and the front door blew inward.

"Go. Go. Go," one of the men in our group yelled, and a flow of members went ahead of us into the mansion.

It was hard to focus on anything other than the space in front of us, ensuring we were checking for traps or anything that could harm us. But the more floors that we cleared, the more we realized the place was empty, but there was no sign whatsoever that Markos was dead.

Henry entered through the back, and within minutes, we'd joined the rest of the party that had arrived.

"Clear!" someone called out from the top floor.

Another shouted from the floor right below it. This carried on until every floor was cleared.

"There has to be another level, or someplace we aren't checking," I said, while snooping around his office. Dark wood covered the floor, and soft cream brightened the walls. There were bookshelves along each wall and a massive desk in the middle of the room. Pictures, in heavy silver frames, lined the bookshelves.

I picked one up and inspected it: a man near my dad's age with silver hair, dark brows, and a rigid jaw line. He wore sunglasses in the image, and he was sipping a drink while a man next to him smiled and pointed at the camera. The man in the picture had a tattoo on his hand that looked like an hourglass with a knife cutting through it.

I knew that tattoo.

My mind flipped around memories of where I'd seen it, but I couldn't place it at the moment, so I continued down the shelves, seeing image after image of this man who had to be Markos in each and every one.

He liked to see himself, that much was clear. In a few of the pictures, it was just him.

Kingston tore open the desk drawer and dumped out all the contents. He did the same with the other few drawers until the surface was littered with all Markos's items. We began sifting through everything, seeing if there was any information that would lead us to him.

"Bag all of this up." Henry walked into the room, holding an assault rifle. A few of our men moved around the room and began doing exactly that. I watched as they started packing things away, but saw something that caught my eye.

"Wait!"

Kingston glanced at the man who had frozen with his hands on a pile of papers.

Walking closer, I plucked the picture out of the pile and

inspected the blonde woman inside it. There were several images being held together with a paperclip. I could feel my rage begin to unfurl as I sorted through picture after picture.

The blonde woman walking on a college campus, pregnant.

The blonde woman smiling at a guy wearing a hockey letterman jacket. He wasn't looking at her, but she was staring at him.

The blonde woman walking with the man, his hand around her waist.

My brother came around my shoulder and watched as I flipped through each and every image, then set down his gun, and by the way he picked up each image I dropped, I knew he was just as angry as I was.

"Why the fuck does he have all the pictures of Mom and Dad?"

I looked up, catching my twin's gaze. Dad had mentioned that Markos was intended to marry our mom... Presley had mentioned that her dad killed our mom's father because he was a bad man. He must have been the one who had orchestrated that arrangement. I could understand wanting to make good on an arrangement or even someone promised to you, but these images...

"He was stalking her."

Kingston grabbed another picture. "Not just her...he was watching Dad too. Even before he took over El Peligro."

I stopped looking when we came across an image of our mom in a bathing suit. That was enough, especially if he'd creeped on her privately.

"But why would he keep these after twenty years?"

My brows cinched in, mirroring my brothers who was trying to work out the same thing.

Henry leaned closer, trying to help. "Do you think he considers the pictures a trophy?"

That was possible, depending on what kind of sick fuck he was. He'd stalked her, so that part was already clear...

"Dad said he'd confirmed Markos was dead..." I said it only loud enough for King and Henry to hear. Both of whom watched me silently. We had to figure out how our dad knew, and what intel he had that we might be able to use, but more than that, we needed to figure out where Markos was if he wasn't dead.

I ENTERED THE MANOR, and the habitual silence felt suffocating. I wondered if Kingston felt this when he walked inside, or if it was just me.

It was ironic that the tables had turned so violently, and now we were stuck in some sick version of purgatory where we paid for the sins we committed. Each time I felt a memory surface of running through these halls as children, or when I thought I heard her laugh, sorrow would threaten to drown me.

I bypassed the wing closest to where Kyle and his family resided and headed straight for the Eastern side of the manor, where my family was.

"Gio!" Scotty called somewhere behind me, but I ignored him.

"Giovanni!" He tried again, but I wouldn't be giving that fucker a single moment of my time. Now that Presley wasn't here, I owed him jack shit.

I was closing in on the front door to our section when Scotty spoke up again, but this time his words stopped me in my tracks.

"She called me this morning."

I slowly turned around, clenching my jaw. The halls were dimly lit by bronze sconces and a few lamps, but this section near our home was still cast in enough shadow that it made Presley's great uncle look every inch the villain he'd always been to me and King. Scotty wore a black turtleneck with a pair of black slacks. He had gun holsters over his chest, and his dog, Reaper, trotted next to him with his ears alert.

Scotty stepped closer. "It's normal for her to call once a week or so. She checks in, always lets me know if there's anything I need to be informed of."

Fire ignited in my blood, boiling me from the inside out to hear that she was communicating with him, and not me.

"She never has anything to report other than that she's happy and Adrian treats her well." Scotty continued to advance closer.

My chin dipped to my chest because I didn't want Scotty, of all people, to see the defeat in my eyes. I felt like he'd ordered Reaper to attack me, my heart somewhere torn on the ground.

"Except this morning..." Scotty paused, then came to a stop a few feet away from me.

My eyes lifted, latching onto his, trying to decipher what that meant.

"This morning, she said the ocean was beautiful, but the sky was dark."

Reaper's nose nudged at my hand, silently demanding to be acknowledged. As much as Scotty disliked it, his dogs were both soldiers and pets, and they'd been around my brother and me long enough that they were fond of us.

My voice was soft as I inquired, "What does that mean?"

"That means," Scotty started and then snapped his fingers, ordering Reaper back to his side, "something triggered her there enough that she's on alert. She'll be playing double agent until whatever it was that triggered her has either come to a head or stopped. That might mean she's in danger, or might need back up, either way, I know to be on high alert."

I heard two more dogs making their way down the hall, their nails clicking along the marble. "Why tell me?"

Scotty smirked, and it was the same gesture he made whenever he witnessed Presley best us in the training ring, or when she'd show us up on her precision with the blade or gun. He was proud of her, but so were King and I. We never cared that she beat us; in fact, we preferred that she did. Scotty was the only person who got a sick satisfaction at seeing his little protégé beat us.

"Just wanted to see if you still cared if she lived or died. You and your brother talked a big game about taking sides against us, but you'd still do anything for her, wouldn't you?"

I didn't respond.

He already knew, and there was no use in making myself look like an idiot.

His laugh trailed down my spine and curled inside my gut, making me want to punch him.

"Which means I can still use you as I see fit. If I asked you to go there right now and pull her out of Adrian's arms, you'd do it, wouldn't you?"

My lip curled back as I stepped closer. "Not because you asked me, you motherfucker. I would do anything to protect *her*! Let's just be clear, it's not because you asked me to. I'd let you die if I could."

He stood toe to toe with me now. "You're never going to be the fire in her life, Giovanni. It'll never be you. You're a safety net. Stars she once looked at and thought were mesmerizing, but mark my words, she'll choose your brother."

"What's going on here?" The door opened behind me right as my fists curled, and I stepped closer to Scotty. I wanted to hit him.

I wanted to kill him.

My mother's voice, however, was soft, and it reeled me back with a sharp tug. I'd never do any of that in front of her. I stepped away from Scotty and left him standing there in the hall, while the anger in my soul surged like a thunderhead and buried all the hope I'd somehow gathered when my brother promised to relinquish his hold on her.

"Gio, are you okay, honey?" My mother slid her hand over my back and rubbed soothingly.

She'd done that gesture ten thousand times since I was a little kid, but for whatever reason, now it just hurt.

"I need to talk to Dad."

My mother's blue eyes narrowed on me, but she nodded. "He's in the study."

Walking through our living room, and beyond the stairs, toward the kitchen, I found my father tucked away in a small office. My entire life, the room had been bloated with books, packed along each shelf, and even a few piles had littered the floor. Green vines of plants stretched along the glass windows, and a beautiful view of the back property stretched for miles, all green grass and tall trees.

Now, it was bare. All the books packed away; the green vines had withered and died. Even the view outside his window was bleak. Still, he sat at his empty desk with his laptop open.

"Dad."

His amber eyes lifted and softened as soon as he saw me.

"What's wrong?"

I glanced around the room. "You're already packing?"

His chin dipped as he slid away from the desk and stood. "We need a fresh start."

"Kingston and I are staying, we told you that," I argued as that anger surfaced and threatened to explode.

My dad didn't take the bait; he merely sighed. "I understand that, but this place is too big for us anyway. It's time we start looking out for our own family."

"This is our family," I argued, "You raised us to—"

He waved his hand in the air. "I know how I raised you, and I'm telling you it was wrong. My sister, her husband, and kids, that's our focus. My mom and step dad. My family. Your family. That's what's important."

I shook my head in disbelief. "Kyle has nearly died because of his loyalty to you, several times over if my memory serves."

Dad stepped closer. "Kyle has nearly died because of his own actions. He chose to involve Scotty in this, who brought in the Adessos. I'm cutting ties. We're out."

The silence between us stretched as I watched him slowly move back to his chair. I wanted to scream a million other things at him, but none of it would matter. All that mattered was ensuring Presley was safe.

"What proof do you have that Markos is dead?"

His head snapped up, his thick brows curving into a line against his forehead. "What do you mean?"

I tugged at the hair tie around my wrist, lightly snapping it against my skin.

"I mean. We went to his home, and nothing was there. No sign of struggle or forced entry. No blood. Nothing except some pictures..."

I watched carefully as my father's eyes tapered and his mouth twitched. Did he know about the stalking or the pictures? Why wasn't he letting us get close to this?

"Markos Mariano was a twisted and very dangerous man. I told you he's dead, please trust me on this."

Seeing that my father wasn't going to budge only infuriated me more.

"Why won't you help us? If we can find Markos, then we can try and extract information regarding Adrian. We can help protect Presley."

My father suddenly stood and leaned over the desk. "You need to decide which side you're on, Son. One second you're against her, the next you're with her. She doesn't need any more allies. She needs space. We can give that to her by leaving."

"I love her, Dad. I'm in love with her. Help me protect her!" I screamed as all the built-up rage came tumbling out.

My father's face didn't shift, or change even the slightest bit, until he scoffed and his head shook.

"And you're just going to share this love you have for one woman with your twin?"

"Kingston said he's over her." The lump in my throat was difficult to swallow past, especially as laughter spilled out of my father.

"You believe that, do you?"

He rounded the desk once more and stood in front of me. "Do you know that Kingston used to sleep outside of Presley's window? He'd forget that he'd done it because he'd wander up on the roof to make sure she got to sleep okay, but I would go up there and bring him back to his bed. But he'd just run back up there first thing in the morning to check on her, regardless of the weather or the temperature. He used to throw away his homework if he discovered that she was still doing hers, just so he had the excuse to sit and do his homework next to her. He used to name his plants in the garden, and each one of them was Presley. Your brother has loved Presley long before he even understood it was love."

That gutting feeling returned. Being hollowed out, forgotten. My mouth didn't seem to work as the sentiment from Scotty and now my father slammed into me. I wasn't sure if my dad noticed or not, but his words were more effective than blades in cutting me down to the bone.

I took a step back and then another, slowly gathering my resolve.

"Where is Markos?"

My father's features only changed marginally, but he still didn't relent. "I've been doing this longer than you, Gio. Markos is a dead end. Drop it and move on."

I wouldn't be doing either, but for the sake of my sanity, I did leave his office and slammed his door in the process.

CHAPTER 6
PRESLEY

Adrian's smile couldn't be brighter as we swayed around the dance floor.

It felt like he was branding himself on the entire room, and not a single soul refused it. He was happy, charismatic, and joyful. I felt myself trying to keep up with him, continuously grinning as I greeted new people and shook hands. I wore a beautiful green dress that swept over the floor with graceful wisps and swooped down to my navel, revealing more skin than I was used to. My hair was down in silky waves against my back, and I wore makeup that hopefully aged me a bit beyond just my eighteen and a half years.

The reminder of time passing had me thinking of the twins' birthday that had passed. They were twenty now. I hated the curiosity that had curled along the edges of my mind, wondering if they'd celebrated or if they'd thought of me while they did. Two years in a row without me...perhaps this was just the new normal for them.

"To the future Mrs. Adesso!" someone yelled across the room, and everyone around me cheered while lifting their glasses in the air.

A strange, choked feeling stuck itself in my throat like honey.

Too sweet. Too sticky. Too much.

Adrian gently squeezed my hand, and I held onto him as I lifted my arm in celebration, silently agreeing with the sentiments shared around the room. We were celebrating our engagement with some of Adrian's closest friends and employees. There were a few familiar faces, but most of the people around the room were strangers to me.

"Do you want to at least FaceTime your parents?" Adrian offered by speaking closely. His lips slid along the shell of my ear, and it made the fine hairs along my arm stand up. I tried to relax into his embrace and fight the strange gut feeling I had that the twins had been right. I didn't want them to be right, not when they'd stood so firmly on their reasons to eviscerate my heart and piss on everything we'd been to each other.

Searching for my phone, I tugged it free and did exactly as he suggested. I had given him a lie that they'd been tangled in something that prevented them from flying here to Italy. He was under the impression that I'd have a separate party back home at some point. The truth was, I didn't want my father here, just in case there were enemies lurking everywhere, and I just didn't realize it, but Face-Timing would give me the opportunity to have him see who was here and ID a few people.

"That's a great idea, darling." I leaned over and kissed Adrian on the mouth briefly before pulling away and standing up. I called Scotty, knowing he'd ensure my father and mother were carefully protected as I walked around the room, recording.

It rang twice before Scotty's face appeared, and seeing him in the mansion made me immediately homesick. He wasn't in our family wing, but in the shared space near the foyer that held our joint dinner table, and the various spaces to sit, leading out to the terrace.

"Presley! Congratulations, *Lánya*," Scotty cooed approvingly. Reaper's face appeared next, and I had to fight the tightness in my throat that threatened tears to the surface.

"Hi! I wanted you, Mom, and Dad to be able to see how beautiful my engagement party is."

My uncle smiled and then shifted the phone the smallest bit. "Let me get your parents, hang tight."

He disappeared, and for a few seconds, it was just the empty room in the manor staring back at me. The emptiness felt odd, like visiting the grave of an old friend and hoping they'd somehow speak to you, only to be met with silence. My focus moved to the space around me. Glowing lights from the room created a soft ambiance, along with the various teardrop chandeliers and gorgeous marble that shaped the historical building. Every feature shouted opulence, as did the entire guest list with suits, dresses, and expensive jewelry.

I wasn't paying attention to the phone screen when I suddenly froze at the voice coming from it.

"You look beautiful."

My gaze slid down right along with my heart. Kingston's handsome face came into view as he carefully took the seat Scotty had sat previously. He wore tattered clothes, covered in dust and bits of paint, while his hair was longer than I remembered, but it was messy and unstyled.

My mouth parted as my entire soul seemed to freeze.

"I always wondered what you'd look like when you danced at your engagement party. Guess this answers that question. Perfect and yet..." He shook his head as if he couldn't believe it. "Somehow, you still look like you're ours."

"Well, I'm not," I snapped harshly.

He studied me then dipped his face. The chaotic rapping against my chest was concerning, to say the least.

King's voice came out quiet and calm as he replied, "Sorry...not ours. Gio's. You look like you're my brother's. Even as you pretend to be Adrian's, there's a part of you that will always be his. I hope you don't ever forget that, Elvis."

He stood, slowly slid his hands into his pockets, and walked out of the room, somehow taking the air with him. Even though we were in different locations and in different countries, my chest felt empty, and my lungs felt weak.

Scotty was back moments later, a smile on his face, but the wetness against my face had me swiping away the evidence that Kingston had any effect on me.

Elvis. He didn't say it sarcastically, or in that tone he'd used a thousand times, as if he were jealous that Gio called me it. He said it as though that were my only nickname, and he was trying to erase something that was once there.

What did he mean?

"You okay?" Scotty asked, curving his brows.

I nodded. "Just a big night. I feel a little emotional without everyone here."

My uncle glanced over his shoulder and then faced me again. "Show me around the room, *Lánya.* Your mother and father are here next to me."

A new thickness was in my throat as I did as he said and moved around the room, smiling and playing the part. Gliding from one couple to another with gratitude and thanks for their attendance, all the while my mind was stuck on my best friend who had told me I looked beautiful and then reminded me that I was no longer someone in his life that he deemed worthy of keeping.

It cut me in a fresh way that I wasn't even aware he had the power to unleash.

Yet my body radiated with pain.

Elvis.

Elvis.

Not, Mi Reina.

An hour later, my phone was nearly dead, and Adrian's hand was on my hip as he guided me out of the party. My left hand had a gleaming diamond that shone under the dim lighting of the exterior lights that guided us to our armored car. Renzo and Benni met us there, like usual, but instead of having a driver, the two guards took up the places in front while Adrian slid into the back, pulling me with him.

Benni began driving, and I tried to calm my nerves.

"Where's Viktor?" I stroked over Adrian's hand, but he gripped my fingers and pulled me into his chest, where our mouths slid against one another.

Benni answered from the front. "He's enjoying an evening off."

I relaxed the smallest bit, knowing that it was typical for Adrian to give his staff certain days and especially holidays off. It was something that had endeared me to him.

"So, Presley. Did you enjoy your engagement party?" Renzo asked, while keeping his head straight, eyes on the road.

Adrian's hand wrapped around my waist and slid me even closer to him.

"I did. It was beautiful."

"You're beautiful." Adrian's whisper heated my neck as he kissed me there. I wasn't against showing affection in public, but he was starting to get more handsy than normal, especially when his hands slid up under my dress and he stroked over my thigh—dangerously close to my firearm strapped there.

"Adrian." I held his wrist in place, unsure why he was being so bold in front of these two men, brothers or not. I still wasn't sure, but I didn't want anyone else to be present when I did physical things with him.

He immediately relented and let me go with a bit of a groan. "I'm sorry, *Bellissima*. I'm drunk, and horny as fuck."

I heard the two men speaking Italian in the front:

Is she too shy to let him touch her?

Benni laughed and then replied in Italian*: I doubt it. She wasn't too shy to let two brothers fuck her at the same time.*

My breath caught as Adrian tipped his head back against the seat. I glared at the two men in front, feeling a fresh wave of heat hit my chest. Did they see me with the twins?

Had Adrian had me followed, or were they simply assuming?

If I replied, they'd know I was able to understand them even though I was nearly positive they already did. My mind was all over the place, still lingering on the boy back in North Carolina who rejected me and somehow found a way to reject me again.

Who was he to tell me I was only Gio's?

Anger stirred in my veins, making me frustrated in all new ways. Ways that had me wanting to get on the first plane back home just so I could fight with Kingston.

The car came to a stop outside of an unfamiliar home, and it seemed Adrian was nearly asleep. The two men in front exited the car and slammed their doors hard enough that it jostled the man next to me awake.

"Oh, we're here." He yawned.

I glanced around, seeing the modest single-story home, layered in white brick with a steep roof. A small garden fence bordered the yard, along with various pear trees.

"Where are we?" I asked, sliding out after Adrian as he opened his door.

Renzo came around the vehicle and smiled. "This is our—"

"Father's home," Adrian cut in while grabbing my hand and pulling me toward the entry gate.

"Your father's home?" I glanced over my shoulder at the two men following us.

"Fuck," Benni whispered while Renzo cursed at Adrian in Italian.

You idiot. We agreed to wait until you were married before you told her.

"Told me what?" I asked in English, which made them both stop in their tracks. Meanwhile, Adrian continued to pull me toward the gate. I spun out of his embrace and pulled my gun out and aimed it at Adrian while I took two large steps backward.

"Tell me what the fuck is going on right now."

Adrian froze, and the way his face went white as a ghost made something in my heart crack the smallest bit.

"Bella—"

I slammed my eyes closed and cut him off. "Just tell me!"

"It's harmless, Presley. We just had to be sure you were serious about this alliance before we shared that we were his brothers," Benni said, while raising his hands as if he were trying to calm me down.

Renzo mimicked him. "Adrian never wanted to. He wanted to tell you from the start, but we outvoted him, and then with the final say coming from our boss...he had to keep it from you."

The twins were right.

Fuck. Fuck. Fuck.

"Who gets the final say?" I heard a twig snap behind me, so I quickly side stepped and adjusted my aim so I could see who was approaching.

A middle-aged man with silver hair and a narrow jaw walked up. He wore a fine linen suit and had sharp blue eyes and tan skin. My stomach sank, all while my arm rose, and I aimed my gun directly at this man's head.

"Who are you?"

He smiled at me. "I'm Markos Mariano. It's nice to finally meet you, Presley."

I pulled the hammer back on the gun with my thumb.

The man's smile only grew. "You might not want to shoot me just yet."

"And why not?"

He turned the smallest bit, looking over his shoulder, and that's when I realized there was someone standing near the front door. The shimmery blonde color had me audibly gasping as the woman made her way over to Markos. Within a single breath, the ground seemed to slip from beneath my feet.

"Alex?"

CHAPTER 7
KINGSTON

My fingers ached as I slid my thick work gloves off.

I'd been repairing the top floor of the farmhouse for the past week, pushing out images of Presley wearing that dress, wearing her hair down like that. She looked like something from a dream, a dream I couldn't wake up from. One where, in the end, I knew the girl I loved wouldn't be mine.

"Kingston!" Gio roared from the lower level of the house.

He'd been elusive and absent this past week as well. I hadn't told him that I saw Presley on FaceTime through Scotty's screen. I hadn't told him that she wore a massive ring on her left hand that didn't look like anything she'd ever pick out for herself. I hadn't mentioned that she was forcing her smiles upon the room of strangers she was floating around in, and I certainly hadn't shared that I told her in no uncertain terms that she still looked like she belonged with my brother. And not me.

"Yeah!"

I heard his feet slam against the stairs that I had recently rebuilt, and then his head popped up. He'd gotten a haircut, and it looked as though he'd just showered because it was still wet as he ran his hand through the ends.

"You aren't answering your cell." My brother glanced down at my jeans that were covered in dust and paint.

"Been busy. What's up?"

Gio shoved his hands into his pockets and wandered around the open floor. He saw the three bedrooms framed with drywall already nailed in place and the extra set of stairs leading to a third level.

"What's this for?" He ran his palm over the railing, tilting his head back to take in the steps.

It wasn't easy to build a house while not knowing jack shit about it. I had hired three contractors to come and help me, but there were a few things they'd told me I could do that would move things along a bit faster.

Lifting my head to gesture, I explained, "Figured you'd want to star gaze... I built this so you'd have that option from the top level."

Gio's face fell. His hands slid from the wood, and he shook his head.

"Why? She's not coming back. You need to stop doing all this shit, acting like you're building this life for me and Presley. It isn't happening."

I ignored him and set my tools back in the bucket that I'd carried up here. I had been hanging drywall all morning, so I didn't have a ton of things to pack up.

"Kingston, I'm serious. You need to stop." Gio crowded me with a shove.

I shoved him back, making everything tip out of the bucket I had packed things in.

"Gio, stop!"

"No. She doesn't want me, King. Fuck. Why can't you see that?" He seethed.

I refused to see it because I knew better. I had witnessed the two of them interact and fall in love, my entire life. Gio was good for her. He always made her laugh when all I did was make her sad. He taught her how to read the sky for fuck's sake. He'd permanently tattooed that sky on his back just for her. There was no way I was fucking this up for them any more than I already had.

"Let me do this," I begged him while he came at me again, ready to punch me.

He paused, and I caught something in his gaze that scared me. Something that made me want to reach into his chest and check over his heart to make sure it was still beating. I carried my dark clouds and demons with me everywhere I went; Gio was always sunshine and happiness. If his came out, they'd try to kill him.

His voice was quiet as he whispered, "Why do you want to?"

Because I'm not good, not like you, and not like her. Because you always made her smile. Because all I do is ruin things. "I fucked it up. Let me fix it."

My brother shook his head before turning away again, pacing the length of the floor.

"Dad is lying about Markos. He's dead set on leaving, and based off how much has been packed in the house, I think they might be going soon. I need help convincing him. He knows more than what he's saying he does."

Gio was coming to me as a last resort; he knew Dad wasn't going to budge, even if I got involved. But I could tell my brother was desperate.

"Then we motivate him," I suggested. My brother's eyebrows lifted as he watched me grab the rest of my things and head downstairs.

"I don't want Mom to get upset," Gio said as we pulled to a stop in front of the house.

My head dipped in agreement. I had no plans whatsoever in bringing my mother into this or my sister, but that actually had me wondering where she was. I hadn't seen her in over a week.

"Where has Alex been lately?" I shoved the parking gear into place and pulled the small box from the back seat before exiting.

I had no idea if Kyle and Rylie were around, as I'd been avoiding the manor for the most part. The first time I had come over was last week when I caught the FaceTime call. If I did run into them, I planned on being pleasant, or as pleasant as I could be. Unfortunately, my decision to draw a line in the sand between our families made everything fucking awkward when we showed up, or anyone was caught in the same vicinity as us.

Well, me. Just me...Gio was probably on good terms with everyone since living here and being in the family wing.

Gio fell into step next to me as we pushed through the manor doors and made our way down the hall. "I haven't seen Alex in a few days...maybe a week?"

Exactly how long it had been for me. My mind raced with where she might have gone to and I mentally reminded myself to text her as I adjusted the weight of the box under my arm.

Gio paused right as his fingers wrapped around the door handle leading into our family space. "He's going to lose his shit when you do this."

I shrugged. "Then maybe he'll be properly motivated to talk."

Pissing my father off wasn't exactly something I enjoyed doing. While I knew I had become rather good at it these past few years, I actually hated being a burden. I detested this wall that had been erected and all because he refused to help us protect Presley.

It angered me past empathy. Which was why I didn't exactly feel remorse as I walked to his office and allowed my actions to speak all the necessary words.

Dad sat at his desk, and glancing around, I saw that most of his office had been packed up. The only thing that cluttered his desk space was his laptop. His amber eyes flicked up to watch as we entered, and I hated how a flicker of hope or excitement shone there.

"Boys."

"Hey, Dad," Gio said warmly.

I shot my brother a quick glare before pulling the box out from under my arm. We didn't need to give Dad a false sense as to why we were there.

Dad's eyes narrowed. "What's that?"

I nudged my brother's shoulder, so he'd get out of the way. Then I dumped the contents of the box on his desk, covering his laptop. "This was everything found inside Markos Mariano's office. We just wanted to know if you were aware that he stalked our mother?"

Pictures littered the waxed surface of his desk with image after image of our mother. Close-ups, invasive images that Gio and I both had to ensure Henry packed and not us. But there was more than that. He had pictures of Mom when she was a little kid. T-shirts that seemed to belong to her, a perfume bottle, and hair spray. There were ultrasound images of Alex tucked inside the box, as well as pictures of when Alex was at an ice cream shop here in Rake Forge. Another one appeared of Alex when she was swimming at the lake one summer.

An eerie feeling swam through me, making the hair along my spine erupt.

I watched as my father surveyed the mess in front of him. A reddish pink flare filled his cheeks and neck. I cleared my throat and pressed on the gaping wound that had seemed to split open at the memory of this man apparently stalking our mother.

"If he's dead and you put the bullet in his brain, then great. Let's burn all this shit," I warned.

Gio stepped closer, adding, "But if he's not and there's even a chance that he could be alive, then we need to find him, Dad. He needs to pay."

I watched my father carefully as he scanned the things in front of him. The muscle in his jaw flexed, and he looked as though he were about to say something, but then his gaze snagged on a photo in the pile of our family laughing while at the beach. In the image, Dad was holding Gio while Alex was struggling to hold me. She was five or six, and we were just toddlers. The beach behind everyone was white sand with turquoise water.

"This was after..." Dad's voice trailed off as he plucked the image from the pile of other photos.

"After what?" Gio asked.

Dad slowly stood while staring down at the picture before digging in the pile once more. I glanced at my brother to see if he was piecing anything together, but his brows were furrowed as if he were just as lost.

Clasping another image, Dad sank back into his seat and stared at it. The picture was of our mother, in college, from what it looked like. She was out at a shooting range, or somewhere similar...she was all alone, and had a white BMW that wasn't meant for off-roading.

"Son of a bitch," Dad rasped, scowling so hard at the image I thought he might begin to cry.

A door clicked shut from inside the house somewhere, and Dad's head snapped up.

"Shut the door. I don't want your mother to see any of this."

Gio covered the space quickly and quietly slid the door closed, then locked it.

"Dad, what is all of this? After what?"

"Markos was injured, badly, by Kyle. He scared him enough that we honestly assumed he'd slip out of the life and disappear. Any images that he might have collected, I assumed, might be prior to that specific day. The beach image was years after, which means it's possible that he's been keeping tabs on our family ever since."

By the looks of it, he was particularly interested in Alex.

Anger spurred me into action. I began gathering all the images and putting them back into the cardboard box. "No shit, he's been keeping tabs on us. Gio and I told you that he and his little demon godchildren are hell bent on destroying us. All of us. He has an especially dark interest in ruining Kyle. But no one fucking listened to us."

Dad's jaw flexed while he helped put all the pictures away. The second the box was back together, he walked over to the fireplace and pulled the zippo lighter out from his pocket, then lit the box on fire.

Peering over his shoulder, he warned both Gio and me, "I don't want your mother to know how badly her privacy was invaded. She had no idea...and this would frankly scare her. This is why I just want to fucking get out of here. Get you kids and just leave."

Something tugged at my gut, worry or concern. I wasn't sure, but it seemed strange that I hadn't seen Alex in as long as I had.

"Dad, where is Alex?"

His somber gaze traveled from us back to the fire before he jumped up and ran out the office door.

He tore down the hall in a light jog while calling for our big sister. The way his voice pitched with fear had my own stomach tensing and flipping. Gio had his phone up to his ear, likely calling her. I decided to help Dad look by running out of the wing and checking all the other family wings.

Aunt Mallory and Uncle Decker hadn't been back in months, and this time, Carter had decided to join them. She was here four months ago when Dad's sister had come, but after that she decided to stay with her parents. Deep down, I knew it had something to do with what Gio and I had done and how unhinged we'd become after Presley left.

Still, I rummaged through their family wing, consisting of three massive suites, the kitchen, bathrooms, and then I took the door that would lead up to the fourth floor. Taking each narrow step one at a time, my stomach tensed for an entirely different reason. Seeing the space in the daylight did nothing to dim the memory of what I'd experienced in the room all those months ago.

There was still a blanket on the floor from when we'd slept there. No one had been up here since that night.

I glanced at the chaise lounge in the corner and swallowed past the thick lump in my throat. We'd taken her virginity here and given her ours. We'd ruined her here.

There was nothing left in the room, and yet I lingered, even knowing our sister might be missing. I stayed rooted in that spot, staring down at the blanket on the floor, feeling fresh tears gather along my lashes.

What the fuck was wrong with me? Why was I so petty that I ruined the best part of my life?

"Kingston?" someone yelled from below. It shook me loose of my dark thoughts and had me leaving the room and the memories behind.

———

I SAT NEXT to Gio as our father paced in front of us. Our mother was on the couch across from us, her face was tear-stained and utterly broken.

"She sometimes just goes on trips...she's an adult, there's no reason for her to be beholden to us about everything," Dad justified with a broken voice.

He was wasting his breath. Didn't fucking matter, all that did was that she was gone.

"Juan," Mom warned. Our father snapped his head over, and the two spoke silently before a rugged sigh sailed past Dad's lips.

"Not to break up the party, but what is the matter?" Scotty suddenly appeared inside our doorway. His shoulder was set against the frame, nonchalant, and as if he didn't have a care in the world.

My jaw clenched as I glared at the man who had fucked up so much of this for us that I very seriously wanted to kill him. It was Dad who spoke up and explained what was going on.

"Alex is missing."

Our mom's expression was too open, too easily broken, for how she looked at Scotty for help.

Like this madman would ever assist us in any way.

Scotty glanced down at his nails and then rubbed them against his coat. "Oh, that. I know where she is."

Mom stepped closer, her eyes watering.

"Be careful, Scotty," Dad warned, while slowly sliding a blade into his palm.

Presley's uncle searched the room and then snapped his fingers. Reaper, Max, and Rue all appeared from the darkened hallway, a low rumble rolling through the group of dogs as Scotty whispered something in German, which had the dogs' ears lying flat.

Fucker.

"We outnumber you, Scotty. You'd risk the lives of your pets?" I asked, gripping my own knife.

"I trained them to protect me, so yes, I'm ready to risk that."

"Please." Mom walked directly in front of Scotty's line of sight. "What do you know?"

Scotty searched the room before his jaw seemed to tense, and then his gaze dropped to the floor.

"Alexandria approached me about a week ago and asked what I thought of her going to help Presley. She just wanted to be an extra set of eyes and ears, keep Presley safe if she could. Presley had used a code word indicating that there might because to be on alert, so when Alexandria asked, I said yes."

Dad's eyes were huge as he stepped forward. "So you're telling me that you sent my daughter to Italy?"

Scotty's dark brows caved inward as he searched our faces. "She'll be with Presley at Adrian's residence. If Presley is there, then your daughter will be safe."

I caught Mom glancing at Dad, and silent tears trailed down her face.

"Except it isn't safe."

Scotty tried to gauge what was going on from our reactions. By the way his dogs whined and shifted, I'd say he seemed unsettled. "Why?"

Dad swallowed thickly before his voice cracked. "Because Markos is alive and from what the boys just showed me, he's been watching Alex just like he used to watch Taylor."

I wish I hadn't been there to see my mother's face fill with horror at that news. I wish I hadn't been there to see the way her eyes rounded or the way her hand fell to her stomach as a small sound of shock slipped past her mouth.

"So, he's in Italy." Scotty's eyes flicked to mine, and I knew right then that he realized he was wrong. That he and Presley had fucked up in a major way. That he sent his precious *Lánya* right into the arms of a monster.

"I missed the connection," Scotty admitted, lowering his chin to his chest.

Gio snapped at him angrily, "You didn't trust us. Now we're all fucked."

Scotty pulled out his phone and made a call, but whoever it was he'd called didn't answer. Somewhere, deep down, I knew it was Presley, and even further down, I worried she'd be hurt or worse. My only hope was that Alex being there did, in fact, help her in some way.

CHAPTER 8

PRESLEY

Adrian pulled my hand into his lap and stroked his finger down the center of my palm. My eyes were trained on the man across from me, who was sitting right next to Alex. The man in question was smirking, and Alex looked like a plastic doll sitting next to him. Frozen in fear with her golden hair piled on top of her head, thick black lashes, and startling blue eyes.

Markos sipped his wine while Benni and Renzo filled in the rest of the spots around the table. If there were any additional soldiers, they weren't visible. My stomach churned with nerves as I watched Alex for any sign of distress or abuse. Her skin was flawless, no bruises or scratches. Not even her eyes were puffy.

"So tell me, Presley." Markos got my attention by setting his glass down and settling his gaze on me. "My Adrian is quite taken with you. Do you feel the same about him?"

The twins were right, and I wasn't even sure how to process it. This man was dangerous, and I knew that Alex being with him wasn't on accident. It was a threat, but I wasn't sure yet how to approach it or what to say because she could get hurt, so instead I squeezed Adrian's hand under the table and smiled.

"Of course I do. It took some time to warm up to him, but I couldn't be happier about our impending marriage."

Alex's blue eyes lifted to mine and held my gaze for a few seconds before lowering them again to the table. Benni and Renzo helped themselves to the pasta dinner that was in a clear dish near the center of the table. A large green salad filled another bowl, along with a silver tray of fresh bread. There were no maid staff, no chef, no one else seemed to be here...it almost made me wonder if Markos had actually made this meal himself.

Markos glanced first at Adrian, who was sipping coffee, then next to him at Alex. "What do you think, Alexandria? Do you think Presley is fond of Adrian, or do you think she's still smitten with your twin brothers?"

My pulse jackhammered as I watched Alex's eyes plead with me for something I had no way of giving her. Before she could reply, Adrian cleared his throat.

"That's enough, father."

Hearing Adrian confirm his connection to Markos felt like a rock plummeting into water. How could he have kept this from me? Even if this wasn't his biological father, according to the twins, this was the man who had raised my fiancé.

Sliding my chair out, I cleared my throat. "Excuse me, I'd like to talk to Alex alone, please."

Markos tipped his head back the smallest amount, revealing a devious smile. "Of course."

Alex slid out of her spot and gently set her cloth napkin down while she walked toward the hall. I met her halfway, feeling everyone's gaze on our backs. We kept walking until we found a spot far enough away that I knew no one would be able to hear us.

My fingers intertwined with hers instantly as her eyes began to fill with tears. "What are you doing here?"

"I came to help you. Scotty said it would be fine, but when I arrived in Italy, this guy picked me up. I assumed Scotty had set it all up for me, so when he said he was one of Adrian's drivers, I didn't give it a second thought. I just got in the car. I've been with Markos ever since."

"So he kidnapped you?" I asked, pulling her closer.

Alex nodded briskly. "He hasn't hurt me, just said we'd be reuniting after your engagement party. I wanted to be there for that, as protection. I know you can take care of yourself, but I wanted to ensure you had some backup. I tried using my phone, but I think he has a signal jammer going or something."

I flung my arms around her as hers came around me. For two seconds, I allowed myself to be nostalgic and think of home. To remember what it was like to see her every morning and to train with her in the evenings. Alex was always like a big sister to me, and seeing her here really did make me feel better. Although, this would also be difficult because if Markos had half a brain, he'd know that Alex meant something to me, and he could use her as leverage.

He just picked up a hostage, thanks to Scotty.

"We'll figure this out, I promise." I released Alex and stepped back.

We'd have to get back to the table and act like nothing was wrong. Before we did, I gripped her hand once more. "Did he say anything to you, anything that would help us understand his motivation?"

Alex released me and stepped closer. "His motivation? Presley, come on, you know by now that my brothers were right. This is all an elaborate job to get revenge on your father. They'll kill us because we're allies and...well, there might be more."

"More what?"

She flicked a quick look over my shoulder before leaning even closer. "He said something weird about my mom...like he knew her or something."

"Presley, darling." Adrian appeared behind us with his hands loose at his sides.

I turned and saw his worried expression.

"Yes?"

He reached for me, gently. "Come. Let's go back and sit down."

His hand was shaking, which told me he was nervous or possibly afraid. Glancing over my shoulder at Alex, all three of us walked back into the dining room and resumed dinner.

Markos was sipping his wine again while laughing with Renzo and Benni. Adrian's hand moved to my thigh, where my gun used to be before Markos had kindly requested I leave it behind. I wouldn't have, but he used the excuse that I had already threatened him by pointing it at his head.

Reluctantly, I had relinquished it.

Guns were not the only way I knew how to defend myself, but something was digging in the back of my mind that there was more to this sudden appearance of Markos. While Alex might be right about the plan to eradicate my family, I had to think there was something deeper going on here. Why else go through this ruse and not just put a bullet in my head? Adrian knew where my father lived; it wasn't like he couldn't just dump my body on their doorstep.

"I wanted to give you an engagement present," Markos said, pinning both me and Adrian with a heartfelt stare.

"You know you don't need—" Adrian started.

Markos waved his hand. "Nonsense, it's my pleasure to gift something to my sons, and by extension, their new partners."

My blood froze in my veins as I heard footsteps in the hall.

"Years ago, I actually ran within the same circle as your parents, Presley. I had the pleasure of meeting your mother and your father. In fact, I was very close to your mother for a short time."

He was lying. My mother would have cut his dick off before getting close to him.

"There was someone back then that stood in the way of your mother's happiness, Presley. Someone who was nearly responsible for her downfall. I've kept tabs on this person for years, and I'm happy to say that I have finally managed to bring him to justice, and my gift to you is that you'll get the honors of dispatching him."

What the actual fuck?

Before I could say anything, there were sounds of a struggle in the hall, and two bulky men were dragging someone in, so their feet were scuffing the floor. A man in his late sixties was tossed on the table, over all the glassware and food. His groan of pain and outrage echoed around the room. It made me jump from my seat briskly, just like Adrian and Alex had.

"Please. Take your seats," Markos requested, with a wave of his hand.

Adrian helped me back into my seat, but I didn't scoot near the table. This entire situation was weird. The man wore a simple white t-shirt and flannel pajama pants. His hair was thinning so much, he was nearly bald.

His blue eyes landed on me, and immediately his brows lifted to his hairline.

"Rylie?"

I had no idea who this man was, but he knew my mom...

I shook my head to answer the man, and then Markos loaded a pistol across the room before walking over to me.

A singular bullet.

"Do you know who this man is?"

"Markos," Adrian warned.

Markos ignored him and took a few steps around the table. There was glass that had punctured the man's skin. Blood was seeping onto the tablecloth, but the man didn't seem to even register that he'd been hurt other than emanating a few groans.

"Rylie," he moaned in pain.

My stomach flipped as panic set in. Alex gripped the silver butter knife that had been discarded on the table. She glanced around to ensure no one saw her lowering it to her side but she didn't have to worry because everyone's gaze was locked on me for some reason.

"Who is he?" I asked.

Markos tilted his head. "You don't know?"

The man on the table moaned in pain again, but I studied his face, seeing a similar nose and forehead to my mother's. He'd said her name...surely this wasn't her father.

"Is this..." No.

She hadn't ever told me about him...there was supposedly some attempt that he'd made to reach out after I was born, but we were traveling a lot. I didn't know if it was because we were in hiding for so long or if it had something to do with him, but I knew Mom and him were estranged.

"This is your grandfather," Markos remarked.

Benni picked up a glass of wine that hadn't been smashed and tossed it in my grandfather's face. "He's also a dirty, rotten Fed."

My grandfather was FBI? Well, that sort of explained a lot, but why didn't my mom ever tell me anything about him?

"You really didn't know?" Markos asked.

"I've never met him before."

My focus was still on my grandfather, now soaked with wine and bleeding from the glass. I tried to summon some sympathy for him, to care that my blood relation was on the table, bleeding out, but the only person in the room I was worried about was Alex.

"Prove it." I heard the sound of a gun being cocked, and then the cold, metal silver pistol was set on the table next to me. "Shoot him in the head."

My glare snapped up to Adrian's adoptive father. "What?"

"This is your gift. Your grandfather never left the bureau. I was going to kill him myself or allow Benni and Renzo to have their fun, but I figured as his granddaughter you'd prefer to extend more of a merciful kill."

No. I didn't know him, but he was my family.

"Markos, stop this," Adrian seethed.

So, my fiancé wasn't in on whatever this plot was, that or he just didn't like it.

Markos's mouth twitched as he met Adrian's gaze, but he didn't waver.

"Take the gun and shoot your grandfather in the head."

"Where is Rylie? Please, I want to see her, you said I could see her
—" My grandfather began thrashing and screaming, but Benni
stepped closer and placed a cloth napkin in his mouth.

Adrian began yelling at Markos in Italian. I caught pieces of it.

Outrageous. We just got engaged. Why are you doing this?

Stop this now.

I could only stare into the eyes that I'd more than likely inherited.
Blue like the ocean. Blue like my mother. *Blue like her father.*

"Is this not a gift?" Markos barked in response to Adrian.

The two continued to argue while my grandfather gaped at me.
Tears leaked down the side of his face, and his thrashing around had
resulted in even more cuts from the glass. The more they argued, the
longer this man was stuck inside this agony. There was no way out
for him, and perhaps that was the message Markos wanted to send
me. He could get to my family and even force me to harm them, and
he'd leave me with no other choice because if I used the gun on
Markos, I knew someone in the room would kill Alex.

I was stuck, and this man, who was related to me, was trapped
here, at my mercy.

Standing from the table, I leaned closer and stroked my fingers
through my grandfather's thinning hair. "Shhhh."

There was no exit strategy for me. If I didn't do this, then they
would torture him, and for whatever reason, I couldn't stand the
idea of him being harmed in such a way.

"I'll do it."

Adrian paused his rant that had increased in volume. Markos
continued to glare at Adrian as if he were angry and disappointed
that one of his adopted prodigies would go against him. With the
cool steel in my hand, I wrapped my finger around the trigger.

"Pres," Alex whispered from across the table.

Adrian's warm hands found my face as he turned me away from
the sight of my grandfather lying there. "You don't have to do this.
I'll fix this."

I was moved by the redness in his eyes and the way his hands shook. This upset him, greatly. Even if he knew I wasn't desensitized to this world. To the harsh reality of being among men like Adrian and his brothers, it still bothered him. Something in my chest melted a tiny bit more for this man I was bound to marry. While he didn't have my entire heart, he had my loyalty. I slid my palm against his cheek and muttered, "I can't stand the idea of him being tortured. Let me end this for him."

Adrian's eyes moved across my face in panic. "I didn't know."

I believed him.

Pulling away from Adrian's hold, I stood at the edge of the table and stared down at the man crying there.

"What's his name?" I gently pulled the cloth out of my grandfather's mouth and then brushed his hair back. He continued to silently cry.

"Paul," Markos replied coldly.

"Hello, Paul. I'm Presley, your granddaughter. I don't know why I never met you, or why I never heard anything about you, but you should know that my mother is healthy and happy. I'm their only child, and I'm sorry that you have to die. I'm sorry that this is the beginning and end of our relationship."

Paul waved me closer while his breathing began to become labored.

Leaning in, I heard him whisper, "I have stage four cancer. I only have a few months left to live anyway. Please don't feel any guilt over this kill."

"Enough!" Markos yelled.

I stroked his forehead one last time before pressing the barrel of the gun between his eyebrows, and then I pulled the trigger.

CHAPTER 9

PRESLEY

"We're leaving."

Adrian's voice boomed throughout the room, causing Renzo and Benni to look at us. I stood immediately and reached for my fiancé, allowing him to pull me to his side. He then walked around the table and gestured for Alex to join us.

"I arranged for you to stay here tonight, Son," Markos remarked blandly while putting his phone to his ear. He spoke in Italian for someone to come clean up the mess in the dining room.

I refused to look at Paul. I had set the gun down next to his body as the blood from his head leaked over the table and dripped to the floor. Which is why I was so grateful for Adrian's declaration of our departure.

"No. We're leaving. Now."

Alex moved directly next to me, crowding my shoulder. It took all of my strength not to hold her hand and ensure we didn't get separated again.

"Surely allow Alexandria to remain here, her things are in her room, and she hasn't had a chance to pack," Markos replied, flicking a quick glance at Renzo and Benni.

Alex spoke up, boldly and clearly. "Thank you so much, Markos. I'd like to be with my sister."

A tremble worked through me at her declaration and claim on me. My fingers threaded through hers, silently telling her that I too, considered her my sister. My family. I'd do anything to protect her, even if that meant going home and facing all that had destroyed me.

"We're going, Father. You cannot expect me to stay after what you just pulled."

Markos smiled while spreading his hands wide. "My gift?"

"Fuck off," Adrian scoffed, while pulling me behind him toward the door. I held on to Alex for dear life as we exited the house. Benni and Renzo remained in their father's house, and I preferred that, especially after they'd tossed wine in my grandfather's face. The anger of the incident hadn't settled into my bones yet, but once it did, I was going to enact a little vengeance.

Adrian immediately settled into the driver's seat while I got into the back with Alex. We huddled together while the car sped out of the driveway, kicking up gravel behind it. I didn't look behind me to see if any lights followed us, but Adrian quickly pulled his cell up and began ordering his men to follow him.

"I'm so sorry, Presley. I—" His voice cut off with emotion before he slammed his palm against the steering wheel. "Fuck, this was never supposed to happen."

"What was supposed to happen?" I asked.

His eyes caught mine in the mirror, but he didn't respond. Within half an hour, we were driving through his gate and surrounded by armed men.

"This is his home?" Alex whispered while glancing out the window. It was too dark to make anything out other than the armed men and a few gas lanterns lit outside the home.

"Yeah, it's safe." I tried to reassure her, but I didn't actually know if it was or not.

Adrian parked and immediately exited the car. He started ordering his men to take up posts and positions around the perimeter. As Alex and I exited the car, I caught a few pieces of Italian where he mentioned Markos and his brothers. He didn't want them to be granted access without Adrian being notified.

"Come." Adrian walked ahead of us and waved us inside. The lights of his home immediately welcomed us with soft lighting, and a warm fire that his staff had already lit for when we'd arrive.

"Alex can have your room if you're comfortable with that, Presley," Adrian offered.

I gently gripped his wrist. "I don't want Renzo or Benni here until Alex leaves."

He didn't even hesitate before agreeing. "Understood."

I was about to walk past him when his hand came to my hip. "I understand your need to settle your friend in, but please come back to me tonight. I think we need to talk."

Yeah, we had a lot of things to talk about. I nodded solemnly before walking up with Alex toward the guest suites where my old room resided. There were no guards on this floor, and I appreciated that. I didn't want Alex to feel like she was trapped or being held hostage like at Markos's house.

The second we entered the room, Alex pulled her cell out and began dialing. She paced the room while she waited for the phone to connect, and I immediately went to the closet where I had hidden a few weapons.

"Dad. I'm okay." I heard her rushed words, on the verge of panic. I pictured Juan's face and how he'd probably pulled Taylor over so they could both hear what was happening with their daughter. Thinking of them, however, made my mind wander to the twins, and a sharp pain pierced my chest just like it always did.

The words they'd said in that room after they'd taken my virginity. After they'd taken something so precious and all so that Adrian wouldn't have it. How they'd pulled a gun on Scotty when they said we'd have to choose where we stood.

"Can you tell them not to come. I mean it. Presley and I will figure this out, but if you or anyone comes, it could make things worse. Just lay low and let me be here for Presley." I heard Alex say to someone on the phone.

I paused mid-pull as I removed the box that had two handguns inside.

"I mean it, Gio. Please do not come here."

I slammed my eyes closed and continued to pull on the box until I had it out and was checking the two guns inside. I heard Alex say her goodbyes, and then it was quiet again.

"Here." I handed her a pistol. "Keep this on you. There's pepper spray in here and a knife."

Alex glanced down at the weapon and gently set it on the bed. "I didn't sleep at Markos's house aside from maybe nodding off."

"When did you arrive?" It had to have only been a day or so.

She toyed with the edge of the comforter on the bed and yawned. "A week."

I swung around, my mouth agape. "A week?!"

She nodded. "I was so scared, Pres. I kept thinking that it would lead me to you, but then another day would pass. I was trying to plan my escape, but I knew it was going to take some time."

Silence stretched between us while I bit down on my tongue. I was so angry.

How had I allowed this to happen? The twins had warned me, and I went with Adrian anyway, and now their sister was—

"Stop blaming yourself. I know you're doing it," she joked, light heartedly.

Tears burned the backs of my eyes as I moved to the dresser and pulled out a few clothes I still had. Alex was taller than me, but I had shorts she could wear and a few baggy T-shirts. Most of which were her brothers at one point, but I wasn't going to mention that or say anything about it. I doubted she would either.

"Here's some clothes. The bathtub in there is divine, and after you're done, I can talk to Leon, Adrian's chef. He makes the best food, and he's so sweet. I can have an entire meal sent up to you so you don't have to leave the room if you want."

Alex nodded and then pulled me into a tight hug. "I'm serious, Pres. Stop blaming yourself."

"How?" I choked out. "How do I not blame myself? This is exactly what they warned me would happen."

Alex pulled back and swiped at my tears. "Adrian didn't even seem to know it was going to happen, so I'm not sure my brothers had the whole story. Also, at what point were you going to tell me that things between you and my brothers got romantic?"

My face flushed so pink that I had to take a few steps away.

"I mean, I always had a sneaking suspicion that you had a crush and I knew at least one of my brothers liked you, if not both, but I never assumed—"

"It was complicated," I blurted, mortified. "It started when I went to high school, and I just wanted a few typical experiences. I didn't know the twins would refuse to allow just one of them to—"

"Oh my god, stop. I'm okay without knowing all the details. I just wish I would have known that your heart was broken beyond just the best friend left behind. I would have tried to be there for you a bit more, that or I would have gone to hunt down my idiot brothers."

I sat on the bed, letting out a sigh I felt like I had been holding since that fateful night when I was sixteen. "Your parents knew."

Her head snapped to the side, inspecting me. "They did?"

"I overheard them talking the day of the twins' eighteenth birthday. I think they got sent away because I refused to train anymore...they hated that I was training so hard and for this future." I let out a pathetic laugh.

"A lot of good any of that training did me. Scotty never told me what to do if my enemy had a family member on the table while worrying about protecting another."

Her fingers came around mine in a tight squeeze. "I'm sorry you had to do that tonight, Pres. I'm sorry if me coming here has made things harder."

"No." I shook my head. "I'm glad you're here. More than you probably know. I've missed you."

Alex began wandering around the room, touching little trinkets and necklaces. "Christmas felt weird this year. Do you remember when we used to do those tree decorating contests?"

A laugh bubbled up out of me as I took a seat on the edge of the bed. "Gio and Kingston always tried to win by teaming up."

Alex smiled as she turned toward me and took a seat next to me. "So me, you, and Carter would team up to beat them."

"They used to get so upset when our parents would come out and judge the different trees." I laughed.

Alex covered her mouth as more laughter spilled out. "Gio learned how to tie bows just so he'd have a chance at winning."

Our joy sobered as we both quieted and I asked. "What was this year like?"

I had spent every waking moment thinking of them as my family traveled abroad. I had traveled with Adrian to spend the holiday with them in London. It helped take the sting out of being away from everyone, but my mind had lingered on Alex and her brother's. Carter too, and everyone else.

Alex shrugged. "We went down to Mexico. Wren and Archer, and the boys came too. It was fun, but it felt different. Like we were missing something."

Yeah, I knew the feeling.

I hesitated with my question but asked. "Your brothers went?"

Alex nodded silently. "They were there, but they were really reserved and quiet. The only time they'd light up or act normal was if they were around my aunt Wren's kids. It's crazy how long ago that felt, but it was only a month. It's partly why I had agreed to come, Pres."

She leveled me with a solemn glare. "You're the missing piece. I can't bring myself to accept that you're marrying Adrian, or that you'll be here in Italy so far from me. You're not just like my sister,

Pres. You are my sister. Through and through. You're my family, and deep in my gut, I don't think you're safe here."

She was right, and I felt it too, especially after tonight. Instead of confirming all that, I pulled her into a tight hug. "You're my family too. I'm so glad you're here, Alex."

I needed to talk to Adrian and begin to sort out the mess that I had willingly stepped into.

Pulling apart, I said. "Text me if you need anything. Adrian's room is on the third floor, last door on the right. Feel free to come and go as you want; his men won't stop you or say anything. His staff is kind, and they're good people."

Alex nodded before tugging the pile of clothes into her hand that I had given her. I exited the room and pulled the door closed before releasing a pent-up breath.

She was safe.

That was all that mattered at the moment. Now I had to figure out how to get her home.

I SHUT the door behind me as I entered Adrian's bedroom.

The lights were low, and there in the center of the bed sat Adrian with his head hanging in his hands. His tie was undone, his jacket crumpled on the floor and his hair looked like he'd been running his fingers through it possibly since we arrived.

"Hey."

His head popped up, surprise forcing his brows to his forehead. "Presley."

Did he not think I'd come back? "Of course it's me."

I smiled at him as I drew closer, all the while I slipped out of my heels and pressed my toes into his plush rug. The doors to the balcony were wide open, letting the night breeze into the room to caress us.

Adrian's gaze seemed to move over every inch of me as if he was worried I'd just slip away at any second or disappear.

"I didn't think you'd come. I honestly assumed you'd stay with Alex."

I sat next to him and pulled his hand into mine, stroking down the length of his palm like he'd done with mine during dinner. I hadn't realized how much it had quelled my anxiety.

"I wanted to come here. I think I'm used to sleeping next to you now." I smiled again, but the look of utter adoration on his face had my eyes transfixed on his mouth. I had been holding off being intimate with him for so long, and deep down, I knew that reason was attached to the twins. I knew I was subconsciously holding out some hope that they'd undo this damage that had been inflicted on my heart. But there was no rescuing what we were or salvaging it.

"I'm so sorry, *Bellissima*, I had no idea." Adrian choked on his words, making room for a sob before he lowered his head to my lap and hugged my middle. "I'm so fucking sorry."

Stroking my fingers through his hair, I tried to calm him by muttering soothing sounds. I knew now that the twins had been right about Adrian's connection to Markos, and about his brothers. I knew Adrian had lied to me. However, he'd also gained my patience and my trust. I didn't know why or how to explain it, but, in my gut, I didn't think Adrian was going to follow through with whatever plan his brothers had orchestrated. I needed more intel; that much was clear, but pushing him away wouldn't do anything but make me miserable.

Not when I was finally ready to have him remove the stain the twins had branded me with. The pain they'd allowed to fester in my soul and rot.

I wanted something new, and I wanted Adrian to be the one to have it with.

"Adrian, I need to know that Alex is safe here." I pulled his face closer so our lips were just inches apart.

His blue eyes searched mine. "Of course she is."

"Markos won't be able to show up and take her, or me?"

His hand pulled mine until it covered his heart. "I swear it to you. No harm will come to either of you. I know I fucked all this up. I know I owe you a conversation. I know...just please don't leave me, Presley. At least not without first letting me explain a small piece of this."

He moved with me until he was in front of me, looking down. His fingers gently held my chin until he was tipping my head back. "I'm in love with you. When we talked about all these plans, all the shit my brothers planned and Markos, I didn't think I'd care because I didn't think you'd matter to me. Then I saw you at that ball, and then I met you, and from the beginning I knew you were mine and that we could figure everything else out as long as that part were true."

His palm slid over my jaw until his fingers were pushing into my hair. "Do you trust me?"

I didn't hesitate. "I do."

His hand found mine, and he gently pulled me up until I was standing in front of him.

"Then let me have you, my love. Be with me, become mine finally."

Our mouths crashed together in a rush. His hands clasped my waist in a tight hold while mine went to his shirt buttons, where I began pulling them apart, yanking the fabric free from his slacks and off his body. His undershirt went next, then his belt.

Heated lips found the pulse in my neck while he kissed and sucked against my skin, and I undid his pants, pushing them down. He was a gorgeous specimen of perfection, with slick lines of muscle and rippled abs stacked on top of one another. I continued to kiss him until he'd stripped me out of my clothing, and he helped me to the bed.

"I've wanted this for so long," he whispered, pressing fevered kisses to my cheek and neck.

My eyes closed as flashes of raven-like hair slipped through my fingers, two sets of lips caressed my skin, and desperate words of need and desire had washed over me. I forced my eyes open to stay in the moment with Adrian and not go back to them.

"Adrian," I rasped while he leaned over me and lined his rigid cock up with my center. I lifted my leg until he hooked his hand under my calf and stared down at my slick entrance.

"You sure?"

I nodded, and within the span of a single breath, he pushed inside me. I could hear the waves crash against the cliffs outside the balcony, and the stars gleaming in the velvet sky seemed to wink a little brighter as if they were merely an old friend hanging above to say hello.

Pushing my fingers into Adrian's hair, I crossed my feet behind his back, taking him deeper.

"Oh fuck," he breathed, while leaning down to take my nipple into his mouth. His hips rocked forward, his cock sliding in and out of me. I turned my head while our chests heaved, and he increased the speed in which he fucked me. The bed shifted, and the sound of skin slapping filled the room.

I would force myself to love this version of reality. Being with one man.

One heart instead of two that wanted to hold mine.

It had to be enough.

My eyes were closed when Adrian came, and when he asked near my ear if I came too, I lied, and whether he knew it or not, he didn't press me. He was certainly capable of bringing me to climax, but I knew that my mind was too muddled to allow it. Too confused about what was happening. All I knew was that I had to get Alex out of here.

Once Adrian was finished and he'd cleaned up in the bathroom, he brought me a warm rag and began cleaning me. It was gentle and soft and so unlike when the twins had taken me, only to discard me immediately after.

"What's wrong, *Bellissima*?"

I kept my eyes lowered as I tried to hide the various emotions at war in my chest. Instead of telling him that I was reliving what the twins had done to me, and there was still shrapnel in my chest from how they'd ruined sex for me, I tried to focus on something else.

"I want to get Alex home, but I don't know how. I'm worried that your brothers will stop her, or Markos will interfere. I want to go with her, just so I can make sure she actually gets there. I won't be able to relax until she's home."

Adrian pushed a few strands of hair away from my face while he inspected me. I was taking advantage of him in a way because I knew he felt guilty for whatever had been sprung on me tonight, but I didn't care. Not when it meant Alex could go home.

He finally pressed his forehead to mine and replied, "I'll find a way. I promise you."

CHAPTER 10

KINGSTON

Fuck, no one ever told me picking paint colors would be so difficult.

Gray seemed like the safest choice, but would Presley want a cloudy color? She should be here to tell me exactly which colors she wanted. Honestly, she should have been here to see the house completely gutted and finally cleared of all the rotted, moldy wood. She should have seen what it looked like when the framing went up and the new rooms were created.

Eleven months had passed since Presley left, and two since Alex went to help her. I'd been going insane nearly every single day, hoping for word that everything was okay or that they were coming back. Yet, when I reached out to my sister, the only thing she'd tell me was that Presley was working on it and that they were safe.

From what I could gather, my sister enjoyed being there with Pres. She seemed to genuinely want to help her, but the stress and anxiety it was creating was enough that I wasn't sleeping and instead, I'd been pouring every free moment I had into the farm-house. Gio had taken over the role with El Peligro, but thanks to Alex, we didn't need to look for Markos any longer. She'd told us he was there, but that it would be too dangerous to go after him until she and Presley were safely removed from the area.

She convinced us to stay put. While Gio and I both wanted to jump in and make him pay, even our dad told us it was smarter to wait. So that's what we'd done.

It was getting closer to spring, and I was staring at a nearly completed house with walls in need of paint, rooms that needed doors, and floors that required finishing. If I could just decide on a color.

"Not gray, King." Gio suddenly appeared and tore down the sample I'd taped to the wall.

Feeling slightly embarrassed, I set the whole swatch down. "Why not?"

My brother drew closer, inspecting the various color choices.

"There's no way she'll ever go for it...she'll want teal or something vibrant."

I had thought that too, but the idea was based on when she was younger. I had no idea what she'd want now as an adult.

"Teal seems too bright..." I muttered, flipping through another few color samples.

"Dad was wondering if you'd join us for dinner tonight." Gio transitioned without looking up at me.

Our parents were holding off on leaving because of Alex. There was too much in the air until she was back. Dad had flown to Italy twice without actually getting close to where Alex and Presley were, simply because he knew it was dangerous. He was pacing the floors of our home, likely just as stressed if not more than we were. At least the farmhouse was keeping me busy; I had no idea what anyone else was doing to keep their minds off things.

I didn't particularly mind going to my parents; it's just that things were still a little awkward. But loneliness had been like a plague too, so perhaps it wouldn't be such a bad idea to go and get away from the farmhouse.

"Yeah, I'll go."

Gio's head lifted, and I caught the smallest flicker of surprise. "You think they'll be home in time for Presley's birthday?"

I didn't want to think about it.

"No clue."

Gio watched me carefully before moving through the house. He flipped on light switches and fans. He messed with the sink in the kitchen, turning on the water and opening all the cupboards. There were only a few since I selected floating shelves for most of the storage. With each room, his thick soled boots would echo over the floor.

"You're practically finished," he finally said, while running his hand along the completed banister.

"Yeah, I guess." I wasn't sure what to say. I knew this house would become Presley's one day, and that she'd finally accept my brother. The two of them would have a future...that was if we could get her away from Adrian and out of Italy. I just needed to get her here, and I knew she'd stay.

"Have you told Kyle or Rylie what you've done over here?" Gio asked.

His eyes were focused on the windows in the bedroom, and the built-in seat I had made directly underneath.

I shrugged. "No."

With a slight turn, he inspected me. "I think you should. I think this might mean a lot to them that you helped their daughter achieve something that was always so important to her."

I doubted it. Kyle and Rylie were not my biggest fan.

"How are things with El Peligro?" I asked while walking out of the house. We took the back door, which led us to a small patch of dead weeds that I'd need to tend to when I had the chance. I envisioned grass out here with a spacious patio, something that would allow Presley to relax while she watched the stars.

Gio fell into step next to me, but I didn't miss how he checked his phone before tucking it into his pocket. "Henry wants to mobilize the men, but there's no word from Alex yet, and I don't want to risk getting her or Presley hurt. He thinks we should move on from Markos and where his location is over there. Alex mentioned that they're in separate homes, but she doesn't have an exact address."

"So what does Henry think you should be focusing on then?"

My brother watched his feet. "There's a new seller for some new street drug down in Florida."

I shook my head, confused. "He's willing to start a turf war; there's about fifteen various gangs between here and Florida that would go to war over that."

"None with ties to the cartel, though. Henry wants to go and establish a presence."

I agreed that they shouldn't move on Markos just yet, but leaving didn't seem like the right move either. It was dangerous, and we didn't have enough intel yet to make a specific play. "Is Henry willing to listen and hold down the fort here, or is he pushing back?"

Gio ran his hand through his hair while we moved through the wet weeds scattered along the hillside. The weather was wet but not as cold as I had anticipated for the end of February. The year prior, it rained like crazy this time of year, but things were warmer than was typical for winter.

"Honestly, I'm not sure. They've been asking about you a lot. I think Henry is sensing a fracture in our leadership, and it's making him nervous. I have a feeling he'll try to test it by forcing us to go with him to Florida."

That wouldn't work. I shook my head while grabbing for my phone. I had a habit that I couldn't seem to break, which was always checking to see if Presley had finally unblocked me and needed help. "If he tries, then we just tell him no. We aren't leaving the area right now unless it's to track down Markos."

We were approaching the manor near the patio terrace for our family's wing. I could see the lights on in the kitchen, and a few lights above my garden flickered to life as the sun began to set. A tiny pinch echoed through my chest as I glanced at my forgotten patch of earth that once was so meaningful to me. The place that used to bring me peace and calm me. I suppose I now channeled that need to help something live into Presley's farmhouse.

Right as we neared the patio doors, someone appeared in our peripheral. Two smaller images at first and then the looming presence of my least favorite human being. Scotty approached with two of his dogs.

"Need to talk to you two."

Gio scoffed while pushing forward. "Pass."

I heard Scotty let out a frustrated sigh, but I followed my brother. Scotty drew closer as the shadows of twilight claimed the terrace. "It's about your sister and Presley."

Gio stopped, and I paused merely because I didn't want to leave him alone with Scotty. If he stabbed him again, his dogs would rip into my brother this time, and then I'd have to kill one, and that would eventually, undoubtedly piss Presley off.

"What about them?" Gio asked.

Scotty was just a few feet away from us when he brought his phone out and showed us the screen. It thankfully wasn't a FaceTime call, but it did show that Presley was on the phone.

"Pres, tell me that again," Scotty spoke close to the speaker.

Suddenly, Presley's voice echoed from his device, making my stomach drop out.

"Adrian has been trying to get Alex out for weeks. At first, it seemed like it would be easy...he called up his pilot and told him to get the plane ready, but within an hour, his pilot had called back, saying Markos had given him a direct order to stay grounded. After that, Adrian let things cool down for about a week, then tried again; this time, he used the excuse that we were going on a vacation, but the result was the same. Markos then took control of the town, all the shops, the cafés, and then his staff started rotating without his approval. We have no idea where these people were taken, or where they went. Adrian and I woke up, and there was suddenly a different person barging into our room first thing in the morning, serving us breakfast."

I felt my brother's gaze slide over to me, but I refused to look.

He'd see it in my eyes, the devastation and the guilt. The horror that I'd allowed her to slip through our fingers and land directly into Adrian's palm, and now Markos. They shared a room...they slept together at night.

Fuck. Why did this hurt so badly when I'd ultimately agreed to let her go?

"Has Markos been in Adrian's home?" Scotty asked.

"After the first few attempts to leave, he started showing up randomly. He's been careful about what he says or does around me, but his presence alone sets all of us on edge. After the dinner, where he made me—" She suddenly stopped talking, but my eyes were back on my brother.

"Made you what?" Gio practically growled.

Scotty glared at him as if he were about to hit him in the back of the head.

"Gio?" Presley's voice was soft but guarded.

He ignored her and stepped closer to the phone. "Markos made you do what?"

"Giovanni, Presley has limited time. This isn't catch up hour. I invited you two to be a part of this conversation because you need to know how to control your monster, El Peligro." Scotty chastised, then pushed on, "Presley, please continue."

She cleared her throat. "So, both of them are—they're both there?"

Scotty brought his finger to his forehead and began to rub as he replied, "Yes. They're standing right here listening. Now continue."

"I was forced to execute someone. Adrian was so angry and acted so erratic, I think it tipped Markos off. For the sake of Alex, I told him that I didn't want Markos or his brothers in the house. At first, he honored it, but yesterday he arrived and demanded to spend time with Alex."

She was forced to kill someone. Our Presley, the ball of sunshine that made our universe worth existing in. The girl who loved petting baby highland cows and restoring an old farm house, all so one day she'd find peace. The girl who loved stars and digging in the soil with me, the girl who had freckles, blue eyes, and felt like home.

I didn't trust Adrian to keep them safe. Not if Markos was now demanding shit of my sister and forcing executions. Gio's worried expression reminded me of my promise to let her go, so I made sure my response was focused in the right place.

I stepped closer to the phone. "Presley, I need to get my sister out of there. It's been two months. I'm done playing Adrian's games. I'm coming to get her, and if you're smart, you'll come with me as well."

"Kingston," Scotty warned, but I didn't give a fuck.

Presley's voice harshened as she replied, "You have no idea what Adrian has gone through to keep us safe, and to go against his brothers. He's doing the best he can."

I laughed. "Isn't he the entire reason you're there? I mean, sure, maybe he got a taste of your cunt, and he decided not to kill you, but make no mistake, he is the reason all this is happening."

"Fuck you!" she roared.

Scotty pressed a button, taking her off speaker phone.

Gio began pushing me away until I was heading toward the house. "What the hell, King, you heard what she's just been through."

I walked inside and slammed the door behind me because if I didn't, then I'd take a knife and jam it in the side of Scotty's head. This was his fucking fault, and I would never forgive him for doing this to her. If I were allowed to share how it impacted me to know that the girl I loved was broken in such a way, I would, but I promised Gio that she was his.

So, because of that, I'd continue being a miserable son of a bitch, no matter how much it hurt.

CHAPTER 11
PRESLEY

The balcony had become increasingly smaller since being trapped here for the past two months. I'd done everything in my power to push this singular thought out of my head, to see this any other way I possibly could, but Kingston was right.

For nearly two months, Adrian had seemingly tried to get us out of here, but he hadn't been successful. He used terminology that always made it seem as though things were right about to shift, with weeks or days, and yet months had passed. While Kingston's hurtful words echoed in my head, abrading my chest like tiny pricks of a needle, I pushed it away as I tried to focus on the point he was making.

Turning from the balcony, I stormed inside, seeing the bedroom empty as usual. Adrian had been so stressed recently that when he did come to bed, he was only there for mere hours before leaving again. We'd had a few nights a week that he'd hold me, fuck me, or taste me. Then he'd let me go and be off again, never telling me more than a few details at a time. I knew he couldn't share everything, and while I trusted him, I was starting to lose my patience.

Pulling out my phone, I sent him a text.

Me: Where are you, need to talk.

Adrian probably wouldn't see it for a while, so I set off to find Alex. I missed Leon and other members of the staff who used to be in the house. Now, I felt like I was walking on eggshells, being watched and monitored by every single person in the house. Markos had ordered the clean out, so all the people now milling about surely reported to him.

Alex was sitting outside by the pool, a book rested next to her while she stared at nothing with a sorrowful expression on her face. The sound of birds flitting in the surrounding trees filled the air as I walked out onto the paved terrace. Alex hadn't seen me yet, which allowed me a few extra moments to study her. Things shifted last night when Markos arrived and demanded to have dinner with her. I had wanted to kill him, but he'd brought too many men with him, and I refused to put Alex in danger.

So we sat through another dinner where we had to consider if we'd be forced to see someone executed or if something was going to happen to one of us. I hated the way the color had drained from her face and how terrified she looked as she stared out at the pool, seeing nothing.

I had to try and give her hope that we'd get out of here. I walked closer and got her attention. "Hey."

Her blue gaze snapped over, meeting mine. Her mouth tilted into a smile as she made room on her lounger for me. I slid onto the cushion and let out a heavy sigh.

"That bad, huh?" She laughed while reaching for her book.

I wanted to ask if she was okay, but I already knew the answer.

I placed my head on her shoulder and began to read over her shoulder. "I'm going to push Adrian to get us out of here, but it's hard to get him to just sit down long enough to have that conversation."

Alex made a humming sound. "You mean the conversation regarding his alliance and the farce that it was?"

My gut twisted into a knot. Yeah, that part.

"I know he deviated from some initial plan..." I started, but she stopped me with a shake of her head.

"Presley, you know better than that. Don't justify his behavior simply because he developed feelings for you."

"You sound like your brother," I mused with a sigh.

She glanced over at me, as if she were waiting for me to continue.

"Kingston said almost the same thing when I called last night. He still hates me, that much is clear."

Alex released her book, allowing it to drop to her lap, and grabbed my hand. "You've developed feelings for Adrian, right?"

Something like guilt twisted around in my chest, but I lifted my chin and owned it, meeting her intense stare. "I have."

"Then why do you care if King hates you or not?" Her brow raised in challenge.

"I don't."

I did, though, and I knew I needed to get a handle on why it mattered so much. The fact that both brothers hated me enough to steal my virginity only to use that against Adrian would be enough to sever our ties forever. It didn't matter what they thought of me.

A ping sounded from my phone, making me look down.

Adrian: Just pulling up now

Sliding out of the lounger, I glanced down at Alex and reached for her hand. "He's here. I need to go see what I can do. But I promise you, if he keeps putting this off, we're going to scale those damn cliffs, I don't care. We're getting out of here."

She laughed as I walked away, but I was serious.

I was done being here.

ADRIAN WALKED into the bedroom with the grace of a ruling monarch, but the bags under his eyes looked as though he carried the same weight as one. He wore a navy-blue suit with a wrinkled white shirt buttoned beneath it. His brown shoes were scuffed and even had a few dark, mysterious blotches on them.

"What's wrong?" I asked, moving from the bed.

He began taking off his jacket and cuff links, but didn't reply. I tried not to take it personally, but it stung. I waited for him to remove his dress shirt and shoes, until he was just in his slacks.

"Adrian."

Finally, he turned to me with those ocean eyes that matched the waves currently crashing against the cliffs below. "I know what you want from me..." He ran his fingers through his hair and let out a heavy sigh. "I've been trying to push things off because I don't know how to—"

His voice cracked, and the vulnerability in his expression had me moving closer. I was in his arms with his mouth at my ear, his fingers trailing through the curls in my hair. "You used to wear this in a crown, always braided...these past few months it's been down. You're nearly nineteen now. I had this idea for your birthday..."

I smiled into his chest, but his severe sigh returned, and he pulled back.

"I know you need to know all of it, from the start. I'm going to tell you, and then I'm going to find a way to get you home. I promise."

He pressed a kiss to the corner of my eye ever so gently, and then he sat down on the edge of the bed, and I sat across from him on the small, tufted stool.

"My father was Lucian Adesso. He was the leader of a smaller mafia outfit here in Italy. His best friend was Markos. While their history is a little exhaustive, the important part is that my brothers and I grew up knowing Markos as our godfather. He was always around, every birthday, every Christmas...he was there. When I was seven, Renzo was ten and Benni was twelve...our dad had been flying to New York more often. Markos would watch over us anytime he'd go, except for this one time. Dad left again on urgent business; there was this man who was making things difficult for his business partners. He needed to organize the muscle or something, but Markos was worried about him, so he chartered a flight and took all of us with him."

Something told me this was going to make me cry. My fingers dug into the fabric underneath me and tried to balance my breathing.

"We arrived in New York, and Markos immediately had us pile into a big SUV. I remember wondering if the television screens worked that were in the back of the headrests. I was so focused on the screen and whether I could find any movies in the car that I missed Benni screaming how he'd spotted our dad. We were pulling up to a restaurant where he was supposed to be meeting his men, but when I looked out the window, Dad wasn't paying attention to us. The moment he realized we had arrived, he ignored whoever he'd been talking to. Instead, he started toward our car, turning his back on the shadows..." His voice trailed off right as my heart continued to bang against my rib cage.

I pictured small Adrian, just like me at that age, and how we'd both been so vulnerable and so scared. I didn't even need to hear him say what happened next; I already knew. Someone had killed his father right in front of his three sons and best friend.

"A man came out of the shadows, he killed my father so fast, it was impossible for Markos to even open his door to get to him. One second, our dad was smiling, walking toward us, and the next, his eyes were too wide and then..." His voice cracked, and I rushed forward, crowding the space by his knees.

"Adrian."

He shook his head, a smile lingering on his lips, but a few tears fell from his lashes. "Markos was so shocked, he didn't even tell us to stay back. All three of us boys ran to our dad. We held his hand while he slipped away. Markos cried, and I remember he didn't even look to see who had done it, as if he knew. Later, when we asked how we'd find who killed him, he explained that he knew who had done it. Then he showed us this playing card, the only thing on it was, The Joker."

My father? No, that couldn't be right.

"Adrian." I wanted to be sensitive, but there just wasn't any way my father could have been the one to kill his.

His hand came to my hair as he began soothing me. "Shhh, it's okay. I don't blame you for your father's sin...although that was the plan."

I sat back on my heels and watched as new emotions worked his features. Agony, guilt...pain.

Tilting my head the slightest bit, I asked, "What exactly was the plan?"

Adrian stroked along my jaw while letting a few more tears slip off his lashes. "I wasn't lying when I said I saw you for the first time at that ball. You were sixteen, I was eighteen, and I knew at that time exactly who your father was, and when my brothers saw that you were present, we began to develop a plan. Your cousin falling in with the Ferro family was just a lucky coincidence for us. It pushed Scotty to start poking around a few of his old allies. Except that's where he went wrong. From the time your father killed mine, Markos had been slowly buying out all of Scotty's old contacts. He was meticulous in finding each and every one. Someone planted the suggestion that Scotty look into me. That I might be a blank slate when it came to choosing sides. We erased every single trace that Markos was connected to me, and then we erased my brothers' connection as well, until all that was left was an opportunity to lure you in."

Just another man who saw me as disposable. An opportunity for revenge, and fuck, he wasn't even right about his vengeance in this case. I tried not to react, so I could hear the rest, but anger stirred so strongly in my chest that I moved out of his space and began to pace.

"Go on," I encouraged.

Adrian's eyes shifted to the balcony, as his Adam's apple bobbed. "The plan was to get you to trust me. Then to eventually fall for me, so you'd agree to marry me. I was told to do whatever it took, be as convincing as possible."

"Then what?" I asked, needing to just finish this.

"Then once we married, we'd force you to carry out the hits on your family."

I lost it and began laughing. He immediately rose and came for me, clasping my arms. "Presley, please."

His tone bordered on panic, but I continued to laugh until I began to cry. "What was to come of me once I dispatched my family?"

"Pres—" He tried to cut in.

I stepped away. "Just tell me."

Another brief silence passed before he replied. "I was going to have the choice of keeping you or letting Markos find someone who wanted you. But, Presley, let me explain why I couldn't go through with it. I didn't—"

"Just tell me what Markos thinks is going to happen now. We've been here for two months, and at this point, it feels like we're being abducted. Have you kidnapped us, or am I free to go?"

"Please, just let me explain why I haven't let you go. I just...I know that I had to explain this to you, and I know that now you know, you'll go and you won't come back and I'll lose you, and I can't —I can't lose you."

I wasn't even sure how to respond, so I rubbed the stress out of my forehead. "So you've kept me here because you've been trying to figure out a way to explain all this to me in a way that would make it so I wouldn't leave?"

"It's more complicated than that. Markos has to think we're following the plan, or else he has a fail-safe set up that will kick in if he thinks I'm going off script. He's already suspicious because of how I acted that night at dinner, and how protective I've been of you since. He keeps trying to push up our wedding date."

"Well, there's not going to be a wedding, Adrian. I'm going home. If you don't allow me to, then I'll scale those cliffs myself. I will become the weapon my father raised me to be, and I'll die ensuring Alex gets out."

Adrian walked closer, tentative and cautious. "I know, Presley. I know you will. I don't deserve your forgiveness, Presley, but you have to understand that it may have started disingenuous, but it changed. I changed. This is real. If you don't want to marry me, then that's fine, we don't have to, but don't leave me. Let me fix this."

"Adrian." I sighed, wiping under my eyes. "I'm going home."

His hands came to my face, gently but securely. His eyes were wide and frenzied as he asked, "Why? I know you care for me; you even almost love me. Why can't we work this out?"

My chest was tight, my instincts about to kick in to physically hurt him, although I didn't want to. Even after everything, I couldn't bring myself to harm him. Instead, I pushed against his chest and explained very simply.

"Because my father didn't kill yours. You blamed the wrong man and punished me for it."

His eyes narrowed in confusion. "What do you mean?"

I eyed the balcony as an escape route. "The twins tried to warn us about you and your brothers. They mentioned the name Lucian Adesso in front of my father and my uncle. Neither of them would have allowed me to enter into this alliance if they knew that your father was someone mine had killed years ago. They would have known, even with you erasing your ties, the name Adesso. I'm telling you, it wasn't my father."

Adrian stepped away this time, creating distance between us. Then, with a scoff, he shook his head. "You're wrong."

"I'm not. But it doesn't matter. I want out of here, Adrian. If you have feelings for me the way you say you do, then get me home."

"Presley." Adrian ran his hand through his hair.

I walked over to the table that Adrian and I had shared a thousand breakfasts. Moments of intimacy where he'd bring me to orgasm. Moments that made me wonder if perhaps I could be happy with him and fall in love with him. For a moment, I glared down at the oak surface and resented how it hadn't changed while everything else seemingly had.

I didn't want to hurt him, but if he—

"Of course I'll get you home, it's what I promised you. Regardless of what happened or why, I do love you, Presley. I fear I'd do just about anything for you, including defy Markos."

My heart squeezed with relief and softened the smallest amount. We stared at one another until Adrian pulled his cell out and began dialing.

"I'll find a way to fix this and then, I promise you, I will find a way to win you back."

CHAPTER 12
GIO

Kingston didn't know I had started sneaking up here at night.

Honestly, I didn't know if he'd even care that I was...he said this was supposed to be for me and Elvis, once she returned. I went along with my brother's bullshit ideas and justifications for pouring all his time and energy into this house, but I didn't buy it.

I didn't think he'd be able to walk away from Presley or this house once she came back. It was just a matter of time before all this blew up again, and if Adrian was still in the picture, then we didn't stand a chance. She's already chosen him. If she somehow came home with our sister, and decided to stay, then I'd let her have this house without the expectation of staying in it with her. Presley deserved to be free of us once and for all, and while Kingston was trying to be noble, it was a wasted effort.

I toyed with the teal hair tie that was still around my wrist and looked out the window, seeing little to no stars. There were too many clouds that had begun moving in; we were supposed to get more rain, and based off what I overheard, it was going to mess all of

Kingston's shit up because he had painters coming to finalize the outside color.

I didn't personally think that Presley would give a flying fuck that Kingston had fixed up the house for her. The second she arrived home, she'd still be pissed at us. It would take a lot of coaxing and convincing to bring her out of her rage bubble. She was hurt, and the only way to undo that would be with slow and measured actions, like with a wounded animal. You couldn't show up with a house for said creature and expect they'd accept the shelter.

My phone vibrated on the window seat next to me with a text. I picked it up and saw a text from Presley. Which meant she'd unblocked me. Hope filled my lungs like fresh oxygen at what this could mean, and what I'd say to her, but then I began reading.

Presley: You're a son of a bitch for saying that.

What was she talking about? I held my phone as my brows caved in, curious and confused, until another text came in.

Kingston: For speaking the truth? You're upset that you didn't listen to me and then got fucked over? If that makes me a son of a bitch, then fine.

Presley: We used to be friends. Do you even remember that?

She'd managed to unblock both of us, but had somehow selected an old group chat thread to text Kingston in. *Did she even mean to unblock me?*

Kingston: We used to be so much fucking more than that and you know it.

It was starting to become more obvious they hadn't meant to add me into this conversation but I didn't stop reading, even if they weren't including me, or had been talking privately, I just kept reading.

Presley: Yes, and you decided that didn't matter either.

Kingston: You didn't decide it mattered to you until it suited you.

Presley: I'm not doing this again with you.

My heart had started to race the more of their exchange I watched. Why did this feel so intimate?

Kingston: Then why did you text me out of the blue, why not text Gio? Why is it me that's on your mind when you're in bed with Adrian?

Fuck, now I felt like my chest was open and they were just being dicks about pouring in the gasoline, and irresponsible with the matches.

Presley: I'm not as angry with Gio as I am you because he didn't say shit that was insensitive and rude.

Somehow, that didn't make me feel any better.

Kingston: Fine that's fair. He is the better brother but answer me. Why are you texting me while you're in bed with him.

Presley: ... why do you care either way?

She asked a good question. If Kingston had truly let her go, and no longer cared either way about her, then why was he baiting her? If anything, he should be kind, hoping to get her to stay when she came back. He was fucking it all up again, and he was doing it because he still cared. In fact, if I went back and looked at everything he'd done, it was clear that he cared too much. While I was hurt, I wasn't so hurt that I agreed to fucking her and then leaving her. I didn't agree to pulling our protection of her, or our friendship. It was something I knew with time we could likely work through, but not my brother.

He wanted to burn every memory, destroy every moment, and erase her.

I was still staring at my phone when a new alert came in.

Dad: Need you and your brother to come to the house asap.

Feeling petty and hurt, I decided to jump into the conversation.

Me: Sorry to break this little heart to heart up, but Kingston, dad needs us up at the house.

With one last glance up at the sky, a tender part of my chest throbbed, wishing for stars. For something that would help lead me back to the way things were before all of this.

It was late when I finally arrived in the family wing. Kingston was already there, sitting on the couch, legs propped up on the ottoman with his phone in his hand. His eyes traveled up to mine when I moved to the spot across from him.

"Hey, I'm sorry about the text thread." He cleared his throat while placing his feet on the floor.

I shrugged. I knew he wasn't over her. He was a liar, and it was better that I realized that now instead of when she got back.

"Gio, I am sorry. I didn't know—"

"Drop it. I don't fucking care," I snapped in return.

Dad walked out of the kitchen with a white ceramic mug filled with tea. He was shirtless and wearing his sweats when he settled in the chair across from us.

"Thank you both for coming so soon." His eyes bounced between us, like he knew we were in an argument.

King nodded while I just watched them both. I just wanted to know what the hell he needed, so I could go sort out all of the emotions I was feeling.

Dad sipped from his mug and then jumped into what happened. "I got a call this evening from Adrian Adesso. Seems he's desperate for help and is asking for us to step in and be the aid he needs to get the girls out."

I didn't look at my brother when I asked, "He can't just place them both on a jet and tell the pilot to come here?"

"Obviously not," Kingston snapped.

I glared over at him, but before I could reply, Dad cut in.

"Doesn't matter, and we're not arguing about it. Adrian needs to get them out, and he said his property is being watched like a hawk, all of his aircrafts and employees are under Markos's direction. There are too many soldiers to just simply have the two of you go in, even if Scotty and Kyle were to go with you."

"So what are you asking of us?" I asked.

Dad sipped from his mug again, then settled it on his knee. "This isn't easy for me to agree to, nor is it easy to ask. However, I'm not too proud to do whatever needs to be done for the sake of my daughter. I need your sister to be safe, so I'm asking you both to lead El Peligro to their doorstep and get her and Presley out."

Kingston slowly slid his gaze over to me, and while I didn't see any reaction there, I knew what he was thinking. So, I asked it.

"What if Presley doesn't want to leave?"

Dad set his mug to the side and brought his hands together. "Adrian was insistent that she'd be returning."

Probably to stay with Alex, or to touch base with Scotty. I had a feeling she'd want to come back with her, but this just confirmed it.

King's brow raised as he sat forward. "You're sure she'll leave with us?"

I replied arrogantly. "Why don't you just text her, Kingston?"

Dad let out a heavy sigh. "I honestly don't know, but based off what Adrian said, both girls will be ready to go, and from the severity of the situation, I don't think Presley will have preferences on who it is that picks her up. You can both stay behind and lead from a distance so you don't have to be around Presley if that's a concern of yours."

The only *concern* was that she might try and shoot us on sight.

"It'll be fine," I snapped, pulling my cell out. Henry would have to start mobilizing the guys tonight, so we could leave first thing in the morning.

"How do we communicate with Adrian regarding the pick up?" Kingston asked.

Dad pulled his phone out and examined the screen before shaking his head. "You don't. There's a location for you to go and a time frame in which to arrive, and that's all."

I scoffed, "You realize this could be a trap."

Dad's eyes burned under the lights, making his amber eyes glow. Sometimes I got jealous that he and Kingston looked so similar. I took more after my mother, with what felt like lighter skin compared to King, and lighter blue eyes, and even my hair didn't seem quite as dark as his. He was like a shadow, everything darker and colder.

"That's why you're going in with the army you built. This is exactly why you have it. A risk worth taking to get your sister out of there."

Kingston sighed heavily and slowly got to his feet. "When do we get to kill Scotty for sending her there to begin with?"

Dad didn't wince or flinch as he looked us both in the eye and replied, "As far as I'm concerned, I never heard you ask, and I have no information whatsoever on anything that might happen to him from here on out. Whatever I may have told you before regarding the rules of this manor and respecting his training guidelines, consider them gone. Scotty James is a threat to this family."

King and I both watched him as he left, and then our gazes locked on one another. I'd wanted to kill Scotty for a long fucking time, but my love for Presley had always stopped me. I wondered if King would still stand by that reason for not murdering her uncle or if he'd finally own up to the lie he'd been telling about how he's over her. This might prove to be a great way to test that theory.

CHAPTER 13

PRESLEY

Adrian kept looking over at me, as if he wanted to say something.

Ever since our little vent session, things between us were strained and awkward. I wanted to move into the room with Alex, but he reminded me that his entire staff was reporting to Markos. We were supposed to be planning a wedding, so sleeping apart wouldn't exactly fly.

I understood that Adrian felt as though he was justified in his vengeance, but he had so much time to come clean and tell me what had happened. Even during those months where I had been visiting him, and I had opened up to him, he hadn't. Even at the dinner, when I specifically asked about his brothers, he'd lied.

I was angry, and I was tired of men treating me like I was an optional tool to pick up and toss back into a drawer when it served them best. So, this morning, when he alerted me that we'd be venturing to the countryside for a picnic and that Alex was welcome to join us, I knew he meant that we'd finally found a way to get home. I packed only my cell, charger, and my gun into my purse, knowing everything else could be replaced. I just wanted to get Alex home.

We took the Range Rover, which put Adrian in the front, next to our driver, while Alex and I were in the back. After an hour of heading farther into the countryside, and away from civilization, I worried that Adrian might have been planning something else other than our freedom. My stomach flipped as I stared out the window at the passing vineyards and low- hanging trees, the green hills, and the cliffsides.

Adrian laughed with our driver about a soccer game and other sports, as if nothing were wrong. Alex tapped out a message on her arm for me to relax, which meant I was noticeably anxious. I decided to make a show of excitement for my engagement by swiping through pictures of my wedding dress with Alex. Ironically, before all this, I really was planning to marry Adrian. Themes had been picked, center piece ideas and even the cake had all been decided. While it made me sad, showing her how gorgeous the details of the dress were worked to take the edge off my stress, until I caught Adrian's hurt expression in the mirror.

He held my gaze for several heavy seconds until finally, Adrian cleared his throat. "Presley darling, will these flowers along the hillside be sufficient for what you'd envisioned for our wedding?"

I made a show of looking out Alex's window and smiled. "These are perfect. Can we pull over so Alex can help me look through them?"

Adrian muttered an order to the driver, and within minutes, we'd pulled over to the side of the road, and I started toward the hillside, holding Alex's hand. I knew he had to do something to take care of the driver, but I didn't stick around to watch. Moments later, Adrian began running behind us as he tossed a needle to the side of the road.

"Hurry, Markos is tracking the vehicle. There's at least two of his cars behind us by a mile or so; we need to disappear into the trees."

We began running, while I asked from over my shoulder, "The driver?"

Adrian's hand came to the small of my back, helping me up the hill. "Ketamine. Markos has ways of ensuring he's alerted if his men are killed or if the vehicle goes off course."

"Who are we meeting?" Alex asked, hiking up the loose gravel that began sliding under our feet. We both wore leggings and closed toe shoes because Adrian had made a big production of how we were going to the countryside to walk and explore, and needed the appropriate clothing to do so. Now I knew he was just preparing us.

My legs burned from lack of training and my regular exercise routine. While I'd done walking, swimming, and some combo drills in Adrian's gym, I wasn't nearly as toned or as well prepared as I used to be with Scotty in charge of my training.

"We're meeting your brothers ..." He trailed off.

Alex swung her gaze over to me as we locked eyes.

The twins were here.

My stomach flipped for an entirely new reason. Hate, hurt, and anger...it all swirled in my chest like a storm, forcing my lungs to ache and a burn to develop behind the backs of my eyes.

I hadn't been home in almost a year, and if I knew they wouldn't be there, then perhaps I'd feel a little bit better about returning, but the fact that I had already texted them sat like a fat elephant between us. I'd unblocked them both when Alex had arrived that first night because I knew if they had to get in touch with me regarding her, I'd need to already have that done. How I didn't realize that I had opened an old thread, when I started texting Kingston, I had no clue.

Embarrassed wasn't even the right word, and not because I was worried about Gio's feelings. I was just ashamed that I had allowed Kingston to get under my skin so effectively.

"There," Adrian said, nodding toward a small stone house that sat in shambles. Large overgrown trees hung low, providing significant coverage. We continued walking toward the house, all the while my stomach seemed to drop completely out. Adrian could be walking us to our deaths, or the twins could decide to snatch Alex and leave me to die.

My eyes were on the ground, not even focused, when I felt Alex wrap her fingers around mine. I glanced up, seeing her reassuring smile, and felt a small wave of warmth invade my chest. It would be okay. Whatever was behind that door, it would be okay.

I heard the small kick of a stone and glanced up, seeing someone in a bulletproof vest, standing on the roof...or what was left of it.

"Stop there," the man shouted.

Adrian paused and tried to reach for me, but I stepped away right as someone opened the door to the house. I froze in place as I locked eyes with a set of cool, gray eyes, followed by a pair of angry golden ones.

Fire trapped behind glass.

I stared, unmoving, while the twins emerged, both carrying high- powered rifles against their chests, covered in bulletproof vests. Kingston inspected me slowly and then moved his gaze to his sister.

"You okay, Alex?"

She nodded. "Just ready to go home."

I didn't like the prick of pain that unfurled in my heart at his obvious dismissal, but I should have known this was the game Kingston would play. He knew he was in the wrong, that he'd hurt me, and yet, months later, instead of acting apologetic in any way, he just kept pushing me away, punishing me for something that didn't require penance.

Gio's attention was on me, but kept going back to a certain man who took up a protective position behind him. Gio spoke in Spanish to said man, but I caught the name, Henry. Moments later, an entire group of men shuffled around the building and began removing tree branches from concealing a helicopter.

"They're ten minutes out," Adrian said, glancing at his phone.

"Got it," Gio replied, while Henry began speaking into a walkie.

Adrian stepped closer to the twins. "They'll shoot at you."

"We'll get enough altitude before they do," Kingston replied, leading us to the side of the helicopter. They'd yet to fire up the engine, so I turned to Adrian, suddenly fearful that this would be the last time I saw him. As angry as I was at him, I was disgustingly attached to the idea of being with him. Of him protecting me from the twins and offering me an out where they were concerned. It was artificial, and yet as Alex boarded the aircraft, I hung back.

"Would you..." I started and saw a vulnerability in Adrian's gaze that made my throat tight. He stepped closer and gently pulled my hands into his.

"Ask me anything, and I'll give it to you."

I felt the twins hover nearby, but I didn't pay them any attention as I stepped closer to my fiancé. "Would you come with me?"

His mouth twitched the smallest amount, so much that it nearly looked like a smile.

"Of course you'd ask that, the one thing I can't give you."

"Why can't you?" I tucked my fingers into a tight fist at my side, hating that this felt like another rejection. Asking him was dangerous; once my father and Scotty realized what he'd done, and to what extent they'd plotted, his life might be forfeit.

"I have to get back and try to keep Markos off your trail for as long as possible. If I'm fast enough, he won't know for a few days or even a week that you're gone."

Someone cleared their throat behind us, and I heard the helicopter engines begin to start up.

"I'm sorry, Presley. For everything." Adrian pulled me into his arms and pressed his lips to mine in a kiss that felt like goodbye. I was about to tell him that I could find a way to forgive him, if we just gave ourselves some time. But someone pulled me away, and as I looked up, I saw a clenched jaw and amber stare that drove a hole into my chest.

"We were told you'd be returning with us," Kingston snapped harshly.

I tried to pull my arm free, but he held firm. "I am, but let me say goodbye."

Adrian stepped closer and tucked a piece of hair behind my ear before closing the space and pressing his mouth there, whispering, "I love you. Promise me, my darling, if I never see you again, then you need to chase the sun. Let it love you the way you deserve to be loved and finally embrace that fire that's been simmering in your soul that you've been too nervous to release."

With one last kiss to my cheek, Adrian placed a note in my palm right as Kingston pulled me away. Ducking my head, I moved to the open door of the helicopter and then settled into the seat next to Alex. Across from me sat Gio, who was staring at me as if I'd stolen something from him.

I glanced out the window and watched as Adrian tucked his hands into his pockets and watched us fly away. Once we were high enough and hadn't been shot down, I pulled out the note he'd given me.

I did some digging. I have a picture of that night, who killed my father. It's been scrubbed from the internet, but I have someone who can find the things that don't exist. I'm going to email you the image. Be safe, my love.

CHAPTER 14
GIO

I used to be jealous that Kingston had something as tangible as soil to touch when he felt anxious. It became something that tied him to Presley when they were younger, too, with the glass jars full of dirt that she'd bring him. It was foolish of me to assume I could ever have something as vast as the stars to share with Presley.

I should have known that we'd outgrow the notion that anything could connect us after our time apart broke so much between us. But for some reason I thought...I had this stupid inclination that the map on my back would be a place holder for the missing days in between us. Now, having her back at the manor, she was close and yet seemed further than she'd ever been.

We'd arrived by jet over a week ago, and she hadn't uttered a single word to us. Not on the plane, not in the car on the way home... she clung to Alex like a second skin and allowed my sister to fill us in on everything that took place. Presley didn't add why Adrian was suddenly kissing her goodbye, or why the fuck she was forced to execute someone. Or who it was. There were so many questions I still had, but I knew I hadn't earned the answers. I wanted to... but I had no clue where to begin.

She'd moved into Uncle Decker and Aunt Mallory's wing of the house after hearing that they'd opted not to return for the foreseeable future. This came after Carter was put at risk those four months ago when we'd fucked everything up by going after the motorcycle club, and that shit followed us here. It was something I was still trying to atone for, and that had several ramifications. One of which apparently included losing my cousin's presence in the manor.

Presley hadn't come out of the wing. Not to train, or to seek out her parents, or to walk outside. Nothing, and while I had caught sight of her mom and dad walking over frequently to visit her, Presley would remain inside, tucked away like a little recluse.

I was ready to test the waters and see if I could get her to start talking to me, but I wanted something that would remind her that once upon a time, we were best friends. Before the emotions and feelings and all the leaving...we were there for each other through everything. I didn't have dirt, and I couldn't capture a star, but I had crushed pieces of our past just rotting away in my chest that had to count for something.

With a silent inhale, I rapped my knuckles against the exterior door to the wing of the house she had moved into. Seconds passed, but nothing happened, so I tried again, this time with more force. Glancing around the hallway, I tried to gauge whether someone would have a front row seat to how embarrassed I was about to be if she chose not to open the door, but it was completely empty. I didn't hear Scotty's dogs or anyone training in the gym. Just dead silence.

Another minute ticked by, so I knocked again.

The door suddenly opened on my third rap. "What?"

Presley gripped the bronze knob while clenching her teeth. Laying eyes on her again after so long made something in my chest flutter. I had seen her in the jet, and on the ride home...but I hadn't had a chance to really look at her, not like this. Where she was unguarded and unfiltered, her raw self that always existed before she left us...before we left her. The blue in her eyes that always reminded me of the hottest part of a fire, warning of total combustion, waged a silent war with mine.

"I wanted to check on you," I mustered a response after feeling like my voice had been scraped clean of all sound.

Her nails dug into the wood near her face, just barely holding the door open. Her teeth literally snapped shut as she replied coldly, "Well, you've checked. I'm still hurt, Gio. Still pissed and angry and not interested in seeing you."

The door slammed shut before I could say anything else.

THE NEXT DAY, I arrived at her door with a bouquet of marigolds. I hadn't heard if she'd ventured out of her room or not, but I had to assume she was still in there. My knuckles rapped against the wooden surface again, just like they had the day before. This time there were less butterflies in my stomach, but seemingly more wasps. It didn't flutter so much as knot, making me weary of another negative encounter.

There was no answer again. So, I continued to knock, until I was pounding against her door. I knew it was rude, but I needed to start making progress with her, and I couldn't get anywhere unless she agreed to talk to me.

Finally, the door swung open, revealing another angry version of my best friend. "I'm going to seriously hurt you if you keep making me get up from the couch."

I shoved the flowers between us, watching nervously as her gaze dropped. Those dark brows raised, hitting her hairline, which gave me a chance to take in her slick hair and how long it had gotten since I'd last run my fingers through it.

Her lips pressed together as she let out a sigh. "Why did you bring me these?"

"You know why." I inched the flowers closer, hoping she'd take them.

We stood there for a few silent seconds before she finally snatched them from my hand and then slammed the door in my face.

Smiling at the polished surface, I considered it progress.

I took a sip of whiskey while I connected the little dipper with my finger, drawing invisible lines in the air. I thought back to the first time I had found it as a kid and how I had been so excited that I could actually find a star system on my own. Mom and Dad didn't even make light of it or explain that it was literally something anyone could see when the stars came out. They were always doing that.

Kingston was the one who broke it to me that the baby dipper was easy, and if I wanted a challenge, I should try to find the star system shaped like a bull. Then he'd tell me to find an archer with his bow string pulled. He'd keep giving me little challenges until astronomy had taken over my life, and it became the thing that I studied more than anything else. The thing that calmed me, defined me, and reminded me that it was possible to be connected to someone, no matter how far away they were.

Which was ironic because my brother was the reason I currently detested stars. It wasn't his fault, but everything inside me still wanted to blame him. I needed him to fix this shit because somehow it was hurting more than the first time we left and were separated from Presley.

"The fuck, Gio?" Kingston startled while crawling out onto the roof with me.

I connected a few more stars with my finger, drawing an invisible line between them. My twin crawled next to me and took the whiskey from me.

"You know better than to drink while you're up here."

Always the buzz kill. I sighed, then leaned back. "King, did you ever think that maybe we're being kept away from the one person we love, simply because we both fell for her, and we crossed some cosmic boundary by doing so?"

He made some grunting sound while watching me. "The hell are you talking about?"

"We shared a womb, and then we shared everything else afterwards. We can't also share the same soul mate. God wouldn't be that cruel." My voice was somber, but I felt the words punch through my chest.

Kingston finally glanced up at the sky, but only for a second before his eyes traveled down to the ground. "Not sure God did this to us, brother."

Me either. Maybe it was a curse...or a dream we couldn't wake from.

"Why are you up here, Gio?"

I found another constellation, but this time I didn't lift my finger to draw the lines connecting it. Instead, I pushed out a heavy sigh. "I gave Presley a bouquet of flowers."

I didn't catch if he froze or looked concerned. I didn't care anymore.

"That's good, right?" he asked.

I laughed while lying flat on my back. "Yeah...she accepted them...but this morning I woke up covered in them."

The memory of the golden petals littering my covers had something punching again in my chest. Like whatever it was needed to get out, but I'd kept it captive, so now there was nowhere for it to go.

"She..." Kingston started, but I interjected again with a laugh, feeling warm from the whiskey.

"Ripped the entire bouquet up and then poured the petals all over me so the first thing I'd see when I woke up was her rejection."

Kingston didn't respond for a few seconds, and I realized belatedly that was because I hadn't stopped laughing.

"She'll come around, Gio. I promise." My brother placed his hand on my shoulder before forcing me back inside the house.

But I couldn't help but think about how easily she'd texted him, even though she was angry; at least she had wanted to speak with him. She wouldn't even accept a bundle of marigolds from me.

Maybe she'd dug into the ground so deep, the only thing she craved was darkness.

Kingston wasn't made up of anything other than shadow, so it made sense for her to crave him. I was always her sunshine, and now she hated my warmth.

CHAPTER 15

PRESLEY

"Try slowly easing into it." My cousin's voice echoed from my phone, where I'd placed her.

My fingers wrapped around the handlebars as I slowly drew my knees up, and then I let out a grunt as the exercise machine began to wobble.

"Presley, you're not even trying. This really isn't even hard," Carter chided while she watched me from the phone screen.

"This isn't built right!" I shouted at her as I toppled off the small exercise machine and rolled to my back.

Carter sighed as if she was the most disappointed coach ever. "I'm going to recommend you stay away from any reformer machines while in this Pilates era that you've stepped in."

"What's a reformer?" I asked, breathless.

Carter held her hands out in front of the screen as if she needed to stop me. "Don't look it up. I'm serious, I think you'll kill yourself, trying it. You need to go back to the boxing ring and gloves and whatever else Scotty drilled into you."

The memory of the email sitting in my inbox came back, making me wince.

I'd been avoiding this for a week. Hiding, like an animal in the only wing of the manor, not inhibited by someone who hurt me, or who birthed me.

I needed space and time to come to terms with everything circling my head. The anger at the twins, the ache I had for Adrian, which was confusing in a different way. He'd been confusingly silent these past few days, where previously he'd been texting me. Especially after I had inspected the image he'd sent, and I came to terms with who was in that photo.

I wanted to talk about it with someone, but Adrian wasn't responding, and the twins were...well, they wouldn't ever be an option again. I could go to Alex, but I was nervous she'd pull her family into it out of fear of how it might impact them. I wasn't sure if it would, and if I was being selfish by not saying something.

There wasn't a clear path forward other than avoidance, which was why I was here, trying to get back into shape by using Carter's mysterious workout equipment that looked as though an ironing board and thigh master had blended into one machine, equipped to tone my thighs, abs, and hopefully my ass.

"I gotta go, you're doing that creepy silent thing." Carter sighed before hanging up. I missed her. But I was glad she was safe and happy, wherever she and her family were at the moment. They didn't want to tell any of us, which hurt...but I couldn't focus on it as I knew it had nothing to do with me, and everything to do with my fucked-up family, and the twins.

I stood from my spot on the floor and glanced around the empty walls that now seemed to cage me in. My laptop sat on the coffee table, calling me back to it as if I could somehow decode what the fuck to do merely by staring at that photo again.

But, as if called by a siren, I shoved the top of the screen up and watched as the image immediately came to life. The grainy image depicted a white building with a lit-up doorway that another man walked underneath. Dark hair and an unmistakable jaw that nearly matched Adrian's was clear in the picture, and there behind that man, carrying a gun, was a man who shaped me more distinctly than my own father had.

Scotty.

A heavy knock at my door had me slamming the laptop shut. "Son of a bitch."

I knew it was Gio based off the knock. He'd been stopping by nearly every day this week, and even after I had cut up and practically shredded every single marigold he'd brought me and tossed it on his bed while he was sleeping, the idiot still managed to show up with that annoying knock.

"Leave me alone!" I called toward the door, hoping he'd hear.

The knocking stopped, which meant he likely had. I sagged in relief, back to staring at nothing while trying to piece together what exactly it meant that my uncle was the one who had killed Adrian's father. It meant he had lied to me and knowingly placed me in danger by encouraging the relationship and marriage with Adrian.

It meant he'd framed my father.

It meant there was a chance he'd lied about other things as well. God knew how many other things. He was my mentor…my trainer. The man who was more involved in my upbringing than my own father was. I felt like I had been shaped and practically formed in his image, and now every piece of me carried some mark of his.

I refused to look deeper into what it meant that he had placed me in danger, or how it began to pull at the thread in my mind of exactly how I was ever going to trust him again.

I was staring off into space with the computer open in my lap when suddenly there was movement off to my right.

"Why are you ignoring Gio?" Kingston stood next to the stairs, with his arms crossed and an angry scowl on his face.

I screamed, tossing the laptop. "How the hell did you get in here?"

My voice came out shrill as I tried to mentally play catch up.

"You know how I got in here." He rolled his eyes.

Yes, the fourth floor…where the balcony leads out to the roof, connecting to the rest of the house. I slowly shifted so I could reach the computer and shield the screen from him.

"*Why* are you here?" I asked.

He took two steps forward, tapering his gaze so that it was shrewd and unforgiving. "I didn't fucking stutter, Presley."

"Neither. Did. I," I replied just as shrewdly in return.

We stared at one another, neither of us moving until he finally broke first, flicking that ire in his eyes to the open screen that was now on the coffee table.

"What is that?" He covered the space between us in less than two strides. I went to reach for the laptop right as he pulled it up.

"Kingston." My fingers wrapped around the bottom, but his instantly covered them, and then he let them linger while he stared at the screen.

"What am I looking at, Presley?"

Fuck. I yanked the device as hard as I could, but all it did was make him lose his footing and fall forward. The laptop dropped to the couch, and his palm landed next to my head, pressing into the sofa. Our faces were inches apart as he glared down at me, ruthlessly and angrily.

My eyes searched his, as if they were convinced, apart from what my mind and heart had warned them of, they could somehow dig through those amber irises and find the boy who once protected us. The one who grew up doing anything and everything to ensure we were safe and cared for.

"You're being needlessly cruel to Gio," Kingston rasped.

I wet my lips, not on purpose, but my mouth was so fucking dry since he'd walked in. He seemed to burn everything when he entered a room. "Why do you care if I'm mean to Gio? I'd be just as mean to you if you gave a shit."

He smirked. "I don't, though. So, perhaps you should give the twin who still does a shot."

"I'll pass. Thanks, though." I smiled up at him sweetly.

He clenched his jaw, obviously fighting through something, but I didn't care anymore. I slid under his arm and shot off the couch, leaving my laptop behind. Damn him–if he looked at the picture, he could put two and two together. I'd already deleted the email from Adrian and only kept the image downloaded to my computer.

My back was to him as I began to scale the steps, one at a time, when I heard him ask, "This is Scotty...he's killing someone who looks—"

"Kingston, drop it."

He paused, glancing up at me. "Tell me what happened."

"No." I turned to leave again, but Kingston stopped me again with his words from where he stood below, "You need protection...if Adrian was desperate to get you out and this picture shows Scotty killing someone... He put you in harm's way, didn't he?"

"You just got done saying that you didn't give a shit about me." I challenged with a bit of a scoff.

His cold gaze flicked over to something in the corner of the room. I followed his gaze to the plant, completely dead inside its planter. Something passed through his eyes when he finally snapped the laptop shut and tossed it to the couch. He tucked his hands into his pockets and shook his head.

"Stop being cruel to Gio. For the record, he never wanted to fuck and leave you. That was all me. He never wanted to punish you. He never wanted to lose you, Presley. Forgive him."

My heart hammered out a warning in my chest.

I should have listened instead of making my way down the steps. "And you did want to do all those things?"

I stood in front of Kingston as he glared at the freckles spread across my nose.

"Obviously."

"Why? I didn't deserve your cruelty." That warning in my chest beat out a steady drum, but I just ignored it and kept pushing.

Kingston's face twisted in pain as he got even closer, until our faces were close. "Why? You broke my heart, Presley. Fucking shattered it, and you don't think you're owed a little cruelty for it?"

"You broke me first, asshole," I seethed.

His head tilted to the side as he smirked. "Well then, let us stay broken, Presley. I know I am."

"I don't believe you." An angry tear made its way down my face.

He watched as it slowly rolled down my cheek, then a shuddered expression took over his face before he wiped up the wetness from my face with his thumb.

"I only came here to tell you to start talking to Gio. You and I, we're over, but you and my brother still have a chance. Don't ruin that."

With that, he turned and walked down the hall until he was exiting the front door.

MY MOTHER and I hadn't spoken since I returned.

At least not in any real depth. I had hugged her, told her I was safe, and then explained that I just needed a little space. She hadn't questioned it, likely because I had kept in touch with her while I was in Italy. While I hadn't shared all the details, I had shared enough that she wouldn't feel like she was completely in the dark.

Today, as I stared at their front door, I tried to remember the soft cadence of my grandfather's voice as he had called for his only daughter, assuming I was her. How as he took his last breaths, it was of her that he thought of. I owed her that information, not only as his executioner but as her daughter. I punched in the code that Scotty had set for our home. It had never struck me as odd that he was the one who set the code or set up all the security measures in the manor.

I found my mother on the balcony that led from the kitchen, overlooking the small stone patio below that was scattered with potted plants and green vines that curled over the stone railing. Her dark hair was in a sleek sheet, pin straight against her back. She wore a set of silk pajamas while she sipped a cup of coffee, and the familiar sight of her had me relaxing. I smiled as I made my way to the chair next to her. The one my father typically occupied when I usually found them out here in the mornings while growing up.

"Hey, Mom." I greeted her warmly, loving how genuine her smile was as she raised her blue eyes to mine.

"Presley!" She set her coffee down on the bistro table in front of her before standing to wrap her arms around me. A burning sensation began behind my eyes as she held me, and a tight knot in my stomach made my breath hitch. I didn't want to tell her.

How did I tell her?

She separated from me, holding me at arm's length before inspecting me. "You okay, honey?"

A tear slid down my cheek. "I need to tell you something."

She reclaimed her spot while I took the one next to her and pulled her hand into mine.

"You knew of a man named Markos Mariano?"

Her brows drew in close, but her chin lifted in a nod. "I remember him."

"He's Adrian's father...well, adopted," I explained and watched her face as I began to explain the story of how I went to dinner that night with him, and Alex was there. My mother stiffened when I explained that Scotty had encouraged Alex to go. My mother did not trust Scotty, not anymore at least. Perhaps she once did, but since handing the reins of my upbringing over to him, and when she pulled that gun on him, I knew something inside her had snapped.

"Markos had a prisoner...it was a test of some kind for me."

I spoke past the ball of anxiety swelling in my throat.

"He was a federal agent, Mom." My voice broke into a whisper as she suddenly shot to her feet.

"No." Her hands came to her face as she began shaking her head.

"I didn't—" I swallowed, unsure how to even continue. "I didn't know him, but he kept calling me you...and he seemed so confused."

A sob escaped my mother as she slowly sank to her knees. "He didn't..."

"I was worried that if I didn't do as Markos said, he'd torture him."

Tears flooded my eyes as a sob scraped up my throat, making it burn. My mother cried in ugly, loud sobs as she shook on the floor, and I moved so I could hold her. Her head landed on my shoulder as I curved around her, wrapping my arms around her back.

"I'm so sorry, Mom. He told me that he loved you, and his last thoughts were of you."

"He..." she hiccupped, "he made you kill your own grandfather?"

I sat back with a tear-stained face and nodded. "He told me it was my grandfather. I knew what I was doing, but based on how they spoke of him...I just—"

My mother's hands came to my face in a gentle hold as she inspected me. "You did nothing wrong, my love. I'm so sorry you were forced into that position. I hate that I wasn't there to keep you safe. I'm so sorry that you were set forth on this path and that I didn't protect you from it. There were so many times I hated myself for allowing you to endure what you have, I always worried you'd resent me."

I shook my head. "Never, Mom. I'd never resent you."

Her face was red and blotchy as she pulled me closer and we rocked back and forth for a few seconds. "I'm sorry I never told you about him. I kept thinking our world would stop being dangerous, but it never did. My dad wasn't trustworthy when it came to intel. I worried he'd leak something that would get you hurt. He refused to step away from his job, even at the cost of losing his relationship with me, but I still should have told you about him."

"It's okay, Mom. I promise you, it is. I love you." I kissed her cheek and then decided to spend the rest of the day resting on the couch with her while she silently grieved a father she resented but still loved. My dad arrived later that evening and didn't ask what happened; he just dropped to his knees in front of my mother and held her face in his hands, pushing her hair back while fresh tears slid down.

I decided to give them a moment while my mother explained what happened and wandered to my old room. Everything was exactly where I left it the last time I had visited. I checked my phone to see if Adrian had texted me, but the second I realized he still hadn't, I turned it off and left it on the dresser. Clicking the main light off, I decided to lie down on my bed and try to process my interaction with Kingston.

He was over me, while pushing me into Gio's arms.

My eyes trailed over to the ceiling of my loft, seeing a few faded glowing stars still clinging to my ceiling. Gio had promised to always be my sky, my way back. He promised to always look for me, and yet I felt so abandoned.

I was so hurt by their actions. I couldn't simply forgive Gio and act as though Kingston didn't exist. I couldn't love Gio and not still want Kingston. It was all connected to each other, and I hated that Adrian had left me to this fate. To them.

He'd delivered me back to the tragic beginning that I had so desperately tried to escape. My humiliating crush on two brothers who merely pacified my attention because they just had time to kill and didn't mind keeping me as a secret. I wish I would have been wise enough to realize that's all I would ever be to them.

A secret and then a regret.

I pulled a pillow into my chest and stared at the dark ceiling until my eyes burned. Eventually, light crept through a crack as my bedroom door opened and my dad gently peered inside.

"Dad?"

He rushed over to my bed and pulled me into his arms. "I'm so sorry, honey. I'm so fucking sorry."

He rocked me as he sobbed into my hair, obviously processing the information he learned about how I had to kill my own flesh and blood.

I didn't resent my mother. I never would. I had seen her silent battle over my training and all the things required of me my whole life, and even that time she angrily confronted Scotty. She even risked her life to defy Scotty.

It was my father I struggled not to resent.

He was supposed to be my protector, and he'd placed me in the hands of my uncle, a murdering, backstabbing liar. I was shaped, formed, and molded by the same monster who created him. He should have known better, and yet he risked me anyway.

I was tired of being gambled upon. Merely a game of odds and how well I'd survive if I beat them. I refused to play any more games for him or Scotty. I was done.

I wanted to break, but as my father sobbed, I realized I'd done enough breaking.

Now I was angry.

Really fucking angry.

CHAPTER 16

KINGSTON

S omeone was knocking on my makeshift door. It was made of barnwood and a flimsy piece of shit, to be honest. He could just push on it hard enough and come inside, but he was trying to be polite.

"Come in!" I called before returning to the duffle bag on my bed.

My brother walked in and scanned the spare space like usual. There was a twin-sized bed with a threadbare blanket, a small dresser, a rug, and a space heater. Gio decided to lean against the dresser, crossing his arms while he inspected all the things left on the bed.

"Where are you going?"

I gave him a quick glance before turning to grab my extra ammo.

"Not sure yet, maybe West."

He turned with me while I grabbed an extra pair of boots I'd brought over from the house. "You're leaving again?"

I wasn't staying to watch him win over Presley, or the way the two of them would inevitably fall back in love. I was strong enough to let him have her, but I wasn't strong enough to allow him to have her in front of me.

"Yeah. I'll talk to Henry about taking over my place in El Peligro, don't worry."

Gio scoffed, "Kingston, I don't fucking care about El Peligro. Why are you leaving?"

He wasn't that dense, so I didn't answer him. He would get there on his own eventually.

"This is about Presley?"

I still didn't reply because I didn't feel like he really needed an answer.

"Tell her you finished the house, Gio. That will be the way to win her over."

"I'm not taking credit for that house. You worked your ass off to finish it, you tell her," Gio argued.

I zipped up my last bag and set it toward the end of the bed. "I'm letting her go, Gio. I thought for a second yesterday that I might be able to try, but I can't. She's too hurt, and it's me who keeps doing the hurting. I think she might be in danger; I want you to keep an eye on things and be ready with El Peligro. Adrian was afraid for her, but I think it goes deeper than that. I think Scotty is connected to it."

My brother's solemn face remained unfazed as he watched me pack. His silence began to chafe as he just stood there, but as I neared the door, he stood in front of it.

"You're saying goodbye this time. Go over there, tell her to her face that you're leaving, and tell her why. We're done doing this toxic bullshit where we leave and don't say exactly what's on our mind," Gio explained calmly.

I gripped the strap of my bag tightly. "I told her I loved her, Gio. Laid it all out there for her, and she—"

"Chose us!" he interjected loudly.

I shook my head, stepping back. "No, she chose him."

"She chose him after we pushed her away. You're not remembering correctly because you're hurt. I get it, but you told her on the boat, and after that, she came to us. She wanted us, even after our time together on the fourth floor...she wanted us, but you wanted to punish her."

That's not how it went. I'd told her I loved her before I realized she had an entire year to get in touch with us. A whole year, during which time my own brother nearly took his own life because of how hurt he was over her silence. We stayed away to protect her, but we had never shut her out. We communicated every day with her, but she refused us.

I had every right to be angry.

I had every right to feel hurt. Presley could have taken the news and realized that we just needed time to fix all of it, everything broken between us, but instead, she chose to marry someone else.

"I'm not moving until you agree that you'll go tell her."

"It's like six in the morning," I argued, clenching my jaw. This was bullshit.

Gio scoffed with a slight roll of his eye. "You know she's up."

I did. Presley was always up the second the sun lit up the sky.

"Fuck. Fine." I sighed, pushing past my brother. "Carry my shit to the front then."

I saw Gio grab my bags from the bed while I exited the barn and headed toward the manor.

Fog clung to the trees stretching along the back property line that bordered the manor, and farm, and a cold chill clung to the air as I walked in just a T-shirt and black cargo pants, and black boots. I'd yet to even lace them up before Gio came barging into my room, and I had planned on slipping into a hoodie before I left, but it was better to just get this shit over with. I had talked to Presley yesterday, so there wasn't much left to say. I'd just explain that I was moving on, starting my life, and letting her live hers. I'd wish her the best and tell her to go see what Gio had done for her on the farm.

I slipped in through the back terrace door, knowing the code to enter the house. I was rehearsing what I was going to say as my heart began to hammer against my chest, but I worked to shove the feeling down. I was doing the right thing.

Expecting to see Presley in her new location over where Carter typically was, I stopped short at the sight of her walking out of her family wing. The bleak morning light came in through the glass windows and terrace doors. Presley looked tired, her eyes were puffy, and her hair was braided back, resting against her oversized T-shirt that cut off at her upper thighs. It was an older T-shirt...*my T-shirt, to be specific.*

My eyes practically burned a hole into her chest from staring so hard at the lettering. She must have noticed because she finally glanced down, and a blush worked its way into her cheeks, under the freckles across her nose.

"What are you doing here?" she asked, tugging the shirt down to cover more of her legs.

My mouth wouldn't shape the words I wanted to say. My tongue seemed stuck to the roof of my mouth, and my throat felt like a baseball was stuck inside it. The knot forming in my stomach had me panicked that I was making another bad decision. Like the one where I agreed to make things seem meaningless when they started, and Presley was just sixteen. Or when we decided to remain gone, gathering the support and strength of El Peligro. Then, taking her virginity and leaving moments after... and here I was still punishing her.

Yesterday, she seemed angry at the idea that I was still angry with her, and maybe if—

"Kingston?" Presley took a step in my direction when there was a playful knock that sounded at the front door, which was just a few feet from where Presley stood. Her head swung over right as her phone made a chiming sound.

She glanced down at her cell and then smiled. "It's Adrian. He's here!"

She might as well have shot an arrow at my chest. I took a half step back; unsure I wanted to explain that I was leaving now. They were about to have a reunion of some kind, and I didn't want to be a part of that. Fuck, I didn't want to see her kissing him. I turned around, about to leave, as Presley swung the door open, and then she released an earth-shattering scream that seemed to rearrange something inside my chest.

I dropped my bag and ran toward the door. Clearing the frame, I found her on her knees on the front porch, hovering over a black bag. Glancing around, I checked for anyone who might be lingering on the property, but all I found were missing guards and an open front gate.

Presley was sobbing as she began moving her hands around whatever was underneath her. I finally looked down and felt my heart sink for an entirely different reason.

Adrian was in a body bag, on our front steps, with a note stapled to his forehead. I slowly got to my knees, next to the girl who once brought me glass jars full of sunlit dirt, and wrapped my hand around hers as she sobbed over her fiancé's chest.

"I can't read it, King. You have to read the note." She hiccupped.

Very carefully, I tugged the note from its place against Adrian's forehead and winced when I realized there was a bullet hole under the paper. I began reading it to myself just in case it was something she didn't need to hear right then.

My DEAREST PRESLEY,

You win. Seems his loyalty was to you and not to this family. So here you go, you can have him. See you soon-
Markos

"WHAT DID IT SAY?" she asked, glancing up at me. She hadn't let go of my hand, and I decided I wouldn't release hers either.

"It says that Adrian loved you."

Her tear-stained eyes searched mine as if she were trying to tear apart each word and decipher a different meaning. She gave me a solemn nod before returning to Adrian's body, smoothing back his hair and pressing a kiss to his blue lips.

She whispered against him, "I'm sorry I couldn't love you the way you deserved."

There was a shadow that appeared in the corner of my eye, making me glance over. Scotty stood there, wearing his tactical gear, glaring at the body as if it were a speck of shit on his shoes. Presley continued to cry while she touched Adrian's face and tried to fix his hair.

"Presley, we need to move the body," Scotty demanded, sauntering closer.

Anger twisted her features as she snapped her head up; her lips wobbled, but her tone was sharp. "You will not touch him."

"And you will not sit here and cry over a corpse. Get up. You were trained better than this." Scotty sneered in reply.

"She's not one of your fucking dogs," I roared back at him.

Scotty scowled at me and worked his jaw back and forth while a few of the guards began flanking him. *Where the fuck were they when this body had been dropped?*

"Kingston, Presley is hysterical, and I can understand her anger. However, you shouldn't be feeling anything other than joy. Regardless, please consider helping Presley by removing her from the corpse. Even you know this is unhealthy."

I hated Scotty with every fiber of my being, but he was right. It was freezing outside, fog was increasing around the property, it was the end of February, and she was in just a simple T-shirt, kneeling on concrete steps while hovering over a cold, dead body. I tried to pull my hand free of hers so I could help pick her up, but she squeezed it, so I wouldn't budge.

"I'm staying," she gritted out between teeth that chattered from the cold. Her dark hair fell over her brows, and her lips were turning blue, but I was inclined to sit with her. I felt it somewhere down in my soul that something inside of her was splintering. I had assumed Presley was broken before, but the way she stared at me, determined with an unfamiliar fire in her eyes, I knew this was different. This was true grief, and it was tearing through her like a storm in the ocean. She was drowning, and regardless of our past, there wasn't any chance I'd leave her.

There was movement behind us, where Gio stepped through the door. He draped a large blanket over Presley's shoulders and sank to his knees next to her, grabbing her other hand.

"That's okay, Elvis. We'll stay with you."

And we did. We sat there in the numbing cold, each of us holding one of her hands while she mourned the man who was supposed to become her husband. The man whom I was positive she assumed would set her free from us.

CHAPTER 17

PRESLEY

I could hear Gio and Kingston talking to one another.

Their voices were quiet, and they were being gentle with the cadence they used. It was starting to get late, and I knew they hadn't eaten or done anything other than sit here with me all day while I clung to Adrian's dead body.

I realized what I was doing was crazy, and perhaps I should consider how I was making everyone around me feel, but I didn't want to.

If they wanted to leave, they could. I wasn't forcing them to stay. I just didn't want anyone to touch Adrian's body. Not yet. Scotty would probably just dump him in some furnace or bury him without caring at all, and I didn't want to do that to him. I needed to protect his body and ensure he had the proper respect given to him. At first, I was worried, I'd be the only person who would fight for that, but after having the twins by my side for the entirety of the day, that wasn't true. Deep down, they were still my best friends.

"What are you guys arguing about?" I finally sat up and wiped at my eyes.

Kingston lowered his chin to his chest, almost like he was afraid to speak directly to me. Gio responded. "We're trying to figure out where to take you. Do you want to go back to your famil—"

"No," I interjected immediately. I refused to go back to my family wing. Not while Scotty was there and had access to me.

"We don't think you should be alone in Carter's," Kingston added softly.

I hated how careful he was being with me, as if I would just shatter into a thousand pieces if he handled me wrong. He'd never been like that with me. My whole life he'd delivered harsh truths; he'd been the patch of shade for me in all of Gio's sun. I never realized how badly I needed that.

"I'll be fine."

"No, you won't," Gio argued.

Truthfully, I didn't want to be anywhere in the manor. My mother would come and check on me, or my dad...they were already worried about me after what they learned, what I did to my grand— a tight ball of emotions suddenly swelled in my throat, making fresh tears want to fall. It was possible that some of my grief for Adrian was also for a man that I was never given the chance to know, but was forced to murder.

Solitude sounded good, along with distance from everyone. My eighteenth birthday flashed in my mind, how up in the loft I had found that solitude, and how I was completely alone until I had called Adrian. He filled the space left void by the twins.

"I want to stay in the barn. I don't want to be here, and I want Adrian's body brought there, put on ice. He needs a proper burial."

Gio brushed a few strands of hair off my face. "Done. Will you let Kingston carry you there?"

I saw his eyes move swiftly over my head, but I didn't catch his twin's reaction. I felt it, though. Kingston moved away from me and made some sound of disagreement.

"I'll handle the body if you get her there, Gio."

Rejection sharp as a needle, pierced some unhealed wound in my heart, directly connected to him. While Gio seemed desperate to get into my good graces, his brother wanted nothing to do with me. Which was fine, he didn't need to want me. My roots were made of unrequited love and pining for a life that would never be. His derision was nothing new for me.

"I don't need either of you to take me there. I can walk. I think the fresh air would be good for me." I slowly moved to get up by placing my palms under me against the cool cement, but Kingston lurched forward to stop me.

"Can you just let Gio take you, please?"

My eyes snapped up, seeing his already searching mine. The familiar amber hue felt like a gut punch, making me immediately drop my gaze.

"Why do you care, Kingston?" I shoved his hands away and got to my feet. I was shaky from not eating anything all day. I swayed enough that I had to catch my balance on a pillar.

I heard Gio curse, and then I was being swept up into his arms and tucked against his chest. "Come on, Elvis. I have a surprise for you."

Without glancing back at the twin who had no love left for me, or the man who'd died because he had too much, I was carried away. Past the front entrance and around the side of the manor, toward the only place that ever truly brought me peace.

Gio walked long enough that I'd closed my eyes and breathed in the crisp winter air. I knew exactly where he stepped by the way his body shifted in elevation or dipped from the messy terrain. However, when I expected him to veer off toward the barn, he changed direction toward the house. That had my eyes flying open, and my head lifting. The last time I had seen the farmhouse, it was still rotted out, full of disarray and moldy pieces I needed to gut.

The house before me wasn't what I had left behind at all.

"Gio," I inhaled as he stopped in front of the renovated home. Fresh, white paint covered brand new siding, while dark green shutters enclosed new glass windows. I could see gauzy white curtains covering them from the inside, which had my mouth lifting into a feeble smile.

My heart twisted in my chest with elation and hope.

Gio set me down, and even on shaky legs, I found a fresh strength hold me up as I stepped over a manicured patch of grass leading to a freshly built porch. I climbed wide steps while holding tightly to the railing. Gio was behind me but gave me enough space that I didn't feel smothered.

A green door that matched the shutters had a black knob and a wreath hanging that looked like it was full of white baby's breath. It was such a delicate touch and one that tugged at a gently folded away memory of playing knights and dragons. I was the queen, and Kingston agreed to be the knight who protected the realm. He had decided his job would be to bring the queen a crown of baby's breath every morning, so she knew he was still alive and hadn't been eaten by a dragon.

I tried the door, and it opened easily as if it were just here waiting for me. The floors were a light oak color, covered in warm rugs. New archways had been designed in places that I couldn't even recognize as rooms before. The walls were a soft eggshell color, but there were a few accent walls with green wallpaper that had little highland cows printed all over them.

Reaching out, I traced a finger over the wall and spun around as curiosity tugged out a memory I had of a time when Kingston had shared a piece of himself with me.

I dream of marigolds too...ones that sit on a kitchen table, plucked from the garden I grew. Wallpaper that has little prints of Highland cows and a pantry full of organic Cheetos. Sunlight soaking into plants in a home that smells like coconut and oranges.

The dining table was circular with five chairs around it, and there on the table was a vase full of marigolds. My breath hitched as I walked into the farmhouse-style kitchen. An older designed fridge was set up between two long counters made of butcher block. A deep, porcelain sink lay under a large window that revealed the barn out front and the fields beyond. I moved to the pantry and tugged the door open.

A variety of food was inside, but I zeroed in on my favorite snack: organic Cheetos.

"Did you do all this, Gio?" I already knew the answer, but I was curious as to why Kingston continued to push his brother toward me and shy away from me himself.

Gio rubbed the back of his neck and cleared his throat. "Bits and pieces. Come on, I wanna show you upstairs where the bedrooms are."

I went with him, still feeling a strange high come over me. My dreamhouse had been completed...the farmhouse I had always wanted and dreamed of one day living in. The small touches throughout were better than anything I could have ever hoped for. There was so much consideration into what suited me that it made me emotional for entirely different reasons.

We crested the stairs, seeing a large book nook take up the back wall. Shelves were built in, along with floor-to-ceiling windows and a long table stretched along the opposite wall acting as an office space. Beyond that, on one side of the room was a doorway that led to a large room, with warm oak floors continued, softened with thick rugs. A large king-sized bed, covered in pink and white bedding, was across the room near the cushioned window seat. The attached bathroom suite had an arched doorway leading to cream tile, a claw-foot tub, and an enclosed shower.

I wandered around the space, gliding my finger along surfaces and feeling sunlight touch little places as if it were all made of magic. I padded back toward the book nook where I could see the other bedroom doors and another slim set of stairs. Holding the rail, I took the steps up to another loft. "This is what I wanted to show you," Gio said, holding his hand out as if to help me reach the last step.

Glass stretched everywhere, which made the room warm as the sun soaked through.

"This would make a good greenhouse," I mused, while sliding

open the door that led outside. There was a balcony that had lounge chairs, a gas fireplace, and a telescope set up.

"No, not a greenhouse, Elvis. Stargazing," Gio said as though I should have known that.

It finally clicked for me that the house had been set up for me, but framed around things a certain twin would enjoy. I saw nothing set up for plants. No greenhouse of any kind, not even a single potted plant in the house anywhere, which meant only one twin intended to stay here with me.

That rejection reared its ugly head once more with a stinging bite. Outrage and a frenzy of sorts seemed to sweep through me at the realization that Kingston was merely toying with me, and now he had every intention of just letting me go.

"I need to shower and eat." I turned away from the space and headed back down to the bedroom I assumed was created for me. It had photos hung of highland cows and stars. No plants, no life of any kind. I wondered if Kingston had purchased new clothes for me, or if I'd need to bring them over. Didn't matter; I could pack all of it up and drive it over. Regardless of how angry I was at the twins, this house was a significant gift that warmed my heart and arrived at the perfect time.

"Are there clothes here for me?" I asked while walking toward the bathroom suite. Somehow, I already knew he wouldn't know if there were.

His staggering response told me as much. "Uh...let me check for you."

I moved to the clawfoot tub and turned on the hot water. Gio returned moments later with a pile of clothes in his hands. "I found these."

Almost a complete replica of the clothes I'd had at home. I didn't wait for Gio to leave before stripping out of the T-shirt, socks, and underwear. I didn't care if he saw me or if he wanted me. My fucks had vanished the second Adrian arrived on the doorstep.

I hadn't even had a chance to process that they'd used his cell phone to text me, to mock me so that I'd open that door excitedly. After days of silence, of fear that something was wrong, of him being upset with me, he had finally reached out, and I had stupidly assumed it was—I had killed him. The realization hit like a stone.

Just like I had killed my grandfather, I was responsible for Adrian's death too.

All because I had demanded we get out when we did. I could have found a way to get Alex out while I remained there with him. I could have protected him if I had just stayed.

Gio cleared his throat behind me.

"I'll just go get you some food and bring it up here." His heated gaze slowly slid down my frame, to my breasts, which were heavier now that I'd stopped training as much. My waist, which was fuller, and even my thighs were softer. I'd never been given the chance to enjoy a softer figure because of how hard Scotty drilled me, and eleven months away from him had allowed me to set my own exercise pace and my own diet. It allowed my metabolism the opportunity to slow down, and my body to hold weight.

When I looked in the mirror now, I enjoyed what I saw. While it wasn't a huge difference, it was enough to make me smile, and when I inspected my hands, I knew the scarring would never leave, but they hadn't been broken open in months.

Once Gio left, I sank into the deep tub and allowed the hot water to soak into my body, removing the grief and the stress. I slipped down far enough that my hair soaked, and the steaming water covered my face, and with my eyes closed, I began to count.

One. Two. Three.

My grandfather's blue eyes flashed before me.

Four. Five. Six.

Adrian's smile.

Seven. Eight. Nine.

Crawling into bed as a child, lying between my best friends.

Ten. Eleven. Twelve.

A shadow fell over the tub, making me open my eyes while under water.

Kingston stood with his arms crossed while he watched from above me. His presence threw my counting off balance, so I emerged from the water with a gasp. He didn't flinch or move in the slightest bit. That familiar scowl, with a deadness to his gaze that set me on edge. I wanted to crawl inside his chest, sort out the mess, and demand he explain to me what the fuck he was doing. Something told me earlier, before Adrian, that he was about to say goodbye. The fear over losing him again had me feeling panicked.

"Are you leaving?" My voice was sharp, accusatory.

He continued to stare until finally his gaze fell to the floor. "Was planning on it."

I knew it. I hated how much it hurt that he was going to leave me again. "Why?"

"What difference does it make? I'll leave you here with Gio; he can help you. He'll stay with you here, and he'll keep you safe."

Frantic, wild emotions swept through me. It felt like he wasn't giving me a choice, as though he'd just exit my life simply because he felt like it was the right thing to do, or perhaps he truly hated me. If that were the case, then it only made that frenzied feeling worse.

If he hated me, then I'd completely take advantage of his hate. I'd ruin him the way he ruined me.

"I want you to stay." I softened my tone. I'd play the grieving fiancée card if that's what it took to have him sit with me, to stay with me. I knew it was wrong, but so was his choice to build me my dream home, then walk away as if it meant nothing at all. It was cruel, harsh, and the sort of poison that would eventually end us one way or another.

I was in love with him, and yet he chose not to love me back. Over and over again, we were cursed to walk through the same door that kept leading back to the room where we knew we'd hurt one another.

"Gio will stay," he softly explained, while scratching the back of his neck.

I slowly stood from the bath and brought my arms around myself, as the cold air hit my exposed skin. "Kingston, I don't want to be away from either of you right now. It's important to me that you stay. I'm in danger...they used his cell phone to text me just seconds before I opened the door. That's how close they were able to get today."

He flinched the smallest amount while glancing away. I reached for a towel right as Gio walked through the door. He glanced at Kingston, then me, as if he were trying to size up what was going on.

"Here you go, Elvis." He looked around for a place to put the sandwich, chips, and water.

Gesturing toward the room, I asked, "Can you set it in there? I'm going to lie down."

"I'm going to head back to the barn..." Kingston trailed off, moving from the doorway.

With the towel wrapped around me, I walked between both brothers and moved to the bed. "I don't want to be alone tonight."

"I'll be here," Gio offered with a smile.

I glanced past him and inspected Kingston. "I want both of you."

Deep down, I knew the thread of that statement was true. I may be toying with Kingston to inconvenience him, merely because he didn't want to be around me, but I did want him. I wanted both of them, and I wanted Kingston to confess that he'd finished the house for me, and I wanted him to tell me about all the things he built and why. I wanted him to tell me if he'd built in anything for his plants or had anything here at all that indicated that he'd one day be living with me.

"Elvis, I don't want to push Kingston if he doesn't—"

"Well, I do," I replied easily, while dropping the towel and slipping under the covers.

Kingston watched me with a calculating expression, where his eyes narrowed and one of his dark brows raised. Gio looked between us but didn't say anything.

"You don't think I know he hates me? I'm well aware that he does." I adjusted under the blankets and then began sipping from the water bottle Gio had brought me. "I simply don't care right now because under all that hurt and hate is one of my best friends. The boy who endured seeing someone murdered, all so he could rescue my favorite stuffed animal for me. The boy who once jumped into a fighting ring full of grown men, just so I wouldn't fight alone. The boy who used to teach me about plants and sunshine. Prove he's gone and I'll leave you alone."

Kingston's nose flared while he slammed his jaw together.

I raised my chin. "Break my heart again, King. Let me know you're out for good and I'll never bother you again."

"She's had a hard fucking day, King. Just come sit next to her so she'll be able to rest. She needs us," Gio finally said softly to his brother.

I didn't like that he needed permission from Gio to stay, but it worked. Kingston slipped out of his boots and pulled his shirt up over his head, which made embers from an old fire stir in my belly. It was supposed to be all ash and dust, but when he began walking toward the bed while unbuttoning his jeans, I couldn't breathe.

"You touch me, even once, Presley, and I'll touch you back. I highly suggest you stay under the covers, and I'll stay on top." I froze in place while he neared the bed. Gio was watching us carefully, but he wasn't moving.

"Gio?"

His blue eyes slid down to me and softened. "You sure you want me in there? Because I'm a little different than King. I want you to touch me, Elvis. I want you to want me, and if you need to be held, I want you to ask me. Is that what you need tonight, or do you only require the bastard twin who's all asshole vibes?"

Kingston settled on top of the covers next to me, then lifted his middle finger toward his brother. "Would you rather me bullshit her?"

"I'd rather you just make up your fucking mind," Gio snapped in reply.

I glared between the two brothers, then began eating my sandwich. There was a television on the opposite end of the room, mounted on the wall. I didn't miss that this bed was king size, where the ones in the other two rooms were both only queens. Someone had selected this size on purpose. If Gio did help at all, I had a feeling that would have been it, but maybe I was wrong. Maybe, deep down, King did have ideas that maybe we could find a way forward.

Kingston didn't reply while Gio began undressing.

"Grab the remote before you come over," I requested while finishing off my food. Both of them had to be hungry, and yet I didn't see them get anything to eat.

Gio slid onto the bed next to me, and while it was a king-size bed, I still felt snuggled tightly between them. They'd gotten bigger in the eleven months we were apart. Their muscles larger and more defined, and I knew they'd had a birthday, so they were both older now. Twenty years old... I was still eighteen for a few more...days. Shit, my birthday was only a few days from now.

The television turned on, and suddenly my favorite movie was playing. "How did you find this?" I asked, snuggling deeper into the bed.

"I pre-loaded movies on your TV about a week ago, while I was up here," Gio replied as the movie started.

"But you guys hate this movie."

Kingston scoffed. "You're naked under the covers, Presley. Don't assume we're paying attention to anything other than that."

I was staring up at him when he finally looked down at me and frowned. "Just watch your movie. I promised not to touch you."

My focus returned to the television as a young talking pig tried to fit in with the other farm animals, and the tight band around my heart that had held my grief all day began to loosen.

CHAPTER 18
KINGSTON

The room was annoyingly dark, save for the glowing stars that I'd pressed into the ceiling above Presley's bed. Gio was asleep next to her, and at some point, he'd turned the television off, thrusting the room into shadows. Presley slept, or at least it seemed like she was. I had stared down at her exactly three times because each time that I did, the blanket had shifted, revealing more of her skin that I didn't need to see.

Honestly, I was grateful once the TV was turned off, just so I didn't have to keep seeing the way her tits had pressed up against the soft duvet cover or how her dark hair looked against her creamy skin. The color of her hair reminded me of the soil I used to run my fingers through. The one thing that used to balance me. I saw that color and thought of my dreams and how they so easily rested against her neck, in silky waves. Removing my finger from hovering over her collarbone, I closed my eyes and curled my fingers into a fist.

I should be in the barn, or on my way to California, literally anywhere else other than lying in bed next to her. But fuck she was persistent. Why couldn't I just let her go, break her heart, and leave her once and for all?

It's what I'd told Gio I'd do... I told him I would, but he had to know what it would do to me. What it would do to her...if the tables were turned, there would be no way I'd ask him to give her up. I'd never be able to live with myself if he ever hurt in that way. Didn't seem to matter though, that I'd effectively carved out a place in my chest that she once resided in. It was always easier for the nice guy to get the girl, not the toxic one, ridden by his trauma and all the bullshit that convoluted his head.

Gio deserved this life. I deserved the shadows his would cast.

Slipping off the bed, I wandered through the room, trailing my fingers over the finished trim and walls. My eyes slid shut as I padded down the stairs.

One. Two. Three. I began counting, remembering exactly how much effort it took to nail the boards in place to finish each step.

Once I was on the bottom floor, my eyes fluttered open as I moved to the kitchen and began finding food. I was starving, after all the emotions of the day and the ones through the night. I located turkey and cheese and made a sandwich, which I consumed in nearly three bites. I followed that up with grapes and a tall glass of water.

By the time I turned away from the fridge, I let a colorful curse fly.

"Sorry," Presley apologized, while tucking her hands over her chest. She had slipped into the shirt I had taken off earlier and had left on the floor. I ignored what that did to me, that she'd been in my shirt earlier when I found her this morning, and now again. I wasn't sure what that meant, especially because Gio's was right next to mine.

"It's fine." I finally replied while cleaning up my mess.

Presley toyed with the butter dish, seemingly at peace with the darkened house. A tiny slice of moonlight flowed in through the kitchen window, and a bit more from where we'd left the curtains open.

"This house is better than I ever imagined."

I carefully set my plate inside the sink. "Yeah?"

Presley tilted her head up and stared. "Yeah...the tiny details especially."

"Well, Gio knows you pretty well," I answered, while gesturing toward the room. I felt slightly awkward because I was still in my boxers, no shirt or even socks on.

Her eyes trailed over my bare chest, and the same old ink that hadn't changed since she last ran her fingernails over each one of them. I couldn't bring myself to add anything that might not ever be exposed to her touch.

"Gio didn't build me this house," Presley said matter-of-factly, drawing an invisible line in the butter dish.

My head was already nodding. "He did—"

She shocked me by stepping around the counter and getting directly in front of me. Her head tilted back once more, those electric blue eyes on fire as she stared up at me. "Stop lying to me."

"I'm no—"

She raised her hand faster than I could process and slapped me across the face. My head jerked to the side as my eyes stung with tears merely from being hit so hard.

"Stop it." Her voice was a whisper, an anguished prayer.

I felt empowered to see how far she'd go to get me to stop. "Gio planned out every detail, hired the contractors, and gutted the whole place by himself."

Another slap landed against my cheek, but I had started walking toward her, making her back up.

"He didn't focus on anything else for months, Presley. Almost an entire year, he toiled in this fucking house. All so you would have a place to finally belong. Because he knew better than anyone that you've never felt like you really fit anywhere."

"There was one place I fit," she whispered on a sob while her ass hit the kitchen table.

I stared down at her. "Where?"

"Between you and Gio, you idiot. You two have been my roots, my wings, my entire origin story. Even when you leave, even when you're not even really here when you return. My soul is still tied to yours, which is why this game you're playing is so fucking stupid."

"I'm not playing a—" She lifted her hand to slap me again, but I gripped her wrist and then automatically went for the other when she lifted that one. Bringing her wrists together, I held them above her head as I leaned forward, covering her body with my own.

My mouth trailed over the column of her throat, hovering the smallest amount.

"Why do you keep hitting me?"

She fought against my hold, but I kept her in place, with her hands pinned above her head.

"You told me if I touched you, you'd touch me back."

I couldn't help the laugh that slipped from me or the way my cock swelled in my boxers.

"You're such a fucking brat, Presley," I whispered against her ear, right before biting down on the lobe.

She lifted her hips the smallest bit. "And you're such a fucking prick, and yet you're hard."

Even hearing her say that had my dick twitch and a groan slipping from my mouth.

"What is it you want from me?" I asked, almost desperate for her to just spell it the fuck out. I knew she was still angry with me for what I did to her last year. I knew she carried so much hurt that she might not ever get over what I did to her.

Shifting her head so her lips were near the side of my face, she whispered in reply, "I want you to stop calling me Presley. I want you to call me your queen again. I want you to stop pretending that you're not going to be a part of my future. I want you to handle me the way you've always handled me."

"And how's that?" I inched closer, allowing my erection to press against her thigh.

So fucking tempting.

She wet her lips and then went lax in my arms. "Like I'm yours.

Broken, whole, hurting, happy. Whatever I've ever felt, you always made room for it."

"And what do you feel right now?" I was even closer, and I knew she could feel my thickness against her thigh because she let out a small gasp.

Her lips lifted again, and this time I pulled her closer to the edge so she could grind against my cock through my boxers.

"I feel desperate. I need you to touch me. I need you to help me navigate this new hole in my chest that Adrian left behind."

My stomach tilted and soured. I didn't want to help her with anything Adrian related, but I had the unfortunate disposition of being in love with her, so I'd do whatever she asked of me. Even if it was to simply touch her, to make her feel so she could grieve the man who took her from me.

My heart shattered the smallest bit as I saw the lone tear slide down the side of her face. I moved so my tongue swiped at it, removing it from staining her skin.

Then I whispered softly, "Okay, *mi reina*."

She let out a sob as I released her wrists, and they came up, wrapping around my neck. Her mouth found mine in a frenzied rush. My hands moved under her shirt and spread her thighs so I fit between them. Using my fingers, I slid through her slick center with a hiss. She was completely soaked and ready for *me*.

Lifting her hips, I tossed her leg over my shoulder and lowered my face until I was tasting that sweet wetness that coated her smooth pussy lips. She let out a sharp cry as I worked my tongue over her clit and then remained there, gently tugging at it and playing with it before pushing inside of her. I moved slow, and deliberately, drawing desperate sounds from her. Ones that would likely wake Gio, but I was doing this for her.

I had to stop worrying that he'd walk away. I had to trust that what she said was true. Her roots started between the both of us; if one of us were to walk away, it would damage the entire integrity of who she is and fuck everything up beyond repair.

My face was soaked as I sucked and took my fill of her cunt, and when she was about to come, I lowered her hips back to the table.

"No. Please, Kingston," she sobbed while still shifting, desperate for friction.

"Relax," I whispered, while pressing a kiss to her neck. "I know you need to come, but I want to know how far you'll go to get your release."

"Kingston," she begged.

I picked her up and carried her with me to one of the kitchen chairs and sat down with my back against the wood, then settled her so she was straddling me. She let out a sultry moan as her pussy pressed against my swollen cock, still concealed by fabric, but my weeping tip had soaked it.

With my lips at her ear, I whispered, "We're going to play truth or pass. You pass, you miss out on getting to rub against me. You tell me what I want to know, you'll get to do whatever you want with me."

"I want you to fuck me, Kingston," she rasped in reply.

Her hands were tangled at my neck as she tried inching closer, attempting to rub against my hardness. I gripped her hip, holding her in place while I smiled against her cheek.

"Be good and I will."

"Fine," she whispered in my ear before sucking along the outer edge of it.

It made me thicken with a groan, but I pushed through. "First, tell me what things you've used to get off."

She kept kissing near my ear while pushing against my hold on her hip. "My fingers, a pillow a few times, and a..."

She hesitated, so I ran my fingers down her ass with a rumbled, "What?"

"A double penetration toy."

I hummed into her neck then whispered, "Take my cock out, but don't touch it."

She moved her hands from my neck and slowly peeled back the band from my boxers, allowing my cock to spring free.

She muttered near my neck, "You're soaked too."

"We're about to fuck, just you and me. I know the only other time you've been with one person was Adrian." I had to pause because even saying that made me want to grip her so hard that she got angry welts on her skin, and then I wanted to fuck her senseless.

"Tell me something you wished he did to you, but you were too nervous to ask for."

"It's a little soon to be going back—" she started, so I began to retreat.

"So you pass?"

Presley let out a tiny breath before slowly dragging her fingers up my arms and then wrapping them around my neck once more. I wanted her to tell me they hadn't fucked.

I *needed* her to tell me they hadn't.

Instead, she pressed her sweet lips to my ear once more and said, "He was perfect. His cock was thick and long, and always made me come—"

I swallowed the tightness in my throat, knowing I needed it confirmed that she'd actually done it. She'd had sex with him.

My hand fisted around her hair and pulled, revealing her throat. "Stop it."

She moaned while trying to push closer. "He liked to fuck me against things, the dresser, the wall, the balcony sometimes. He would fuck me so hard that I'd almost black out."

It wasn't like I had asked her to be faithful to me, or to Gio. We'd fucked her and then rubbed it in her face that we'd only done it to brag about it to her fiancé, but fuck this hurt.

"Presley," I warned. My other hand moved to her neck, where I began to squeeze.

She gasped a few times before she smiled. "Fine. I always wanted him to press his finger to my ass while he fucked me. I needed pressure in both places, but I didn't know how to ask for it."

145

I was a prick, and I deserved the burn I felt along my heart, but it didn't stop how hard I gripped her waist, lifting her and then slamming her down on my cock.

She gasped and held the back of my head, pulling my hair.

"Fuck," I rasped into her neck before I shifted my hips and pulled her against me. Her pussy was hot and tight, fuck even if she had fucked Adrian, she was still just as tight as she was the night we'd taken her virginity.

We began moving in a way that had her breathing labored; my strokes were deep as I pulled her away, before dragging her back with so much force she whined each time. Her nails made tiny little marks against my skin, and I realized I liked that. So I pulled her harder, and fucked her deeper. Her toes reached for the floor as she pressed impossibly closer, which made the chair creak.

"Feels so good, oh my god." She moaned loudly.

I ripped the shirt from over her head, so I could see all of her. Leaning down, I brought her left tit to my mouth and began to suck, then I lifted three of my fingers to her mouth.

"Get these wet for me."

She tried to catch her breath and asked, "Three seems like a lot."

I smiled before kissing her, then once we broke apart, I shoved all three into her mouth and allowed her to suck on them, coating them completely. Then against her ear, I gritted, "One finger isn't going to prepare you to take my cock and certainly not Gio's. I know you're desperate to have us both take you again, so I'm going to prep you to be ready for when we're both fucking you again."

Her hips moved faster as her mouth attached to my neck, sucking and moaning. I used my fingers to prod at her tight hole while she ground down on my cock. Each pass backward, she pressed into my fingers and hissed while shuddering forward.

"Yes, right there."

Movement near the stairs caught my attention. I saw my brother drop to one of the steps while he watched us. I didn't alert Presley or tell her. I just fucked her in the ass with my fingers, while letting her grind against me as hard as she needed. The chair continued to scrape against the floor with loud creaks and scrapes. Her moans grew louder and louder.

"Harder. Please, King, please press harder. I need—" She shuddered against me again, and I said loud enough for my brother to hear, "You're ready for another cock back here. I stretched you so you're ready to take us both, Presley. You want that, don't you?"

Her head tilted back as she cried, "Yes!"

"Say exactly what you want, out loud, so I can hear you."

Her hips rotated faster, pressing harder against my hand, while her breathing came in little spurts. "I want you to fuck me just like this, while Gio fucks me from behind. I want you both to take me in every way you can think of. I want to lose myself over and over between you both. I want to be yours to play with, to lo—" she stopped abruptly as if she caught herself, "I don't care as long as you both are there, and you both stay."

Her last sentence came on a cry as she shattered around my cock. Her body shook as I slowly guided my length in and out of her until I released her ass and gripped her hips as tightly as I could. My release spilled out, and because I was still pumping in and out of her, it began to leak down all over her thighs.

She sagged in my arms while she tried to catch her breath. That's when Gio finally moved, walking over from the stairs to where we were sitting. I worried he'd spout off some bullshit jealousy that he always carried around when it came to Pres, but he surprised me by gently pulling Presley off of my lap and into his arms.

"I'm leaking," she whispered, but he just kissed her forehead and held her closer.

"That's okay, Elvis. I like that he made a mess of you. I want you to sleep just like this under my chin tonight, and in the morning, I'm going to make a new mess inside you."

"Okay," she sighed, but she sounded content, which made something inside my chest release. Before she got to the stairs, she yelled from over his shoulder, "Kingston, you better come back to my bed tonight."

I smirked, then started cleaning myself up.

Once I was back in her room, I lay down where I had been before, but this time, I slipped under the covers. Gio held her closer to him, exactly how he said he would, but his eyes were on me as he quietly rumbled, "Tomorrow, you get to watch me fuck her. Alone. Just like I had to tonight. You'll stay right there and pretend to sleep while I shove my cock inside her cunt, and her tits bounce. While she moans her pleasure and begs to be filled in both holes, you won't move a single muscle."

I didn't reply, but I understood. Same old jealousy bullshit. We'd gotten nowhere and everywhere all at the same time. Didn't fucking care if it meant Presley was back in my universe and my brother understood that I'd be staying in hers.

CHAPTER 19

GIO

Presley's expression worried me.

She had this look in her eye that I had last seen that night she'd pulled a gun on us and we'd threatened war against the family. She stared at Adrian's dead body like that.

Kingston had put his body inside of a long, metal box, and he'd filled it with ice. He was still inside the body bag, but it was unzipped enough that we could see his lips and his face. I stood next to Pres while King stood on the opposite side of the metal box. We were inside the barn, and it was midafternoon, so light cut through the cracks of the weak boards needing to be replaced, and the silence was deafening.

I wanted to touch her, just to ground her because she seemed like she was floating away. Like a dandelion blown to the wind by a careless toddler.

"You okay, Elvis?" I finally asked, stepping closer. The way her eyes fluttered made me regret not fucking her this morning. She'd been sleeping so peacefully under my chin that I didn't have the heart to wake her. I ended up just staring at her for three hours, wondering what it would be like to have that future with her that I had once dreamed of having when we first talked about it. It felt so close now, so close I could see us living in the farm house, see us waking up together every morning. See her walk out through the front door, down those steps toward the barn where she could collect eggs each morning.

"No, I'm not," Presley finally replied while drawing closer to the body.

King stared down with her. "Wanna bury him?"

She shook her head. "I want to take him back to Italy. He deserves to be buried where his family can visit him. He has a family plot in a small village about thirty miles from his house."

My gaze locked with my twin's. She couldn't take a body back to Italy after just barely escaping.

"When did you want to go?" Kingston asked as if this was something we could actually entertain.

She glanced up, hope brimming in her gaze. "As soon as we can. His body won't last. I want to get on the jet, but Markos will be looking for us to enter the country. It's dangerous."

"Yeah." I searched her face and my brother's. "Really fucking dangerous."

Presley briefly glanced at me before zipping up Adrian's bag. "Well, I was hoping we could fly with El Peligro again."

"Of course you can," Kingston replied, right as I said, "Absolutely not."

Presley looked between us when the barn door suddenly opened. Scotty appeared, wearing his typical all black clothes and a grimace on his face.

"This is actually where I'm living if you don't mind," Kingston snapped at him.

Scotty looked around as if he couldn't care less. "Figured you'd be in the house you just spent nine months renovating."

Presley's head snapped over as if she'd been waiting for that little piece of information to be confirmed. I suddenly felt like shit for not being one hundred percent honest with her about that when she asked, but it seemed like King didn't want her to know.

"Well, you're—" King started, but Scotty wandered closer to the body and interrupted him.

"Presley, this is now bordering on obsession. You know what needs to be done, and how time is of the essence. Adrian's out, we need to move on."

Kingston slowly made his way around the box, so he stood between Presley and me.

"Scotty, I'm taking Adrian's body back to Italy," Presley stated evenly.

"No." Scotty shook his head. "You need to focus on meeting with Raul Privosi. He's the head of another family that has reached out about creating an alliance."

Presley looked down as if gathering her thoughts. After a few seconds, she raised her chin and met his stare. "I'm not budging on this. I'm taking Adrian to Italy, and then I'm finding Markos."

Scotty merely picked at a piece of gravel that had gotten stuck to the body bag. "Do you even know how your father is doing, knowing his enemies were within mere feet of where his family slept?"

"I'm sure he's doing about as well as I am. They texted me using his phone, Scotty."

"You were the one who invited them here, Lánya."

Fast as lightning, Presley raised her arm, and the barrel of a gun was pointed at her uncle. She pulled the hammer back, readying it to be fired. Kingston didn't waste a second; his arm was raised with his own firearm as well, backing Presley up.

Was I the only person who didn't walk in with a fucking weapon?

"What are you doing?" Scotty asked, not taking his attention off Presley.

She had the look in her eye, the one that worried me. "You will not stand there and tell me it's my fault Adrian was killed. Not when you're the one who set this all up."

Scotty raised his palms as if to calm her down. "I shouldn't have worded it like that. I'm sorry."

I watched her finger barely trace a line over the trigger as if she were considering pulling it.

"Don't call me Lánya anymore." Her voice shook with the smallest amount of rage.

Scotty waited, but after a few seconds, he nodded. "Fine, but will you at least come back to the manor and talk to your parents about this idea of yours of going back to Italy?"

"We'll take her back." I stepped forward, placing my palm on Presley's arm so she'd lower her gun.

"Don't speak for me, Gio. I'm not a fucking child anymore."

Scotty laughed, then stepped backward. "You're not even nineteen yet, Presley. You've had about six seconds of being an adult; that's not exactly a lot of life experience."

Her gun was back up, aimed at his forehead. "My knuckles are permanently scarred from how frequently they busted open. I got frost bite when I was ten. I dislocated my jaw when I was eleven, fought off six grown men at one time when I was just twelve. Fuck you and your life experience. Fuck you for stealing my childhood and using me however you wanted to use me."

Then, without any warning, she moved as quick as lightning with tossing the gun up and catching it by the barrel, the butt of the handle was used against the side of Scotty's head. She hit so hard, he went down immediately, and he remained there until she stepped over his body and exited through the barn doors.

I STOOD with my back to the wall in the dining hall. The place we ate as a family when the time called for it. Leather couches and armchairs were scattered around the room in a design that looked intentional. I always liked the long vines of greenery that stretched along the glass windows and mixed in with the iron beams along the back wall. Kingston sat perched against one of the long side tables that had copious amounts of alcohol stationed across it.

Presley stood with her arms crossed and her back to the brick wall across the room. She'd never stood there before, during one of our meetings, but she seemed skittish, or like she needed to ensure she knew exactly who it was that was standing behind her at all times. My gut told me she didn't trust Scotty, especially after what happened in the barn.

"Thanks for agreeing to meet," Presley said, meeting the eyes of my parents and hers. Alex was sitting on a leather couch with a bottle of water in her hand. Scotty had woken and made his way here, and now held an ice pack to his temple.

"I'm glad you said something, honey. We need to talk about the breach that happened yesterday," Kyle said from his place on one of the couches. He had his wife, Rylie, under his arm, while she watched Presley with concern etched along her face.

"Yes, well, the reason I wanted to meet was to explain that I will be taking Adrian's body back to Italy to lay him to rest there."

Kyle glanced over at Scotty briefly before his wife slowly got up from the couch and took a step toward her daughter.

"Honey, I know you're struggling with this. I can't even imagine after what you were forced to—"

Presley's eyes slammed closed while interrupting, "Mom, I'm fine. This isn't an emotional decision; it's a pragmatic one."

"This is in no way pragmatic, Presley. You're feeling grief, and it's not logical. Grief will cause mothers to crawl inside graves just to hold their children. It would have you sit in a blizzard if it meant you could feel someone familiar to you. It's why you used to sleep in the twins' beds when they were gone, all those months."

That was why everything smelled like her when we got back.

I hated how pink Presley's face became and how Kingston shifted on his feet, while he glared at Scotty.

"I understand what grief is, Scotty. This isn't that...I am sad that Adrian is gone. He was a good friend of mine. I even loved him in my own way, and I could have been happy with him, I think, but his death isn't causing me grief beyond logic. I'm not so blinded by pain that I can't see if this is a safe decision or not. I know it's not safe, but I'm determined to do it anyway."

Scotty shifted the ice pack, revealing the purple bruise that Presley left him with.

"Well, the answer is no. It's too dangerous."

Presley shrugged. "I'm not asking for permission. I'm informing all of you."

Kyle tapped his hand down against the leather armrest of the chair. "What's your plan to get past Markos and his men? We just barely got you and Alex out of there."

"*We* got them out," Kingston spoke up, pointing at his chest and then over at me.

Kyle glanced our way before over at his daughter again. "Yes, I understand that, but she doesn't have access to El Peligro again. She'll need—"

"She does," I argued, feeling oddly protective of Presley's plan. It was dangerous, but if she wanted to get it completed, then I would help her do it.

Rylie's eyes snapped from Presley over to me, then Kyle spoke up after clearing his throat.

"Just a year ago, you both stood there and said you would go to war with us, and now—"

"We know what we said," Kingston interrupted. "And we're aware of what we're offering now. Things have changed. They came to our home, dropped a body on our steps, and as far as I'm concerned, Adrian left this earth trying to protect Presley."

Scotty's shrewd gaze swung from Kingston to me before he pushed away from the wall and tossed his ice pack. "This is a waste of time." His voice escalated as he yelled, "Presley, you were trained for every situation, and this hiccup shouldn't be something that derails you so much that you're willing to endanger yourself and this family, again. I trained you for this."

"I wasn't trained to murder my family, Scotty! Although, I'm starting to wonder if that would have helped," Presley yelled back.

His brows caved inward. "What are you—"

"I was forced to kill my grandfather in front of Markos, his sons, and even Alex. I had no choice. You did not prepare me for that." Presley stepped off the wall, pointing at her uncle with rage.

The room fell silent at her admission. Kingston's jaw worked back and forth while he stared at Scotty, as if daring him to try and tell Presley even one more time that she should have been prepared for this.

A crack seemed to slip into my chest as I processed what Elvis had gone through, and just how broken she really was. There was only a small version of herself she was sharing with us since she'd returned. I was curious what it would feel like to have her completely shatter and allow King and me to help her heal.

"I'll go with them. I want to help." My mom suddenly stepped forward. She seemed to know how delicate this moment was, but her offering to go with us took me by surprise.

Kingston suddenly turned with the same expression I likely had. "What?"

Dad stepped up behind her, touching her hip. "Taylor—"

Mom closed her eyes, slightly shaking her head. "For as long as I can remember, we have tried to keep the boys away from Presley's fight. We have removed them from being able to step in and aid her in any way. This thirst for violence was indirectly bred into them. It has cracked this family to pieces, and it's time we stop allowing it to. Markos should have been ended years ago. I will go with Presley to ensure her safety and help find him."

Before Dad could argue, our sister said, "I'll go too."

"No. That's enough. We are leaving, or did you forget about that?" Dad yelled across the room, flexing his jaw.

"We have lived together for nearly twenty years, Juan. We are not going anywhere while our family needs us. Your sons love Presley. She's tied to us whether she chooses one of them, both, or neither.

She has earned our allegiance," Mom argued, tugging on his fingers. She did that sometimes when she wanted to get her point across without arguing.

Dad just shook his head.

"So, the family will end with you." Scotty shook his head while glaring at Presley. She glared back in a stance that was unlike anything I had ever witnessed pass between the two of them. He left the room moments later, but Presley hadn't stopped staring daggers at his back while he withdrew.

I knew I needed to talk to Henry about El Peligro going back to Italy and offering protection again, so I pulled out my cell right as Presley turned toward the terrace doors.

"I'll be on the farm," she said as she passed by me.

"We'll be in touch once we get things organized," I muttered to my dad as I followed Presley outside.

I FOUND her shooting at a target set up near the barn. She had unloaded three clips by the time she finally lowered her arms and turned toward the table that held her ammo and case.

"The fucking nerve of Scotty," she muttered angrily.

I walked closer, helping set up the rifle for her to shoot. "He's on a fucking power trip. Always has been."

"Yeah, I think I'm finally starting to see what you and King were always so pissed about." She twisted the rifle scope into place.

Things were quiet for a moment, while the graying clouds seemed to move overhead and the sun fought to break through. Her blue eyes searched over my face before landing on my mouth.

"You said something last night..." Her face flushed the smallest bit, which made her chin drop to her chest.

I used my pointer finger to lift it. "I mentioned making a mess inside you this morning."

"But you never did."

My mouth twitched with a smirk. "You were sleeping."

"I'm not sleeping right now." She tilted her head with a tiny, flirtatious smile.

Something stirred deep in my stomach at her words. Fear kept creeping in regarding her only wanting King, how she might just want to let me go, or only use me if she was craving two of us at once. But me by myself?

I had assumed she was okay with just passing on what I'd suggested last night due to her emotions being high.

"Are you saying you want me to make a mess inside you right now, Elvis?"

She bit her lip and glanced over my shoulder where the barn was. Kingston's stuff was still inside, all packed up for the departure he never took. He'd kill me if we fucked on his bed, or invaded his space like that.

I stepped around the table and pulled her into my arms, sweeping her feet from the ground. "Come on then, Elvis. Let's go make a mess."

CHAPTER 20

PRESLEY

There, buried in my heart, was a wound that I refused to acknowledge.

I knew exactly what I was doing, and I wasn't too proud to do it. Every waking moment that I wasn't distracting myself in some way was riddled with thoughts about Adrian, about Scotty's betrayal. I couldn't even enjoy the fact that I had the twins back in my life because my heart was heavy with worry.

I knew it was some form of grief. I just couldn't pinpoint which thing was causing me so much heartbreak. Was it the murder I'd been forced to commit? The blood on my hands due to my proximity to Adrian, or the fact that my entire childhood had been made up of strings, tugged and knotted by Scotty's fingers.

Each time I toiled with the answer, I'd feel despair, and all I'd want to do was sink into a ball and cry.

I was so fucking angry.

The twins offered an outlet for me that I wasn't too proud to take advantage of. They owed me this distraction after taking my virginity as if it were merely a trading card they stole and wanted to brag about. They owed me for breaking me too many times to even count.

So as Gio carried me into the barn, I reveled in it.

The doors closed behind us with a kick from Gio's boot, and he continued toward the bed. Gio laid me down gently on the cool covers, and I hated how gentle he was. I needed there to be a disconnection between us, like there was with Kingston last night, when I had slapped him multiple times and he'd taken me rough after prying secrets from me.

Gio's lips were on mine seconds later, but he moved down my body quickly, removing clothing as he went. My shirt went, then my bra and jeans, until I was just in my underwear. His fingers moved over my pubic bone and slowly over the fabric of my thong.

"Did you ever clean up the mess my brother made last night?" he asked with a husky voice. He wore a band T-shirt with threadbare jeans and unlaced boots. The way the graying sky spilled in through the small window above the barn loft made his eyes a silver blue. That wound deep in my heart throbbed with an itch to run my fingers through his hair and trace his jaw. I wanted to ask how these months have treated him. How he fared after the humbling experience with his aunt, and how he was forced to heel.

Instead, I ignored my pain and spread my legs. "I didn't."

His fingers hooked under the thin band at my hipbone. "Filthy, Elvis. Such a filthy, fucking mess." He pressed a kiss to my stomach and then my belly button.

"Well, you aren't getting your cunt licked then, because I'm not touching my brother's cum. But why don't you get my cock nice and ready to make that mess inside you."

My thighs clenched tightly together at his command. He stepped back, tugging his shirt over his head, then unfastening his jeans so they parted, revealing his black boxers.

Curling my fingers around the band at his waist, I tugged it down until his swollen length popped free. Tan with a purple hue, his length had protruding veins along the long shaft. He was already weeping at the tip as I ran my thumb over him. Without wasting any more time, I wrapped my fist around his thick base and leaned closer to allow him to skim over my tongue.

My eyes flew up as I watched Gio groan and tilt his hips forward, which had him sliding deeper inside my mouth. Gagging the smallest amount, I started to pull back only to have Gio hold my head in place. He then slowly fucked my throat. "So good, Elvis."

My eyes watered as they tried to connect with his, but his head was tipped back as satisfied moans erupted from him. It encouraged me to hold him tighter while moving my mouth over him. I sucked and licked, and with each pass, he'd pull me closer, suffocating me only to release and pull out of my mouth completely.

"Seems like you're already making a mess, Elvis." His thumb swiped at some spit that remained after he'd pulled out.

"I want you to bounce on my cock while you face the door."

He was doing this on purpose, but I had a feeling Gio had watched Kingston and me last night, so whatever game the twins were playing, I didn't mind being at the center of it.

Standing from the bed, I waited for Gio to sit, and then I settled between his spread thighs. His fingers pushed my thong to the side as he pulled me down onto his slick length. The adjustment was slow at first, the spreading of his heavy cock inside my tight center, but I eased onto it. Gio was bigger than Kingston by a marginal amount; it made sucking his dick a lot of work, but when he stretched my ass or pussy, it was a bit of an adjustment.

Gio hissed while wrapping my hair around his fist, and then with my palms down on his thighs, I began to rock back and forth over him. The sensation felt incredible, the way his length filled every sensitive place inside me. My belly swooped and heated until a moan slipped from my lips and I began moving at my own pace.

"That's it, Elvis." He palmed my breasts, kneading them while lifting his hips to push his length further inside of me. "Bounce on my cock."

I did as he said, fully acclimated to his girth, and I slid against him, desperate for my release as the feel of his cock stoked a fire inside me. Our moaning was nearly in sync as his hips canted briskly and his hands came to my waist, holding me in place. It was when his pace quickened that my jaw went slack and a silent scream seemed to erupt from my chest. My first orgasm slammed into me with a force so intense that when the door to the barn opened, I didn't stop begging.

"Faster, Gio. I need...I need—"

"You're leaving a ring of cream around my cock, Elvis. I'll make sure you get another orgasm, just relax and keep bouncing."

My eyes flicked back up, seeing that Kingston had come inside and shut the door. My mouth was still gaping as another orgasm continued to build, and my nails dug into Gio's jeans. He spoke filthy things behind me, while pulling my hair, forcing my chin to raise toward the ceiling.

Kingston wasn't moving closer, but he also didn't stop watching. He wore the shirt I had slipped into last night, a deep burgundy T-shirt with black jeans and thick soled boots. His hair was askew, and the way he stared with those deep amber eyes had a thrill shooting off inside me. Just knowing he was looking and that he might walk over and touch me. With my eyes locked on King, I rotated my hips, grinding them harder against Gio's lap, and I was still desperate for friction, so I used my fingers to rub over my clit.

Kingston chided from his place in the corner. "You're going to make her use her own hand, brother?"

Gio didn't stop, but he did slap my hand away and replaced my ministrations with his own. I saw King smile as he watched his twin's fingers move over my clit while his cock slid in and out of me.

"Presley, you're making me hard," Kingston said with a sigh as if this were a problem. I heard Gio grunt some curse from behind me, but my eyes were on the other twin across the room, who was now pulling his cock out. He used his fist to rub over the tip and then down the long length.

It made me move faster over Gio's length, while my thighs

clenched, and I felt like I was about to come again. Kingston stepped closer, with his dick in his hand, his eyes burning while they watched me, and right as he got in front of my face, he stood completely still.

Each time I bounced or moved forward, my cheek would skim the silky head of Kingston's cock. His tip was wet, so with each pass, a mess of liquid would be left behind on my face. Having them both touch me again had my insides melting and my core clenching so much that I began crying out as another orgasm slammed into me.

Gio must have found his release shortly after, based on how he froze under me. Kingston gripped my chin and locked his gaze with mine. I knew what he wanted, but he wasn't outright saying it, so I opened my mouth and stuck out my tongue so that the velvet tip of his cock slowly slid over my taste buds. He stroked my jaw, then released a deep groan as ropes of white cum began coating my open mouth and face.

"Now that's a fucking mess," Kingston rasped while catching his breath.

Gio shifted me, so I was leaving his lap, as he pulled out of me. "King, I fucking told you not to interfere."

"I didn't." Kingston shrugged.

Gio glanced at my face. "Really?"

"You both were in my room, fucking on my bed. Forgive me for taking out my dick and walking over to ejaculate."

"I didn't interfere last night," Gio complained.

King smirked while moving to the dresser to pull out a rag. He brought it over to me and gently began cleaning up my face before addressing his brother again.

"And no one told you not to. If I see you two having sex in the house or barn, I'm going to assume you're either open to sharing or I can, at the minimum, release all over her face."

A year ago, I would have worried about them fighting or arguing over me. I would have been concerned for both brothers' feelings and how the tension would affect us. Now I simply didn't care.

They weren't concerned about how it would make me feel when they fucked me, and then said those horrible things to me. When they made me feel stupid for loving them, stupid for always falling for them. I ignored their arguments and continued to clean myself up. I needed to shower and pack.

Right as I stood from the bed, I heard the brothers go silent.

"Presley?" Kingston called for me.

I didn't turn around until I got to the door, and then I glanced over my shoulder.

"Can you please let me know when everyone is ready to leave? I'd like to get going as soon as possible."

Their brows curved inward, conveying their confusion and possibly their frustration. I didn't care if they wanted something deeper from this moment. I refused to give it to them. They were the ones who made it clear that fucking each other could mean absolutely nothing. This was pleasure, and nothing more.

I FOUND my way back to my room in the farmhouse. It was strange how at home I felt here, as if it'd just been waiting for me to settle in. I thought back to all those days I had worked on this house, gutting it; imagining a life inside of it. The completion of such a big dream was still not something I had fully come to terms with, or the fact that Kingston was the one to do it.

A deep sorrow began to fill my chest like loose thread, unspooling and tightening around my organs. I felt so betrayed by Scotty, by the twins, and even my father. Yet, there was this hope that still connected me to King and Gio, this tiny flicker in the darkest part of my heart that whispered of a fresh start. When I closed my eyes, I could see the three of us living here. I had even pictured what it would be like to take it a step further and thought up this delirious idea of one day becoming a mother.

That sadness returned as I pictured Adrian's face, and how he'd looked at me when I had talked about my wedding dress in the car. How there was a future he'd imagined for us as well, and now there was no chance of that ever happening. He might not have ever had my entire heart, but ever since I had fallen for the twins, I had gotten used to only giving away fractions of it at a time. It wouldn't have been fair to him, but it would have been enough for me.

"Presley?" Gio knocked, calling through the door.

I had locked myself inside, needing space and some time to sort out my thoughts. I had fucked both of them, individually—thinking it would somehow fill this gaping hole in my chest, but it did nothing but remind me that they'd both hurt me. Even if what Kingston said was true and Gio didn't want any part of it, he still said those hurtful words after he'd had a hand in taking my virginity. He was still complicit in breaking me.

"I just want to be sure you're okay!" Gio called again with a small thud, likely his forehead falling to the wood.

I wanted to yell at the door that he was wasting his time. The only thing I needed from him was an occasional orgasm. I didn't care if he checked on me or brought me flowers. I didn't care if he was sorry. I wouldn't be trusting him with even the tiniest fraction of my heart any time soon. I was glad we each had separate rooms as I planned to remain in mine, without them, for as long as I felt like it. Eventually, he walked away, and I let out a small sigh of relief.

Eyeing the clawfoot tub, I decided to submerge these feelings and regrets, and most of all release the aching in my chest that hadn't let up since I found Adrian on the front steps.

IT WAS LATE when I finally emerged from my room. I was thirsty and needed a snack, but I didn't want to risk running into the twins, so I waited until it was late enough that I knew they'd be asleep.

As I tiptoed out of my room, I saw that the doors to the twins' rooms were wide open. Each room had the smallest amount of light pouring in, either from a TV screen or LED light of some kind. Gripping the wood trim, I verified that both Kingston and Gio were sleeping. Something about seeing them both on their stomachs in the exact same position but two different beds, completely at peace, had warmth sliding in through the cracks of my broken heart.

It was how they'd always slept unless I was between them.

Leaving them both exactly where they were, I lightly jogged downstairs and ventured toward the kitchen. I had just pulled a cup down and filled it with tap water when I noticed something burning just beyond the barn. Squinting, I tried to ensure it wasn't just something I had imagined, but when the smoke began to billow into the sky, I realized it was an actual fire.

"What the hell?" Who would be burning at this hour and what—

"*No.*" I gasped aloud as I dropped the glass into the sink. It shattered everywhere, echoing loud enough to wake the twins. I didn't care. I was already running toward the front door, throwing it open, and running outside barefoot.

I had on a thin T-shirt and small cotton shorts as I tore through the cold February air. The ground was freezing as my feet slammed into the icy earth and my heart raged within my chest. I heard someone call my name from the house, but I just kept running toward the blazing fire.

It was far enough from the barn that it wasn't in danger of catching, but still the flames licked at the sky, scorching something so hot that even as I neared, I knew it was too late.

Tears slid down my face as I kept running, uncaring for rocks and other rubble, tearing at my skin. I felt some sort of resistance in my skin when I climbed the fence bordering the field, but it didn't matter as I finally drew closer and felt the heat against my face. My eyes searched the space, unwilling to accept what I knew was burning inside.

The metal box was in the center of the flames; the body bag had completely melted away, revealing Adrian's burnt body.

A scream tore from me as I fell to the ground.

There were strong arms that came around me seconds later, lifting me off the cold field. I didn't pay attention to who, but I knew both brothers were outside with me, watching as the man I had considered marrying burned to ash.

Another angry scream scraped up my throat, burning and burning, but I couldn't stop. This one thing I had asked for. Just one, and Scotty couldn't give it to me. I hated him. I hated him so much that I wanted to tear the skin from my bones. I wanted to jump into the flames and burn with the man who had gently tended to my very broken heart.

"Where is he?" Kingston asked. I knew he meant Scotty; they likely knew this had his fingerprints all over it as well as I did. I had defied him, and he found a way to get his way in the end. Now there was no reason for me to go to Italy to bury him, no danger I had to worry about in returning for a senseless task that would have tipped off Markos.

How dare Scotty take this from me. How dare he burn Adrian when I had specifically asked to return him to his family plot.

I was so angry that I pushed out of the arms that were holding me, and I began running toward the manor.

"Presley!" Gio yelled after me as I continued to run.

Kingston must have stayed behind to put the fire out because it was only Gio who ran behind me, and when I came close enough to the terrace doors, instead of using the keycode, I bent down and grabbed a rock and threw it as hard as I could through the glass French doors.

"Fuck, Presley." I heard Gio yell from behind me, but he was too far back to stop me.

I burst through the glass and ran toward my family wing. The door was open as I approached, which meant Scotty was either inside or he'd just left. I wanted him to be inside. My hands shook as my breathing came in and out of my mouth in chaotic waves. My chest ached from how hard my lungs had just pumped cold oxygen into them, and my feet were numb.

The living room was dark, along with the kitchen, but I pushed on down the hall, feeling a strange sense of resolve. I knew I was likely tracking blood from my feet, but I just didn't have it in me to care. Instead, I grabbed one of the handguns that Scotty had hidden in the hallway bookshelf and turned toward his door with both arms raised.

I pulled the trigger without seeing behind the door, and I just kept shooting until the clip ran out. Gio stood to the side with a heaving chest and his eyes blown wide. My father ran down the stairs, holding his own gun, ready to shoot. Gio ran interference and began explaining, but I focused on the door, now shredded with bullet holes.

I kicked the wood as hard as I could, knowing Scotty could easily shoot back if he were still alive, but not caring.

His queen-sized bed was made, his room as tidy as it ever was. His dogs were gone, and I knew if I looked in his dresser, his clothes would be as well. Dropping the emptied gun to my side, I walked farther inside, knowing he left me a note somewhere.

Sure enough, it was pinned to the picture of me above his desk. It was of me when I was little, my head was up through the moon roof of the car my dad drove, and I had my arms out wide like I was flying. The memory had me sucking in a sharp breath.

His words when I was eight came back, reminding me of that happy memory. He'd replaced it with a blood-soaked horror that I blamed myself for years, from that first moment he'd ordered me to kill.

"Presley, honey." My dad said my name as he carefully stepped inside the room.

I plucked the note from the picture on the cork board and let it fall to the ground.

Lánya,

I told you it was too dangerous. Next time, listen.

-Scotty.

My dad drew closer, gently taking the note from me. "Presley, come here, honey."

I spun around to face him and began sobbing.

He caught me as I fell to the floor and began telling him every single detail of what Scotty had done. I explained the photo that Adrian had emailed me, and the burned body. I told him everything, and my father rocked me in his arms like I was a child again. I didn't know where Gio went, but I didn't care.

My dad carried me upstairs to my bedroom, where I eventually fell asleep. When I woke sometime during the night, my father had fallen asleep on one side of me, and my mother was on the other. The idea that they were there to keep me safe, to protect me, had me sinking into sleep once more and subconsciously hoping I didn't wake up.

CHAPTER 21

KINGSTON

The smell of burning flesh still branded my nostrils as I began digging the six-foot-deep grave. I had managed to put out the fire last night and ensure it didn't spread, but it took hours for it to completely die. I passed out on my bed inside the barn for a few hours before returning with a bandana tied around my face to help with the smell.

Rage pushed me each and every time I dug into the soil, ensuring the ash was cleared away from the body. But no matter how much debris I cleared, it was still smoking and charred.

Fuck. I didn't like Adrian, but Presley cared for him, and she'd already lost him. She didn't need salt poured into her open wound like this. Scotty was going to pay for doing this to her, which was the very next thing on my list to attend to.

I pulled out my phone, tossing the shovel aside. The body would need to cool completely before I could properly bury it. I'd already planned to get a casket here and wrap his body up, so he could be laid to rest respectfully in a proper grave. Unfortunately, instead of Italy, he'd be laid here, where his body would remain connected to Presley's future.

Navigating over to my text thread with Henry, I shot him a message.

Me: I want the manor security system completely gutted. All the locks, all the cameras. Every keypad inside and out. The gates. All of it. Replace everything, and make sure you swap out the armory locks as well. I want it all changed, and I want men stationed around the perimeter, all of Scotty's men need to be disposed of. I want them all dead, every single one of them.

Dots were already bouncing around before I finished my text.

Henry: Consider it done.

If Scotty wanted to test the nature of the beast we'd resurrected, then fine. He thought we were heartless before; he had no fucking clue what he just unleashed.

I punched out one last message, going with a hunch I had. I couldn't prove it, but that image I saw on Presley's screen and her ire toward her uncle told me there was a connection to Markos that we were missing. I wasn't entirely sure, but I decided I'd go with it anyway.

Me: I want the bodies of all his men sent to Italy. Dump them in front of Adrian's home with a message inked into each forehead.

Henry: Inked?

I glanced up at the smoke still rising from the body.

Me: Yes, inked. I want you to tattoo the bleeding black heart of El Peligro into each and every forehead. I want him to know we're not just coming for him; I want him to know we're coming to end him.

IT WAS LATER that afternoon when I first saw Presley again.

A car made its way up the mile and a half drive that was rarely used. We typically just crossed the field between the manor and the farmhouse, but there was an actual driveway that was accessible.

Her dad's Range Rover rolled to a stop in front of the house, and Rylie exited the passenger side while Presley came out through the back passenger door.

Her parents tipped their heads back, taking in the view of the house. A tiny kernel of pride and anxiety swarmed my chest as I watched them inspect it. Rylie began gushing over the finalized details, and Kyle even seemed pleased as he tested the strength of the handrail leading to the porch.

Presley, however, seemed completely unfazed as she rounded the car and lifted the back hatch. She immediately grabbed a box and started jogging up the steps.

She was moving in.

Why did that realization send butterflies and knots throughout my stomach? This is exactly what I wanted, and yet the fear that only Gio would have this with her still poked around in the back of my mind.

"Kingston!" Kyle called for me, seeing me near the barn.

I pulled my gloves off and walked over. I smelled like smoke and had ash all over me, but I had enough respect for him because of Presley, not to just ignore him. Once I was close enough, he tentatively placed a hand on my shoulder.

"I wanted to thank you for finishing this house for her. I think she needs it now more than ever."

Presley returned to grab another box, shooting me a glare. I guess we were back to hating each other.

"I'm glad it's something she can feel at home in," I replied, trailing after Presley's dark hair that had lifted with the breeze. She'd jogged up the steps, and I knew my brother was going to kick his own ass for missing the opportunity to help her unload all her shit in the house. He'd been going crazy over how to get her to return to how things were. I didn't know how to tell him that was likely never going to happen...especially after last night.

Kyle gave me one more pat on the shoulder before saying, "It means a lot to me that she has you boys. I know things are complicated between you, but deep in my bones, I know you'll always protect her, and for that, I am eternally grateful to you."

My eyes found the ground, still feeling ashamed of the threat I'd made to Presley a year ago. Hopefully, he really believed that I would have never hurt her and would have shot myself before I would have ever allowed a single hair on her head to be harmed. Somewhere inside, I really *needed* him to believe that.

Thankfully, Kyle moved on, joining in to unload the car for Presley. I decided to give them some space, so I walked back to the barn, grabbed some clothes, and made my way back to the manor to shower. I'd never had to put out a fire that had a burning body inside of it before. I'd never smelled burning flesh in a way that it seemed to coat my tongue and skin. I wanted to scrub for days until the smell left me, but as soon as his body cooled, I'd go right back to smelling like death because he'd have to be buried.

It was just one more thing I'd make Scotty pay for.

HOURS LATER, after I had checked in with Henry and Gio regarding Scotty's men, I headed toward the barn. It wasn't super late, but I was exhausted and just wanted to sleep.

I didn't even have the energy to slip out of my clothes before I pulled the blanket over my body. My face hit the pillow right as someone walked inside the barn.

"Why are you sleeping out here?" Presley asked, sounding irritated.

Opening one eye, I watched as she crossed her arms over her chest, waiting for me. She wore a pair of leggings with a cropped T-shirt, revealing her toned stomach. Her hair was down and the pouty look on her face made me instantly uncomfortable in the position I was lying in.

My mouth was half mashed into the pillow, but I managed, "Because this is where I live."

Her lips pressed together while she took a few steps closer. "I thought you had decided to sleep in the house."

"No. Just that one night."

Hurt flashed across her features, making her lip tremble the smallest bit. I decided to sit up and clarify. "I thought you were pissed at me again, anyway."

"I am, but that doesn't change the fact that I want you in the house."

I stretched and lay back down on the bed. "Tough shit. I'm not one of your sex toys you can pull out when you want to get off and then toss back in the drawer when you're done."

Anger gleamed in her bright blue eyes. Her fingers dug into her arms so tight she was starting to leave white indents. But still, she leaned forward and smiled while she replied. "Rather a toy to be used, than a heart to be broken. Suit yourself, I'll gladly fuck Gio. He's bigger anyway."

She turned around and slammed the door on her way out.

She knew exactly what to say to get under my fucking skin. I should have just stayed in bed and let her go. I should have ignored her barb, because I knew she didn't give a fuck that Gio was bigger; we were both massive, so him being bigger than me wasn't her suffering in any fucking way. Still, her words scraped like talons down my mind and over my heart in invisible gashes.

I tossed the covers off and stormed out of the barn, stomping across the gravel drive way and up the steps to the farmhouse. The door was still unlocked as the automatic bolt hadn't slid into place yet. I angrily turned the knob, pushed it open, then slammed it behind me. It made Presley jump while on her way up the stairs.

Her eyes were huge when she registered my expression.

"Kingston...I was just—"

I pulled my shirt up over my head and pushed my jeans down. My boots flew off as I kicked them and then I ran.

"Wait...I'm," she yelped while darting toward her bedroom, "I'm sorry!"

I ran up the stairs after her and placed my palm up, stopping her door from slamming. "You will be."

"I was just trying to get under your skin," she admitted while backing up toward the bed.

"News flash, *mi reina,* you've been under my skin since we were kids. Since you first brought me a jar of warmed dirt. Since you helped me grow things, and you weren't afraid that I seemed to ruin them. Since your freckles made me smile." I continued walking toward her.

Her eyes watered as I drew closer, but then she glanced away like these words hurt her.

"But tonight, you didn't try to get under my skin. You tried to get out from under it, and I won't allow that." I tugged her hair back with one hand and gripped her by the throat with the other, before slamming my mouth to hers.

Our teeth and tongues clashed together in an angry wave of passion. I continued to pull her hair, while her nails angrily traced my skin and clung to my neck. We moved backward when I finally released her and spun her around. Pushing her face down, I was about to explain what I was going to do to her, but my brother walked into the room.

"What's going on?"

He was only wearing a pair of boxers, his hair was wet, and his expression was completely blank.

Holding Presley down on the bed, I began pulling her leggings down, revealing the thin strap of a teal thong that slid through her ass. "She came out to the barn and told me she was glad I wasn't going to fuck her because you were bigger than me anyway."

Gio smirked. "I *am* bigger."

"Regardless..." I returned my focus to Presley. "I think I should remind her exactly how big I am."

My brother stepped into the room and drew closer to where she was lying face down.

"You want to teach her orally or by using lube?"

Something sparked in my chest. I was worried he'd be against us using her like this, but she was using us. It was all toxic and messy, but it was ours, and at this point, I wasn't sure we'd ever know anything other than this.

"Both." I smiled while slapping Presley's plump, smooth ass. She tried to say something, but Gio moved onto the bed so he was near her head, pulling her tank top off.

"Shhh, it's okay, Pres." He smoothed her hair back. "This is going to feel so good. I promise you."

"I say you remind her how easily you can hit the back of her throat first. That way, while you're fucking her in the ass, she can take me down her throat," Gio suggested.

"Get up on all fours, Presley," I ordered while my brother and I swapped positions.

She did as I said, slowly moving to her hands and knees while glaring at me with that defiant electric gaze. My cock bobbed in front of her face, while my twin brother knelt behind her.

"How do you know I won't bite you?" She smiled up at me. My breath nearly hitched at the way her dark lashes fluttered, and the freckles across her nose took me back to all the times I had watched her and instantly felt like I was home.

"Because you want to get off. Badly enough that you're fucking us without actually forgiving us. So open those beautiful lips and wrap them around my cock while I fuck the back of your throat."

Right as she leaned over the head of my cock and opened her mouth, my brother spread her cheeks open and began licking through her crack. She let out a sultry moan while slowly taking all of me in.

Dragging pieces of her hair into my fist, I began directing her rhythm while she began pulling back and swirling her tongue over the head of my erection. Each time she lowered herself and began choking, and her eyes began to water, I smiled.

"Doesn't really feel like I'm that much smaller now, *mi reina,* does it?"

She moaned again, but she was a mess. Spit had smeared around her mouth and dripped down her chin, all while her eyes remained on me. In and out, I slid through her mouth and hit the back of her throat. Gagging sounds filled the room, while Gio continued to lick and suck through her cunt from his position. She seemed to be handling it well until my brother decided to line his cock up with her and then glanced up at me.

"Let me have her hair."

Releasing her strands, he gathered them up in his fist and then slid inside her in one harsh push.

She released me with a muffled scream, only to reclaim my cock seconds later.

Gio began pumping in and out of her while holding her hip with one hand and her hair with his other. "Still so fucking tight, Elvis."

My orgasm had started to build as she hollowed out her cheeks and began sucking harder than before. I knew my brother was close by the way his hips began slamming against her in rapid strokes. His praises and groans increased as well, and then she released me, only to lower her mouth to my ball sack, where she engulfed my balls in her mouth and moaned.

I didn't want to finish on her face, or even down her throat. I had one thing in mind when I had marched up here behind her. Pulling away from her, I got Gio's attention while he was mid thrust.

"I want back there."

He glanced up, extremely concentrated on where his cock was gliding in and out of her. "Fuck off."

"I'm serious. Come finish in her mouth, I need back there."

He let out a frustrated sound but released her. "You owe me."

We both moved around the bed while Presley sagged into the covers with a moan. "I desperately need to come."

"I'll make sure you do," I promised while I used the wetness from her pussy to coat her tight hole. Gio aligned his length with her face and praised how good she was at taking both of us. He pushed her hair back and then pressed a kiss to her forehead before he gently slid his tip over her tongue.

"This is for being such a fucking brat, Presley." I lightly slapped her ass while I slid the head of my cock inside her. I remained there for a second, letting her acclimate. I knew I probably should grab some lube, but she was wet enough that if I slid through her cunt, I'd be prepped enough to push into her hole.

After pulling back and doing exactly that, I pressed into her with a groan. She was so tight that I nearly burst right there on the spot. I had to stop a few times, ignoring how fast her head bobbed over my brother, so I wouldn't come.

I'd pull back and push in further. She'd gag on Gio's cock, and I'd repeat the process.

Once I was in deep enough, I held both her cheeks apart while pushing in harder and harder. She stretched for me, adjusting to my swollen cock.

"Big enough for you, *¿mi reina?*"

Gio pulled out of her mouth and tipped her chin up. "Answer him, Elvis."

She began shaking as I continued to pump into her, then the begging began. "King, I need—"

I slapped her ass before covering her pussy with my hand, where I began rubbing her clit.

"Answer me. I know exactly how long it took to push into you without lube and how much of your ass my cock stretched. This must burn, *mi reina*, am I wrong?"

Tears tracked down her face as she moaned her pleasure.

"What do you have to say for yourself? I'll accept an apology."

Her fiery eyes landed on mine right as she wet her lips. "I think Gio would be fucking me harder if he were still back there."

Gio took her jaw and shoved his length back into her mouth, in punishing force. He began fucking her with deep strokes that had her gagging and more tears streaming down her face.

She was pushing me on purpose. I knew there was a void she was trying to smother. A pain that she didn't want to feel, so she wanted to feel something else. I knew what she was doing, and I also knew it was complex as fuck. Did I want to be used? No, but did I deserve it?

Yes.

I slammed into her harder, making her jolt forward. Gio cursed while readjusting in her mouth, but I didn't pay attention to him. I focused on the red welts on her ass from my handprints.

My palm came down again against her ass while I thrust, but I used my other hand to quickly move over her clit.

She began to shake again while pushing back against me. Gio must have finally found his release because he was slowing his thrusts while holding her head in place. I heard a few muffled praises from him before he finally sagged back in the bed.

I slapped her ass again. "You swallow all my brother's cum?"

Her head sank down to the bed, but I reached forward and pulled her up by her chest.

"Answer me. Did you swallow?"

I kept pushing in and out of her, making her tits bounce as I held her back to my chest.

"Every drop," she rasped in reply.

"Good fucking girl."

My arm was a tight band under her tits, holding her to me as I glanced at my brother. "Gio, come here. Need you to slide into her cunt, as she mentioned, you're bigger than me. Slide inside her, let her come on your cock while I finish inside her."

He moved without hesitating, sliding his hand over his length to ensure it was nice and hard. Once he was close enough, he began sliding his tip through her soaked pussy lips until he was granite once more.

"I need to come," she begged while her fingers went to Gio's shoulders. I froze in place behind her while my brother sat back on his heels and helped her somewhat straddle him. I hadn't pulled out, so I moved with her as she adjusted over him. She began moving her hips over him while I adjusted myself behind her. Each time she rotated forward, I thrust up, driving my cock deeper. I was seconds from coming.

"That's it, Elvis," Gio praised while pressing his thumb to her bottom lip. "Slide that aching pussy over my cock."

My hands were on her waist, holding her for leverage. The two of them moved slowly, but the way her head pressed back into my shoulder, I knew she was enjoying it.

With my lips at her ear, I whispered, "Make a mess of his cock, so I can hear that pretty, desperate begging sound you make. I'm so hard it hurts, Presley. So fucking hard and so ready to come, be a good girl and go first."

Her breathing was ragged as she dug her nails into my brother's shoulders, but her hips moved back and forth over my brother's cock fast enough that she began to cry out, and right as she did, I shoved my face into her shoulder with a cry of my own. I exploded inside her, and I felt like my soul had left my body while her tight hole caressed my length like a velvet glove.

"Well shit, I'm about to—" my brother said in a rush. With Presley still on top of him, he suddenly thrust up and let out a deep groan, coming for the second time.

We all worked to regulate our breathing as Gio slowly pulled out of her first, and then ever so slowly, I began to do the same.

Once we were out, Presley laid down on her quilt, making her dark hair fan behind her. Her fingers gently touched her pussy, and then farther back to her ass.

"I'm a mess," she sighed.

"Let me get you something to clean you up, Elvis," Gio offered while climbing off the bed. He pulled his boxers back over his softening erection. Presley shifted in bed, crawling up to the pillows, and turning so she faced me.

"You going back to the barn?"

I tucked away a sweaty piece of her hair while Gio returned, and he began gently cleaning her up by lifting her thigh and gently rubbing the cloth through her pussy. It reminded me that while she was only using us, my brother was desperately trying to win her back. I had lost hope that she'd want that, but maybe I could help get things back to where they were.

"Do you want me to?"

She rolled her eyes. "You know the answer to that."

"But I already fucked you with my mediocre dick, what else do you want?" I joked.

Her eyes searched mine, and she was about to open her mouth, but she slammed it shut seconds later.

"Nothing. You can go. Gio will stay with me."

She turned on her side and held her hand out for my brother. "Will you hold me tonight?"

He smiled down at her, completely in love, then slid under the covers with her.

"Always, Elvis."

I knew she was just pushing me away, but it felt too awkward to stay after she'd just said that. Instead, I got up, picked up my clothes, and went to my room in the house. I shut and locked the door before lying face-first in the bed and passing out.

CHAPTER 22
GIO

I finally had her to myself, and I wasn't stupid enough to question her motives or care that she was trying to piss King off.

She was hurt, and playing a game with us. We were the chess pieces, but she was still the queen, and I didn't give a fuck how she wanted us to move around as long as she still wanted us. Or at least me.

I had held her to me all night and enjoyed every fucking second of it.

The moment she began to stir in the morning, she smiled at me for five glorious seconds.

Five seconds where the old Presley came out, ran her fingers through my hair, and brushed her thumbs over my eyelids. She whispered, "My sky fell, Gio. You were always supposed to hold it up."

Sorrow and guilt swelled within me, making me rasp brokenly, "I'm sorry, Elvis. So fucking sorry."

My mouth slowly met hers in a gentle kiss, something as careful and perfect as the stars we used to find. But she pulled back seconds later, completely leaving the bed. She disappeared inside her bathroom, and then the lock clicked into place.

One step forward, and five huge steps back.

I lay back, dragging my arm over my face and letting out a sigh. There had to be some way to get through to her without waiting months for her to get past her grief. I wanted my Elvis back. The one who lived for my smile, all the sunlight I gave, and all the joy I had to offer. I wanted her back. I knew she was in there; I just had to find a way to bring her out.

THE SKY WAS BRIGHT BLUE, with the sun shining in a happy glow. The air was frigid, but that didn't matter. It was March, which meant Presley's birthday was right around the corner, and it was the perfect time for me to execute my plan.

It took some effort and an entire week to arrange it, but it was finally time. The week had been silent and tense, and full of awkward moments.

Moments where Presley would cry, or storm off toward the shooting range and begin firing off endless rounds. Each night, she'd request to be tucked into my arms, but she only ever wanted a sexual connection. At least that's what she'd say, but the very fact that she craved my touch in the form of being held told me she was succumbing to something deeper.

That's what made up the other awkwardness. Kingston was in and out of the house, but each time he chose to stay in the barn, Presley would find a way to punish him by being cozy and romantic with me. It was all bullshit that I knew she didn't mean, but I drank it up anyway. Anything that let me have her in any capacity was worth it for me. Even if that meant we'd fuck loud enough to get Kingston's attention, and she'd occasionally demand I take her in the barn, so he'd walk in and find us.

It should have bothered me. On some level, what she was doing was shitty, but I also knew this was her form of payback to us both, and it was the most effective way to hurt us. She was only giving us the part of her that we deemed valuable.

Any emotions she'd keep back. She was using me to hurt Kingston, and if he was willing, she'd use him to hurt me.

He hadn't touched her since that day the three of us were together. She hadn't asked for him, but during dinner or when we'd watch movies in the living room at night, I noticed how frequently she'd look over at the window that faced the barn. Not having him in the house bothered her a great deal, and I was choosing to ignore it because I finally had her to myself.

Which made this moment worth it. The one where I knew things were going to begin changing.

Waving my arms, I helped the driver of the truck navigate the trailer to the barn. I had moved all of Kingston's shit up to the loft this morning and renovated the pens so they had hay, and were ready for our new visitors.

"Okay, right there!" I yelled as the brake lights lit up. The truck stopped, and the man exited the truck, moving toward the rear of the trailer.

"What the fuck is this?" I heard my brother ask from behind me. I turned around, seeing him lean against the side of the barn with his arms crossed. He wore a baseball hat today, and it took me back to when we were kids. He hadn't worn one in years.

"Okay, where do you want the first one?" The rancher walked toward me, holding the rope for one of the highland cows.

"Just in here." I guided him while Kingston groaned in frustration behind me.

"Gio, you didn't."

I helped the rancher settle two more of the cows inside the barn before I paid him. The rancher ensured I had the right food and the proper setup so the cows would be cared for properly. It took almost an hour before the man drove away. I figured my brother would have left by then, but the second I turned back toward the side of the barn, he was still there.

"This was a stupid decision, Gio."

I walked past him, heading toward the side pasture gate. "She's going to love it."

"No, she's not," he argued.

The cows had begun shifting around in their stalls when my brother took off his hat and began cursing in Spanish.

"Gio!" he yelled and pointed toward the cows. "What the fuck?!"

"She loves cows. It's going to help bring her out of her funk, I know it will," I argued back.

"She hates us. Why don't you get that? She hates us, and she's grieving. You have to let both of those things happen. You can't rush them or stop them."

He was wrong. We could stop it if we just put some effort into it.

"You aren't even trying to get her back, so what the fuck would you know about it?"

His dark hair shifted in the wind as he laughed. "She does not want to be won back. You're not getting it. We broke her, Gio."

Getting in his face, I pushed him back a step. "No, you broke her!"

"You were there too. You said those words to her, too. You stood next to me. You agreed to it. So yeah, you broke her too."

A piercing pain eclipsed my chest as he continued to talk. Somewhere in the back of my soul, there was a painful nudge, something I had ignored and refused to see. Simply because it was too fucking painful to do so.

My sky fell, Gio. You were always supposed to hold it up.

"I have to try," I rasped in a jagged breath.

Kingston gripped me by the shoulders and pulled me close until we were nearly hugging. "Us trying is being here. You were the one who said you'd be a wraith here, haunting everywhere she goes until she's ready. That's what you become. You stay back, come close when she calls, and then you leave her alone. She's hurting, Gio, and until she gets revenge on Scotty and Markos, she's not going to begin to heal. A few fluffy cows aren't going to change that."

I knew he was right, deep down I knew it, but there was a stubbornness in my soul that I didn't want to recognize or give any attention to.

"Maybe she just doesn't want me. I know if you started to try, then maybe she'd start to come around. It's always been you, King, and I'm okay with that if it means she still wants me," I lied. It wasn't okay, it fucking devastated me.

My brother twisted his face like I had just said the most asinine thing he'd ever heard.

"Gio, she wants *you*. There is no wanting me without wanting you, and vice versa. We're connected in that way, and I'm sorry for it. I know you wish she only wanted you and she was only yours, but right now, she's neither of ours. We have to give her time to work through her shit. I promise you she'll come around."

I agreed, but deep down, I couldn't shake the feeling that I was right.

CHAPTER 23
PRESLEY

"You have farm animals!" Alex arrived in a flourish of blonde hair, sun kissed cheeks, and baked goods.

"I saw them." I hesitated while welcoming the twins' sister inside. I had no idea why there were highland cows in the pasture, but they felt like a trap.

Gio had to be behind the livestock appearing because Kingston would never do something so obvious in his attempts to get my forgiveness. He still hadn't told me himself that he'd restored the farmhouse or explained why Adrian's body was currently wrapped protectively from being viewed or picked at by animals. He hadn't explained who had put the fire out or had dug the six-foot grave next to the scorched, burned earth. I knew it was all him, and yet he refused to confess.

Alex set her baked goods on the kitchen counter while examining all the small details. "Well, they're cute. So is this place."

"What have you been up to?" I avoided confirming that this place or the animals were, in fact, cute. We went upstairs so Alex could snoop as much as she wanted. She was peeking in at her brother's rooms, flipping on and off switches before venturing back toward the books where I was waiting.

"I've been bored. I think I wanted to come help you in Italy because it was supposed to give me purpose. Now that I'm home and you're here...I just feel a little lost."

"Maybe you should come spend your free time over here. We have the cows now, and well...there's all sorts of things to keep up with." I wanted to have more enthusiasm for her, but I just couldn't summon it. My mind was frozen in place, continually seeing the flames burn against the night sky. The smell of his flesh burning seemed stuck in my nostrils.

Alex moved so she was in front of me, gently holding my shoulders. "Don't do that. You don't have to worry about me. I just came to see you. I miss you."

"I miss you too."

"Then let's just hang out, even if it's in silence or even if you need to shoot something. I'm here for you, Pres." Her long arms pulled me in close, and her scent settled in some painful place inside me that kept flaring with angry jabs. Alex was safe. Alex had never hurt me.

I wrapped my arms around her and hugged her back. The two of us sat there for untold minutes until we finally broke apart with tear-stained faces.

We ended up sitting near a backfield, picking flowers. It reminded me what we acted out that day in Italy when Adrian had—

"A flower crown, Pres." Alex pulled me from my thoughts and handed me the foliage shaped in a beautiful circle.

Right as I leaned forward to take it, we both froze at the sudden appearance of someone in the field, watching us.

"Who is that?" Alex asked, leaning closer to me.

The man wearing a boxy white T-shirt and black cargo pants waved, and I realized who it was. "That's Henry..."

"Oh yeah, he was there the day in Italy." Alex kept her eyes on him, "Why is he out here, though?"

"No clue." A warning shot off in the back of my mind, but I shut it down. Everything seemed to set me off, lately but there was no reason this guy appearing should feel any different. The twins had men everywhere. I was just making something out of nothing.

LATER THAT EVENING, I ventured over to the manor to see my family.

Mom had texted and asked if I wanted to go over for dinner. I had turned her down three times out of fear that Scotty might try and show up. I had no idea if my father was still loyal to him or not, but after an entire childhood of him allowing me to be handed over to his uncle for training, I had to assume he was. I didn't mind if they came to the farmhouse, but the twins were around...well at least one of them was, and that one liked to play house too intensely for my liking.

It was a struggle not to fall into the idea of Gio being with me in my dream house, but not in the way I had always imagined. I would quickly remember that night where everything broke between us, and things would slide back into perspective for me. I wanted to get to Markos, and I needed to find Scotty, but I had no idea where to even begin, which was another reason I had agreed to finally venture over for dinner. I had hopes that my father might have some idea of where his uncle was hiding.

The back terrace doors had been replaced, but the keypad Scotty had once set up was gone, so I simply pushed down on the handle and walked inside. The manor was dark, only lit up by the natural light from the windows. The eerie feeling of the empty house seemed to chase me as I quickly made my way through the open dining hall and foyer, toward my family wing. Once I was inside, I released a tiny pent-up breath of relief.

The kitchen smelled of my mother's cooking. Tonight, she made a chicken pot pie from scratch, and my mouth watered as I took a seat. I eyed the empty fourth chair, usually occupied by my uncle, with a shrewd gaze and then stroked the handgun strapped under the table.

"So, how are you settling in, honey?" my mother asked, bringing over a pitcher of lemonade.

I removed my hand and tried to relax. He wasn't here. I was safe. "Fine."

Dad smiled warmly at me before glancing at my mom. That was their signature look when she had asked him to be nice about a specific subject. "How is it with the twins being there?"

Ah, yes, the twins. I was surprised when he was kind to Kingston that day, during my move-in. He'd paid him a compliment, which was huge considering he wanted to kill him at one point.

"Good. They come and go." I took a bite of my dinner, hoping to move past that subject because I knew for a fact that the twins' mother had once spilled the beans about the three of us dating, and so my parents likely assumed what we were all doing over there.

Mom took her seat and sipped her drink. "How are you doing, though? Are you sleeping?"

This past week, I had tried, but even being curled up in Gio's arms, I was too aware of not being in Kingston's. The last time I remembered sleeping through the night was when both brothers slept with me.

"Yes."

Mom's gaze slid to Dad's, and the two of them were silent for a moment before Dad cleared his throat.

"I think Scotty might have been working with Markos."

My fork clattered to the plate. A barrage of anger and feelings of betrayal invaded my chest, making it burn and ache.

"Working how?"

Dad's eyes were so full of anger and sadness that it made my own begin to water. "Honey, I'm not sure exactly, but after you told me about the hit on Lucian Adesso and how Scotty had framed me...I've been going back, trying to find a reason for him to have done that. I discovered that Markos slowly bought out all the contacts Scotty would have had. I think Scotty was asked to kill Lucian by Markos."

That didn't make any sense; Lucian was Markos' best friend. "Why would he do that?"

Mom was the one to speak up this time. "Markos was a sick man, honey...I mean the way he dealt with his jealousy over Juan and Taylor. Lucian could have done the smallest thing to upset him, and Markos would have all the power to end him. Think about it, he never did find a bride who gave him heirs. Yet, he inherited three the moment Lucian died."

That was true, and by ensuring they witnessed it, he guaranteed their desire for revenge.

"Which is why Scotty would have left your calling card..." I said to my dad, working through the possibility, "So that it all led back to getting revenge on you."

One thing didn't seem to make sense, though. "Why not leave the calling card for Juan if he hated him that much?"

Dad shook his head while cutting into his meal. "I might be the reason Markos could never have heirs. When he demanded your mother's hand in marriage all those years ago, I nearly castrated him."

Oh. "I thought Scotty was joking about that."

He shook his head. "No, I nearly made it so he could never..." Dad cleared his throat before adjusting in his seat. "Let's just say I guaranteed he'd never have kids or be able to procreate. He would have been very motivated to get revenge."

I took another bite, considering everything and linking all the tiny connections.

"Why wouldn't Scotty just defy him, though? Even if he did do the hit and framed you, why not go against him now and protect us? Why did he go along with the alliance and marriage? Why send me to Italy and put me at risk?"

Mom took another sip before she replied, "My guess is he made Markos swear that you'd never be harmed."

That would make sense as I had never been harmed physically in any way. Renzo and Benni had never harmed me, and even through everything, Markos hadn't either.

"If that's true, then what was his end game... Adrian said the plan was to kill off my family and then either keep me for himself or sell me off. There's no way Scotty would have been okay with that."

"That's true, but the fact that he hasn't told me any of this makes it clear cut for me," Dad said calmly while glancing at Mom. "He's a threat and after what he did to you...our ties with him are officially severed."

A shard of ice seemed to seep in through my chest cavity as I sat there and processed those words. I knew my mother would kill Scotty on sight, no questions asked, but my dad loved Scotty. He was the only father he ever knew; he had trained him and shaped him. He always seemed to have some reason behind what he was doing. Even now, I could sense all the various ways Scotty could be twisting this alliance to fit his own agenda.

I wasn't sure what he was doing, but he'd gone too far. My life was not a poker chip to be gambled. My heart was not merely an organ to be pushed in training. Scotty had risked my life and had effectively ended Adrian's.

With the somber feeling in the room, I added to it, "If he shows up, we can't trust the guards or the locks... Scotty was the one who set everything up."

My dad was mid bite when he glanced over at my mother. A small smile tilted her mouth up while she moved her food around her plate.

"Kingston ordered for all the locks to be replaced, and all of Scotty's men were...taken care of."

That had me curious, but it also had some place inside swelling with pride.

I needed to talk to him and update them on what Dad had shared with me. If it were possible for Scotty to be working with Markos, then perhaps that's where he was currently hiding.

THE COWS WERE STILL in the field when I walked past at sunset, but I remained firm in my resolve not to pet them. Gio was going to have to work harder than just playing the doting brother and pushing all my favorite things in front of me.

I had no idea if Kingston was in the barn or if either of them were in the house, which was my fault for never asking, but I knew they'd come around if I simply asked them to. Well, Gio would...which left me with that stinging rejection invading my chest again. Climbing the steps, I punched in the code the twins had set up for the front door.

As soon as the door locked shut behind me, I nearly sighed in relief. The house was clean, quiet, and peaceful. Warm light filtered in from the open windows, and soft music played from a speaker in the kitchen. Secretly, I loved this place and felt like it was the one place on earth that was designed just for me. For my soul to find rest, and my weary heart to finally heal.

Food had been made from the delicious smell, but from the empty counters, it had been cleaned up.

"Hey." Kingston suddenly appeared in the kitchen with a white rag in his hand. His hair was wet, his shirt was gone, and his jeans hung low on his hips. He looked relaxed and at home. Greedy claws emerged from my heart, desperate to cling to the image and hoard it for later.

"Hey." I set my phone down and slid off my shoes. "Where's Gio?"

Kingston's expression shifted the smallest bit. It was fast, but I caught the hint of anger that slashed across his features.

"He's with Henry and El Peligro tonight. They're going over a few things regarding safety protocols around the property."

That was nice of him to engage in trying to keep the property safe. Although, that was also to keep his family safe.

I wanted to tell him about what I'd just learned at dinner, and how Scotty might be double crossing us. I wanted to tell him that my dad had officially cut ties with my uncle, and I wanted to process that with my best friends, and yet I couldn't figure out how to push the words out. I was still so hurt, and while Gio had apologized and I could see myself talking to him, Kingston still hadn't.

I must have been staring off into space because Kingston let out a scoff.

"You could pretend to care that he's not here."

My brows drew in as I tried to make sense of what he meant. "I do care that he's not here...why would you even suggest that I don't? I'm still pissed, but I thought I had made it pretty clear that I care very much that you're both here."

Kingston's thunderous expression pinned me in place. "Oh yes. Sorry, you're right...we're your disposable cocks to be pulled out and used when you see fit, then tossed away the moment one of us gets sentimental."

Oh, this *asshole*. Pointing at my chest, I argued vehemently, "Sort of like that moment you took my virginity, then rubbed it in my face that you'd only done it to defy Adrian. You used me first."

"Would it even make a difference to you if I apologized because based how you're treating us...how you're treating Gio, it wouldn't make a fucking difference."

Memories of that night painfully flashed through my mind. "I wouldn't know, Kingston. The only person who has tried is Gio. He's the only one who has tried to get sentimental or apologize or do anything."

"That's fucking rich, Presley." Kingston tipped his head back and laughed, then turned for the stairs and began climbing.

"It's true!" I yelled at his back as I began to follow him. "Gio has been sweet and kind and cares."

"You want sentimental?" He suddenly spun on me and reached for my hand. Yanking me forward, I practically tripped as I followed him to my bedroom, where he dropped down to the floor.

He pressed his fingers into the wood floorboard until one of them pulled up, and inside was a lock box. "This is an exact replica of the gun you started carrying around at the ripe age of fucking eight years old. There's one of these in every room, so you always feel safe," Kingston snapped before revealing the back of the board. It was a picture...a familiar picture burned into the wood.

"The photo you made when we were kids, the one of the farm...I had it turned into a stencil. For every room in this house, there's one of these under the boards if not more."

He dropped it back in place and then stood, searching the room with a frantic expression. "I made sure your bed would have slide out drawers so we could keep wedge pillows underneath it. There's practically an entire sex store under there if you look. I made sure you'd have everything to make you comfortable for when the three of us—"

He trailed off, and it made my temper flare.

"See, that's just it, Kingston. You lied about who finished this house for me. You didn't put a single plant anywhere in sight, as if you were trying to erase yourself from this house...from me. You made an entire floor for Gio and stargazing and not a single greenhouse on the property for you. There's no garden anywhere. How was I supposed to know you'd done anything considerate where the three of us might be concerned?"

He rolled his eyes and walked to the side of the room. "Well, if you'd drop that wall around your heart, then maybe you'd learn."

I was starting to feel that familiar rage when he'd piss me off, and to get his attention, I'd say something shitty just to get him to lose control and fuck me. But I was tired of our toxic circle. My heart hurt, and while I previously settled for his touch, now I needed his love. Unfortunately, I was well aware of how that would go.

"Drop it so you can get away with what you did and not have to apologize?"

He blew out a heavy breath while looking down at the floor. "I figured the house would have been apology enough."

My hands came up, roughly tugging at my hair as I stepped back.

"Again, you didn't take credit for it, King. You didn't walk me through the house and show me all the tiny things you did. I didn't know about the stencils, lock boxes, or anything else. You keep pushing me away."

"Because you push *me* away," he yelled. "Every time I think you want to get close, you do something that shows you're only doing it out of spite or to use me for something physical. I know you're punishing me, but how fucking long do you plan on doing it?"

His words stung so badly; I felt numb everywhere.

My voice rose but cracked, "You pushed me into Gio's arms. You told me that I looked like I belonged to Gio, not you. You were cruel to me, and when I did arrive, you didn't even want to stay. You still don't. You keep going to the barn or sleeping apart from me, and it hurts. It all feels like rejection. Like I'm still in that room watching you pull up your jeans after you just had your cock inside me, taking my virginity only to completely ruin me moments later."

A sob had worked its way into my speech, which made me embarrassed. Especially when he just stood there staring at me like I was pathetic.

"So, what is it that you want me to do, Presley? Want me to move in, fuck you every night, sleep with you but not expect you to like me, or want to be my friend? You going to shove your relationship with Gio in my face again? Make me hear you have sex first thing in the morning when I wake up or walk down into the kitchen and see you spread out like a fucking buffet, but only for my brother to enjoy?" he yelled, but a sob caught his words too.

"I want you to care! I want you to apologize and to move in, and to give me space to work out my hurt. If that means no more sex, then fine. We won't touch anymore."

He stepped closer, and I saw the way his eyes watered as he traced the space near my ear. "Touching you is all I have, it may hurt, but fuck, don't take that from me."

His eyes shuddered, and then a lone tear slipped down his face, which had my stomach clenching. I wanted to say something, but he stepped even closer and whispered, "All I do is care. I care so much, I can't sleep. I can't think. I am eternally frozen in this place where I broke you. It was the worst thing I could have ever done, and I'm sorry. You have no idea how sorry I am. I know I can't fix it. I can't go back...I know you relive that moment each time we touch you. But you have to know how badly I—"

His mouth snapped shut, leaving me reeling for what he was going to say. Instead, he took a step back and ran his hand over his face.

"I need to know what you want from me."

My shoulders lifted slightly as my own tears finally fell. "I don't know how to communicate that. I don't want you to leave me, but I'm also not ready to trust you. I don't want to have to tell you to fix what's broken. I just want you to find the pieces and put them back together."

A fluttery panic swept through my voice as I confessed my insecurities to him. I hated how vulnerable I was being with him again, even after all that he'd done to me. Instead of anger or cruelty, he slowly nodded as if he finally understood.

"Then I ask that you stop hiding all of it. Let us see where you're hurting, and all the shattering you've done since we broke you. Don't keep it bottled up. We can't help unless we know how to. Stop trying to hurt us by using us the way you are. We care about you, Presley. We're still fucking in love with you. The way you just want to fuck us and forget us or pit us against one another is shitty and you know it."

With one last solemn glance, he turned around and walked out of my room.

I didn't lock my door, but I did shut it, and then I curled up in a ball on my bed and I cried. He was right. I needed to stop self-sabotaging and start healing.

It was a terrifying idea because it meant I had to trust them again in order to do it.

Was that even possible? The truth scared me more than I wanted to admit.

CHAPTER 24

PRESLEY

It was early when I snuck out of bed.

Gio had come to my bed at some point in the night, but he hadn't pulled me into his chest or put his arm around me. Which worked for me as I didn't want to wake anyone up. My conversation with Kingston had kept me awake all night, making me toss and turn and mull over what we'd said.

It was the first conversation that we'd had that didn't end in angry rhetoric or angry sex.

Which felt like progress. Yet, I pulled on my running shoes, threw my hair up, and quietly exited the house so that I could go for a run because I still felt too much pain in my chest. I started for the woods that I used to run as a kid.

Early morning fog clung to the branches, and moss covered most of the fallen logs. It felt good to run again, and while I wasn't wearing my weighted vest, the cold air on my lungs gave me a rush of adrenaline. I thought over all I had learned yesterday about Scotty and his possible connection to Markos.

I played the night I met Markos in my mind, all the words and the way he said them. I played the two months of fear we lived in after that night and all the tiny things Adrian had said, or didn't. I hated that Markos had killed him, for many reasons, but the lack of information was one of the biggest reasons.

Why bring Scotty into it? Why had Scotty agreed to any of it?

We'd been in hiding; we were safe. Why make up this imaginary idea that we could find an ally with the Adessos?

I thought back to how Adrian said he'd first saw me at that ball on my sixteenth birthday. I realized with a start that Scotty had been the one to suggest we attend under fake names and flutter around our enemies like butterflies just to see if anyone knew any differently.

How long had he been playing us?

My breathing was labored as I pinned my hands to my hips and began walking back to the farmhouse. It was still early, but an hour had passed or so, and the highland cows were out in the pasture, eating squares of hay. One of them lifted its heavy head to watch me approach, its golden-brown hair covered its eyes, but its wide mouth moved to the side as it chewed.

Glancing around, and not seeing either twin, I decided to climb the fence and go visit the burly creatures. An infectious smile worked its way up my face as I began running my hands through the smallest one's fur, brushing back its cute mane from its eyes. Then I fed it some more hay while the other two made their way over.

"You're awfully handsome," I said, giggling as the white one with spots began to nuzzle me. There was one more golden than brown that I began petting next. "You remind me of Gio. You're all sunshine and joy."

"Don't worry, I won't tell him you like his gift." Kingston suddenly appeared behind me, carrying a two-by-four over his shoulder.

Spinning around, I watched as he smirked but kept walking toward the area where the earth was still blackened from the burning body. I wasn't ready to see that space, or the grave that had been dug, so I headed back for the house, ignoring the butterflies in my stomach. Glancing one time over my shoulder, I saw Kingston watching me before his gaze snapped back to the pieces of wood on the ground.

I smiled while I walked inside.

AFTER MY SHOWER, I made my way downstairs. The delicious smell of bacon and toast fluttered in the air, making my stomach growl. I found Gio at the stove, making scrambled eggs while he sang along to a song playing from the speaker in the corner. He only had on a pair of boxers, and for some reason, I loved that fact. His eyes lit up when he saw me, and it made that fluttery feeling return to my chest.

"Morning."

I smiled in return while sliding in next to him, where the coffee pot was. "Morning."

He was back at the stove when he happily said, "I made you eggs, toast, and bacon."

"Thank you." My smile hadn't waned as I watched him cook. Sipping my coffee, I looked over the mug and said, "I met the cows today."

Gio shifted toward me with a brazen smile that lit up his handsome face. "You like the spotted one best, don't you?"

It felt good to release a genuine smile again as I laughed. "Actually, I like the golden one; he reminds me of you."

Gio set the skillet to the side and began laughing. "How, there's nothing golden about me."

"Yeah, there is, Gio. Your soul is pure sunshine."

His face fell as he turned away from me and began to get my toast prepared. His voice was somber as he replied, "I didn't mean to overwhelm you by getting them. King said I pushed it too fast."

I moved until I was behind him, wrapping my arms around his chest and placing my face against his back. "Gio, you've always been my sky. My constant." I pressed a kiss to his skin and then whispered, "Don't give up on me."

He spun around and gathered me into his arms and gently held my face. "Never."

His lips gently landed against mine, light as a feather, then my arms were up around his neck as I added, "And don't give up on *you* either. I love you, Gio. I might be mad as hell still and hurt, but make no mistake..." I kissed him again. "I still want you."

I was lifted to the counter as he moved between my legs, and our kiss continued and became heavier, more intense. His fingers traced up my back, leaving a trail of goosebumps behind. My lashes fluttered shut as I allowed the sensation of his touch to linger, and for once, I allowed myself to enjoy it. This was different than the times before when I'd push for his touch merely to shut out something I didn't want to feel. Now, I wanted his touch so that he was all I'd feel.

His mouth moved over mine in a searing kiss, his tongue pushed into my mouth in deep strokes, and because I didn't want this to be like all the other times, I gently pulled away. I pressed my forehead to his chin while our breathing regulated, and then I lifted my eyes and asked, "Will you come with me to name them?"

He laughed. "Of course I will, but no arguing about what I pick."

Once he helped me down from the counter, I grabbed my breakfast and began eating it while Gio ran upstairs to get dressed. While I was standing in the kitchen, I glanced around, now curious what other tiny details Kingston might have put in when something had me stopping, mid chew.

There, by the kitchen sink, was a brand-new plant that hadn't been there the day before. It was a spider plant with perky green blades sticking out of the dark soil.

The smile spreading across my mouth was instant because I knew this was no simple plant; this was *Kingston*.

IT WAS LATE when I slipped out of bed.

Gio had fallen asleep almost as soon as the movie had started that he'd picked to watch. We had a good day, full of laughter and real smiles. After we'd named our cows: Marvin, Lola, and Georgia. We even worked together to organize the barn for more animals. I wanted chickens, and he thought horses would be a good idea. We agreed that goats were a must, but I took issue with horses. I told him they were expensive, but he just laughed at me.

Sometimes I forgot that he and his brother still led a dangerous gang tied to the cartel, likely with unlimited funding. I wasn't sure I even wanted to be connected to the danger that made up their world, but it was easy to pretend none of it existed while we were on the farm. I knew there were extra men patrolling the property; I saw them near the manor, and while they were spread a bit thinner near the farmhouse, I still saw them.

Wrapping a knitted sweater around my shoulders, I crossed my arms over my chest and ventured up to the top story. I wanted to see the stars, and I still couldn't sleep without both brothers with me, so it was an easy way to pass the time. I wanted to check on Kingston to see if he was in his room, but I felt too embarrassed seeking him out. I had put my heart out there and told him I missed him sleeping next to me. I knew he was taking baby steps with the plants, and I had found three more spread throughout the house, but part of me had hoped he'd come to me tonight.

I knew I wouldn't find him up on the balcony that was designed for stargazing, but when I walked out onto the wide veranda and glanced up, there were almost no stars. Instead, the full moon cast a white sheen over the darkened farm. Pressing my fingers into the overlook that came up to my chest, I examined the barn below and wondered if Kingston was still sleeping out there. But something behind it caught my eye.

There was a floodlight set up, shining on a board being moved upward. It looked like someone was building a small house back there or something. I knew it was Kingston, but I had no idea what he was doing. He'd carried a two-by-four out there earlier, but I hadn't followed up on what he'd done, and where we were in the field, I couldn't see him.

It was almost two in the morning. Why was he still out there?

Deciding I'd find out, I made my way downstairs and pulled on a pair of mud boots before walking outside. As I approached, I saw Kingston with a pencil behind his ear and a light on a set of plans that were drawn up for whatever project it was that he was building.

"Hey." I got his attention while placing my back against the barn wall.

His eyes flicked up in surprise, then he seemed to relax. "Hey."

"Why are you out here?" I didn't look at the structure as it was still too close to where Adrian had been.

He moved around me, gathering some plans and clicking off the light.

"I was just finishing up."

His amber gaze slid over to me again. "Why are you out here?"

"I can't sleep," I admitted, while kicking at a tiny clump of mud near my boot, but it was frozen solid, so nothing moved.

"King, it's freezing out here."

He smiled while cleaning up a few other materials. He wore a thick jacket, jeans, with a beanie on his head. Even all bundled up, his breath still came out in little white clouds.

"No shit, you should go back to bed."

"I can help you if you're still working. I don't mind." I'd have to go find better clothing than my flimsy pajama shorts and tank top covered with just the knitted sweater, but once I did, I'd be fine.

Kingston moved from the workspace and had me moving with him until we were stepping inside the functional part of the barn, where all his tools were situated. "Here." He shrugged out of his coat and slid it over my shoulders. On instinct, I pushed my arms through, nearly moaning at how good the heat felt against my skin.

"You need your sleep, Pres." Kingston began putting his tools back in order.

I picked up a random pair of plyers and toyed with it. "Yeah, I'm sure you're right. I just can't seem to get any lately."

"You seemed to sleep like the dead the night I—" he started but stopped and then studied me as if he had just figured it out.

He told me not to hide the brokenness, so I decided not to. "I can't seem to sleep unless you're both in bed with me. That doesn't mean I'm trying to guilt you into—"

"Stop, Pres. I know..." His hand came out, waving the idea away, but his focus remained on the tool in his hand. "I'm glad you told me."

He moved toward the work table, putting things away while I stood there in his jacket that was three times too big for me. I wasn't sure what else to say since he wasn't engaging with me regarding anything else, so I turned around and exited through the side door.

My walk back to the house was quick because humiliation seemed to bite at my heels. I showed him the broken pieces, but he just stood there and stared.

I slid his coat off in the entry way of the house, leaving it on the floor next to my boots, and then I went back to my room and crawled in next to Gio. The warmth enveloped me like a hug. My eyes were closed, fighting off tears, when I heard the door downstairs shut and then boots on the stairs.

It was fine.

I was fine. I kept telling myself that for untold minutes. I heard him in his room, and the water running from the shower on that side of the house.

I'd finally gotten warm when I felt the blanket lift, and his warm body slide in behind mine. His arms came around me and pulled me flush against his chest. His mouth was warm at my ear as he whispered, "Did I fuck up again, *¿mi reina?*"

"No, I'm just impatient," I whispered back, turning around so I could bury my face into his neck.

He stroked down my back while holding me tightly to his chest. I breathed in his fresh scent, realizing he'd taken a shower before coming in. His mouth came to the space right below my ear, pressing a heated kiss there. He moved down the column of my throat, increasing the pressure and speed of which his tongue swiped over my pulse point and then up into my waiting mouth. We moved together in the same way Gio and I had earlier, in a fresh way that had all the same hints of what we once were.

It felt like he'd picked up a broken piece of my heart and kissed it, gently setting it back in place. Just like with Gio, I didn't want him to think I was still using him, so I pulled back.

"It's okay if we don't. I'm not doing this to—"

His mouth covered mine again before he rolled on top of me. "I know, *mi reina*. I can always tell the difference when you're offering yourself freely with hope to be loved in return and when you're merely using your cunt to punish us."

A molten fire stirred in my belly as his mouth moved over mine, as his tongue slid against me in sensual strokes. He began rocking his erection into me, and my legs parted automatically. I lifted my hips to meet each thrust that he made into my pajamas. Neither of us seemed to care that Gio was asleep right next to us. I hoped maybe he'd wake up and join in, but I wasn't going to look over and check. Not when Kingston reached under the covers to pull my shorts down, and not when his velvet smooth cock prodded at my entrance.

"Can I have you?" he asked, and the request shot off like a beam of moonlight inside my chest. I kissed him again, then encouraged him by crossing my ankles at his back to drag him closer.

"Yes."

His hardened length retreated the smallest bit only to push forward in one solid thrust, which had me gasping.

"Shhh, just relax and adjust. Maybe not as long, but fuck am I just as big, *mi reina*."

Before I could laugh, his lips were on mine again. He fucked me slowly, with deep, purposeful strokes, and his mouth only left mine to move to my breasts, where he worshiped each one by licking and sucking each bud. Even as slow as he moved above me, rocking into me, the bed shifted, and the headboard knocked against the wall.

"You're going to wake up Gio," I whispered. My left thigh was hooked over his arm while he continued to draw his erection out, only to thrust firmly back into my core.

His kisses lingered around my heart before he whispered in reply, "I think you'd like it if he did."

"I would."

Kingston's expression turned feral while his hand reached up to grab the headboard, and his hips flexed forward. "Then I'm not holding back."

Suddenly what was sweet and slow, turned carnal and dominant. His hips jolted ruthlessly, his grip on my hips would leave bruises, but I loved how deep he went, how firm and more than anything how desperate he made me sound. I was begging him to fuck me deeper when Gio woke up.

"Well, shit, looks like I have some catching up to do," he sleepily drawled while he shoved at Kingston's shoulder. "Put her on her side and pull her thigh over yours, so she's nice and spread for me."

King moved us without pulling his cock out of me; he just continued to fuck me in languid strokes, while we turned to the side and did exactly as his brother said. All while Gio poured a generous amount of warm lubricant down my crack and coated my hole. Kingston slowed his thrusts long enough for his brother to line himself up with me, and with Gio tilting his hips a few times while prodding at the tight space, he began inching his way in. I was instantly full, being rocked into by both brothers. One had his mouth on my neck, and the other kneaded my breasts.

"Is this what you always wanted, Elvis?" Gio asked huskily at my ear. His fingers gripped my ass cheek while he thrust and thrust and thrust into me. My mouth gaped with a silent scream, but Kingston forced his fingers inside until they were gliding across my tongue.

"We want to hear your answer, *mi reina*. Is this everything you imagined when you used to touch yourself in your bed late at night, full of shame because you were aching for not just one cock but two?"

"Yes," I answered around his blunt fingers.

Once he removed them, his hand slid down between us, and he began quickly rubbing them over my clit. Between being filled and touched and their demanding words, the sensations were too intense.

I came hard, closing my eyes and screaming out a litany of curses. The twins didn't stop; in fact, they pushed harder and began losing themselves entirely.

"Shit, Elvis, hold onto Kingston because I'm about to fucking lose it."

Suddenly, my ass was spread wider, and he began pounding into me so fast that I shook. The bed was moving so much that the headboard hadn't stopped slamming against the wall in angry thuds. I began crying out as another orgasm ripped through me, and with how fast Kingston rubbed my clit.

"King, stop. I feel...I feel like I'm." I began babbling while trying to catch my breath. I pushed at his shoulders, but he didn't stop.

"You're going to squirt for me. I'm about to come, but I want to do it to the feel of you gushing all over me as I fuck you." His thrusts began increasing in speed, just like Gio's had, and suddenly the sensations were so intense, something gushed out of me and spread all over Kingston.

He groaned deeply near my ear, then froze while being buried inside me. "That's fucking beautiful, all over my cock just like the brat you are."

"I'm there, fuck." Gio groaned into my hair while his thrusts finally stopped, and his hands were around my tits, pressing them together.

I couldn't seem to catch my breath as they both stopped and slowly withdrew, dragging their cocks out of me.

"Perfect." Kingston pressed a kiss to my forehead while Gio stroked gently over all the places he'd gripped so firmly. I smiled as I felt more kisses against my skin. Someone came back with a rag and began cleaning me up, but the second I felt both brothers settle back in and surround me, I fell asleep.

CHAPTER 25
KINGSTON

Presley knelt in front of the large ottoman with her hands spread out over various images and papers.

Gio and I sat next to each other on the couch while we watched her sift through them and explain herself. Her hair was down and she wore one of my T-shirts with nothing else. It had made me hard earlier, which resulted in me pulling her into my lap during breakfast. She bounced on my cock while Gio took a call. He watched her intently while the bulge in his pants increased, and then as soon as I released inside her, he put his call on speaker phone, then bent her over the table to fuck her himself.

Now, actually having fed her food, she explained she needed to talk to us about something.

"Do you guys have access to hackers?" she asked.

Gio nodded. "Best of the best."

She straightened out a map of Italy. "Our engagement party was being held here." She circled a spot on the map with a red pen. "We drove for exactly twenty-five minutes. I remember because I checked my phone when we left, and when we arrived."

I leaned forward. "So, you're wanting hackers to try and locate where he is based off that night, or just listings around?"

"I remember every detail of his house. I want a hacker who can see if there are any traffic cameras that—"

Gio shook his head. "This part of Italy is less progressive; you won't have traffic cameras out here."

"Well, we can start with a radius then," she argued.

"Elvis, we've been on this for months trying to pinpoint exactly where he is. I'm not sure hackers are going to be able to help," Gio explained softly.

She sat up taller, leaning back on the balls of her feet. "You didn't have me before."

I inspected her research, seeing the photo I did previously, of Scotty, knowing this was where all this was really coming from. "What's the plan though...you're planning on going or what?"

Shrugging the smallest bit, she explained, "The plan to go to Italy hasn't changed. Even though we don't have Adrian anymore, I plan to confront Scotty and take out of Markos."

"Just confront Scotty?" Gio asked.

Her brows pulled in tight. "Well, no...I want to—" She trailed off again as if she couldn't say it.

"You pulled the trigger that night, Elvis, when you were in front of his door. You didn't know if you'd kill him or not. I know you have it in you, but do you know you do?"

Her mouth opened and closed, but there were also angry tears beginning to well up in her eyes. "We didn't even have a burial for him. Scotty robbed me of that...he's behind all of this. Did you know he framed my father by killing Lucian Adesso? Did you know he knew what he was sending me into when I was just seventeen, meeting with Adrian?"

Gio's gaze fell to the floor while his expression turned somber. Mine, however, turned sharp.

"We knew most of this, yes. It's why we warned you."

Gio swung his gaze up and then shoved me in the ribs with his elbow.

"Don't be a prick, King." Presley swept away a few tears while sniffing.

"I'm reminding you because it is what it is. I need to know what you want to do moving forward. Boss us around, tell us what to do, but don't hesitate on what you want to do to Scotty James. He's a threat to you, so he's dead."

Her lips smashed together while her eyes shuddered. "Yes. He's dead. I want the hackers to try and locate Markos, and then I'm going."

"We are too, then," Gio advised.

She shook her head. "I can't ask—"

Leaning forward over the mess of everything on the ottoman, I gripped her chin firmly and kissed her. "Stop it. We're fixing things. We're here. Use us."

"Thought you didn't like to be used," she snarked back.

With a laugh, I nipped at her lip. "You can use me as often as you want, just make sure you're also willing to be kept while doing so."

She rose up on her knees and began kissing me back, and when our kisses turned heated, I pulled her over the ottoman and set her between my twin, and then we allowed her to use us for the rest of the morning however she needed to.

I watched over the next few days as Presley continued to acclimate to the three of us. We were slowly getting back to how things were, and I had no doubt that every one of us were panicked over one small mistake ruining the entire thing.

Gio brought marigolds for her every morning, and the two would take time together that didn't include me, where they'd go off in Gio's room and I'd hear giggling sounds or the sound of them fucking. Later, I'd see them in the barn, putting up chicken wire and installing feeders. My brother was happy, and in turn, that made me happy.

This was all I wanted for him, but it was never just Gio that Presley sought out. She'd spend plenty of time with him, and they'd act like the most in love couple that I had ever seen, but anytime I began to withdraw, Presley was there demanding time from me as well. She wanted darker things from me, and I discovered, I enjoyed giving them to her. While we were sentimental, and I was in love with her, I liked when she crawled into my lap and took off her shirt. Any time we spent together ended with us fucking, and I wasn't sure if that was a good thing or a bad thing. I wanted to be like Gio, I really did, but the second I got her alone, I craved the taste of her.

I was obsessed with being inside her, and in her own way, she was inside me, growing like a flower that begged for the darkness and basked in the moonlight. It wasn't often that my brother and I took her at the same time, which I preferred. While I would always do it for her, I loved when I had her to myself, and I knew my brother felt the same way. Regardless of that need, we were both in her bed every single night, holding her so she'd sleep.

Yet, there were times she seemed sad or like she wasn't quite past everything that had happened. I felt like it was less about what my brother and I did, and more about what Scotty and Markos had done to her, and all the things she didn't get to say to Adrian.

Which was why I had finally put the finishing touches on my project at dusk and shot off to see Presley. I found her in her room, swiping through her phone while blinking away tears.

"Hey." She looked up and gave me a wobbly smile.

I walked in slowly. "You okay?"

"Not really. My birthday is tomorrow, and all I can think about is how last year, Adrian was the one who showed up for me and made it so special."

That was a barb in the fucking heart, but I understood why she'd said it.

"I'm sorry, Pres."

She swiped at her eyes. "I don't think I was supposed to fall for him, but my heart was so wounded by you two it was like it had been rescued by him...I was happy with him, King. He wasn't the love of my life, but I'd already cut my heart down the middle for the two of you, what was one more chunk reserved for someone else?"

I sat next to her on the bed and put my arm around her. "Adrian was a good guy, in the end...and I don't doubt that you cared for him. But, Pres, baby...you'll never be able to chop up your heart and serve it to various lovers. Your heart would have never beat properly for him. It would have failed over time, and deep down you know that. Your heart was split in two, and we've never given it back to you. We might have broken it, but you were never in possession of it again."

Her head found the spot between my shoulder and neck while she cried.

"If I can't say that I loved him, then what do I have?"

I pressed a kiss to the top of her head. "Getting the chance to love you, Presley James, is quite the gift. If you haven't realized it yet, you're worth starting a war over. You're worth being loyal to, so much so, you defy familial ties. You don't just encourage love, baby, you demand it with each breath you take. Every smile. Every time you find something that gets you excited. You're like consuming sunshine. Fucking addictive."

She sniffed while more silent tears slipped down her face. In the quiet, I finally decided to tell her. "I did something for you. I know..." I struggled to push the words out, but I swallowed around the nerves and tried again. "I know I'm not as good at big gestures as Gio, but I feel like I have my own way of showing how much you mean to me and how serious I am about fixing what I broke."

She sat up and swiped at her face. "What did you do?"

"I need you to put on something nice, but warm, and it should be black." I kissed her on the nose, seeing her freckles and blue eyes.

Home.

"Okay." She watched me as I left her on the bed and wandered downstairs.

I HAD SHOT a text to my brother to join us, and a few minutes before Presley walked downstairs, he joined me by the front door.

"What are we doing?" he whispered.

I watched Presley walk down in a black lace dress that revealed her plump cleavage but wrapped around her shoulders and wound up her neck. She looked like a gothic princess, a pure stroke of midnight that had my breath catching in my chest.

"We're grieving," I replied, while holding my hand out for Presley. I handed her a bouquet of red roses, which she held tightly to her chest.

She joined us as we walked outside and past the barn. The sun had set, casting shadows over the field, which was perfect for what I had set up. We rounded the barn and approached the space where Adrian's body had burned. Presley jolted to a stop as soon as she registered where we were.

"What did you do?" she inhaled.

Her eyes tilted up, taking in the structure I had built over the grave, and then she searched all the flickering flames inside.

I pulled her hand so she followed me inside. "I built a greenhouse."

She inspected the glass windows and the various wood shelves I had built for the hanging plants that covered every surface. In between the plants were candles lit for the memorial.

"But..." She looked down and saw that the subfloor was built around a patch of dirt that would eventually have grass, and the three-foot-tall headstone sticking out from the freshly leveled earth. "You..." She dropped to her knees; the dark soil would stain her clothes, but with them being black, no one would even notice.

Tears glistened in her eyes as she looked up at me.

I decided to kneel down next to her, careful not to touch Adrian's grave. "You needed life, and I realize now that you needed that from me. Gio will always be your stars, your dreamer, but I'm your reality,

213

and you need that reality filled with life. So this greenhouse is my apology to you, and my promise that I'm staying here with you. I'm not leaving you again."

She viciously swiped at her eyes while releasing a small sob. Gio was next to her, pulling her into his chest for support.

"And the grave?" she asked.

"Adrian's end was ripped from you in the worst way. It forced you to feel stuck in the past. I made a space where Adrian would always be a part of your future and surrounded by life."

She couldn't say anything as more sobs crept up her throat and broke free.

I grabbed a candle and held it over Adrian's grave. "This is his memorial service, *mi reina.*"

Using the small book I had found used for leading funerals, I began to read through a few verses, all while Presley began to break all over again. She cried and cried, even lying down over his grave at one point. Once I was finished, Gio curled up behind her and held her, and then she reached for me, and I got to the ground and faced her. I began to tell her in Spanish how proud I was of her.

Me sienta muy honrada de que seas mía.

I'm so honored that you're mine.

Te amo.

I love you.

We stayed like that for what felt like hours, but by the time we finally got up, Presley had fallen asleep on top of Adrian's grave. I carried her back to my bed, full of soil and death, and held her through the night.

CHAPTER 26
PRESLEY

I woke up feeling extremely warm.

Shifting out from under the sweltering heat, I looked around. I was naked, under a heated blanket, while in Gio's bed.

"Good morning, Elvis." He pressed a kiss to my mouth.

I tried to remember the previous night and sucked in a sharp breath. "Where is my dress?"

How did I get into his bed, and did I fall asleep last night?

"It's being cleaned. King took you to his bed last night and let you sleep for as long as you could, but when you started waking, he had you brought here. I stripped you, cleaned you as much as I could, and then you were shivering, so I put this blanket over you."

"Stripped me...what was wrong with my dress?" I asked, still trying to gauge everything that had happened. My heart felt like it was throbbing as I remembered the greenhouse and the gravesite and finally burying Adrian.

Gio held out his hand for me to take. I followed him, naked, over to Kingston's bedroom, where the bed was covered in dirt and mud.

"Oh." I must have fallen asleep on Adrian's grave.

"I prepared a bath for you." Gio pressed a kiss to my neck and guided me to my room.

In my bathroom was the cutest bath set up I had ever seen. A wooden bath caddy sat across the tub with my phone set there, a cup of coffee, and a candle.

"Happy Birthday, Elvis," Gio said, helping me into the tub.

The water was hot, and the bubbles smelled divine. I nearly forgot...I was nineteen, finally. How did a whole year already pass? How had I only known Adrian for a year and yet it felt like I had grieved an entire lifetime last night.

"Thank you, Gio." I squeezed his hand, then pulled him down for a kiss.

He smiled into my mouth, then stroked my jaw. "I love you, Elvis."

My heart pinged with a softness and a joy that I could only seem to find in Gio. "I love you too."

He released me and moved to the door. "I'm going to go get your breakfast and then we're going to get ready to go."

I didn't even get a chance to ask where we were going when he left. I sank down into the tub, expecting more grief to assail my chest or to torture my mind, but something had shifted. It felt like I had some form of closure now that I had said goodbye to Adrian in an official capacity.

So instead of sinking under the bubbles, I picked up my coffee and sipped it while flipping through my phone, checking my texts.

Mom: Happy Birthday, my sweet girl. I love you and I'll call you later.

Dad: Happy Birthday, honey. I can't believe you're nineteen. Your mom made that one cake you like with the raspberry filling.

I smiled as I continued to scroll, feeling lighter than before.

Kingston: Happy Birthday, mi reina. I'm so glad I'm here for this one.

Alex: Happy Birthday, little sis. I hope this birthday is the best one yet. You deserve a good one.

Carter: HAPPY BIRTHDAY COUSIN!!!!!! Love you! Ps. Tell Scotty he's a dick. I have no idea why he showed up here to see dad, but it seemed really off. Like also, how the fuck did he find my dad? Also, are you still using the reformer? I have a new one I found on a TT shop that I think you might actually be able to use.

Shit. I sat up, letting water woosh around me as I brought up my cousin's contact info and pressed call.

It rang a few times before she sleepily answered.

"Presley, why do you hate me?"

"Carter, hey. What happened with Scotty last night?"

Something crinkled in the background while she yawned. "He wanted to ask my mom something more than Dad...even though he said he was there to see Dad, he asked about my grandpa's company and the various locations that he was operating in. My mom was really on edge, and even my dad seemed uncomfy."

"How could you tell?" I asked, taking another sip of my coffee.

Carter yawned again. "Mom and Dad made immediate plans to leave. I guess my dad finally called yours and found out we're finally on the outs with psycho Scotty. So, now we're leaving again."

That meant my dad might have been given more intel if Uncle Decker had called him.

"Okay, well, I'm sorry that you guys are having to leave again."

She sighed heavily. "It's fine, how are you doing though? You're back home now, right?"

"Here, Elvis, wanna eat in the bath or come out and eat it here?" Gio called from my bedroom.

Carter gasped into the phone. "Oh my god, is that Gio? Are you hooking up with one of the twins?"

I smiled into the phone while toying with a few bubbles. "Uh... not exactly."

"King, we're doing breakfast up here!" Gio yelled downstairs, but it echoed into the bathroom.

I heard Carter practically wheezing before she started screaming, "PRESLEY JAMES, YOU'RE HOOKING UP WITH BOTH OF THEM?"

"Gotta go, love you."

Gio appeared in the doorway as I was stepping out of the tub. I reached for my terrycloth robe and wrapped it around myself, tying it off at the waist.

"Who was that?" His jaw moved to the side as he tossed a blueberry into his mouth.

I smiled while feeling a small blush surface. "That was Carter."

Gio smirked as things began to click for him.

"She heard me yelling."

I nodded. "She did."

"And she heard me call for King."

Reaching for my coffee, I took it with me into the room. "She did."

"So she knows?" Gio followed me to my bed. There was a tray set up with flowers, breakfast, and more coffee. I smiled as I settled against my pillows.

"She guessed that I'm hooking up with both of you."

Kingston walked in holding more flowers and a wrapped birthday present.

"Good morning."

I smiled at him around my toast. "Morning."

"What is Gio smiling about?" King moved to press a kiss to my forehead.

Gio replied, "Carter found out Presley is fucking us."

Kingston stole a piece of toast before humming. "Scandalous."

I searched their faces, curious why they didn't seem as nervous about our family finding out as before. It was expected with them living here that their parents and mine marginally knew what we were doing, but no one had outright said anything about me being a couple with both brothers.

"You guys don't care?"

Kingston laughed while stealing my second cup of coffee, and Gio did something similar. "We're planning a future with you, Elvis. One day, we'll have holidays together, and they'll see both of us kiss you at different times. They'll see you curl up and lay your head on our shoulders or dance with us. They're going to know that you're with both of us, so no, that doesn't scare us."

Kingston added, "The sooner they find out, the better."

I smiled into my cup, feeling a sense of joy that I hadn't thought possible since I was naïve and sixteen.

"Hurry up and eat, we have other birthday things to attend to," Kingston said, before exiting my room and walking into his.

"Where are we going?" I asked as Gio took my hand and guided me to a familiar black Camaro. A thrill of excitement shot through me at the idea of being in the car again. I wasn't sure exactly why we were using this car instead of the SUV that typically was used, but it was my birthday, and I wasn't complaining.

Kingston opened the passenger door for me and then shoved the seat forward. "It's a surprise." He smiled and then handed me a blindfold.

I crawled into the back seat as memories assaulted me, all good ones. I clung tightly to the reminder of all the things we'd done in this car. I felt like this was where our story officially started.

Gio crawled in next to me and helped secure the blindfold in place. "No peeking, Elvis."

The smile on my face refused to budge as the car started and we began driving. Gio's grip on my thigh was firm, and since I was wearing a pleated skirt with black tights, his fingers played a game of tracing lines up my thigh, dangerously close to where my core clenched.

My hair was down and curled. I wore makeup and a black,

cropped, long-sleeved shirt with my skirt and cute platform boots. It was a huge contrast to how I had spent my eighteenth, holed up in my room with no makeup while I stuffed my face and ate copious amounts of junk food.

"Okay, almost there," Kingston said from the front.

I tried to listen for any sounds of where we might be going, but I couldn't make anything out.

The car came to a gentle stop, and Gio began exiting the car while telling me to keep the blindfold in place. I felt his hand guide me until I was clear of the roof and door, and then suddenly I heard a loud, "SURPRISE!"

My blindfold was lifted and there on the front steps of the manor were my parents, Juan, Taylor, and Alex. There was a banner that said my Happy Birthday across it, and Alex held a bundle of balloons for me.

"You drove around to the manor?" I laughed as Kingston walked over and pulled my hand in his.

Gio did the same on the other side. "Nothing but the best for our queen."

I rolled my eyes and followed everyone inside, for the first time ever showing that I was proudly with both brothers. If anyone noticed or made a face of disapproval, I didn't see it. Everyone just seemed happy to be celebrating me.

The dining, lounge area past the foyer was decorated with black and white balloons, with gold ribbons and streamers. Sinatra played over the speaker system, and there on the massive table, where our families used to gather for meals, was a display of tiered foods, drinks, appetizers, and my favorite cake in the middle.

I was moved by how much work everyone had put into things. Alex came over and began gushing about the food and all the different things I needed to try. It truly felt like the worry over Markos and Scotty had been put to rest, but I kept glancing over at my father, trying to sense if he felt it too or if he couldn't seem to fully enjoy himself because he felt the threat lingering over our heads.

I needed to know why Scotty went to visit Uncle Decker.

Kingston walked over and pushed a few pieces of hair out of my face before pressing a quick kiss to my mouth, and it took me by surprise. So much so that I blinked up at him, shocked. He'd just kissed me in front of our families...did that mean Gio wouldn't be able to, or were they going to rip off the band-aid right here, tonight, on my birthday?

Kingston must have realized my surprise because he leaned in close and said, "I told you. The sooner the better, *mi reina*."

He pulled away and wandered off toward the corner his siblings were in, and I decided to head toward my dad. He surprisingly didn't seem affected by what he might have witnessed, which only made me want to ask him about it.

"Are you having a good birthday, honey?"

I grabbed a stuffed mushroom and popped it into my mouth before nodding. "Really good."

"Good." He set a few more pieces of food on his plate before moving to the side.

"Does it weird you out?" I moved with him, speaking in a hushed voice.

Dad glanced around like we were spies. "Does what weird me out?"

He even used a fake whisper to play along. I rolled my eyes while letting out a bit of a relieved laugh. "Just...um, me with them."

How did one ask their dad if it freaked him out to see his daughter showing PDA to her boyfriends?

My dad smiled down at his plate of food. "Do you remember how often you'd get in trouble for sneaking into their bed as a little girl?"

"Yeah." I smiled, remembering he even took away my favorite stuffed animal to try and punish me over it.

"Yet you just kept wandering back to them. You said it was where you felt the safest."

That was true. Gio and Kingston were my pillars, and whenever I felt the anxiety of my father's world, or Scotty's, the twins would be where I found stability.

My dad held his plate while tasting a piece of chicken, then continued, "It was never my fear of them falling in love with you that made me so worried, honey. It was only ever what would happen if they fell for you but couldn't have you. That happened, and somehow, someway, we're here now. We made it through. If they treat you well, and you're happy, that's all I care about. Besides, I couldn't really have hoped for better. They would do anything to keep you safe. I know that now."

My eyes burned, but with happy tears. I wrapped my arms around his middle and squeezed him. "Thanks, Dad."

I was going to ask him about Scotty when my mother swooped in and pulled me over to the table of presents.

"Okay, we're doing gifts, everyone!" she called out.

The first one was from Juan and Taylor. It was a barnwood frame painted white, and inside was a photo of me, Gio, and Kingston. I had no idea where or how she got the picture. It was the three of us in a group, but while I looked at the camera, each brother decided to look at me. This was the second photo I had seen captured like this.

"Mom, you found another one." Gio groaned.

Kingston laughed while tossing a wadded-up napkin at him. "We really never stood a chance."

"We all saw it for so long, way before any of you," Taylor joked, but it warmed my heart.

The next gift was from Alex. A gift box of all farmer related things. An egg apron, a sun hat, gardening gloves, warm socks, chicken feed, and a few other items that made me laugh.

"Thanks, Alex."

"It was mostly selfish because I want to come over and play with all the farm animals you eventually get over there."

The room erupted in more laughter and smiles while I went for

222

the next gift. This had plain wrapping paper, but the box was huge. I began unwrapping it and then lifted the lid.

There, folded inside, was the dress I had picked out to wear during my wedding to Adrian. The air seemed to be sucked out of the room, the sound dulling to a ringing. "Who sent this?" I rasped while plucking the card up. I knew I shouldn't read it, and yet, I couldn't seem to stop myself.

Lánya,

Enjoy your time on the farm.

It's about to come to an end. You've already managed to kill one suitor off, I encourage you to release the twins before they take up any more space in that back field. I have a new alliance for you to prepare for.

-Scotty

The twins were behind me when I finally released the note. Anger soured my tongue and had me leaving the table in a rush. I heard people yelling behind me, but I ran to my family wing and rushed into Scotty's room.

No one had touched his things yet. He was meticulous about what he took, what he kept behind, and how he taunted me. Even now, I knew he was testing me. I knew this was a test and I was failing, but I also didn't care anymore. I wanted this stupid game to be over.

I began pulling everything off his bed and pushing the mattress up. There was a photo of me and my dad together when I was small. I grabbed it and then began rifling through anything else left behind. He had boxes of photos, of notebooks, and memorabilia. He left behind suits and a few clothes, along with his prized baseball bats that had been signed by players in the MLB at some point. I began grabbing whatever I could and piling it in the middle of the room.

The twins appeared in the doorway seconds later. Kingston was holding the box that had the wedding dress inside.

I turned away from them and grabbed another box, tossing it into the center of the room. I wanted them to argue with me, to pull me away and tell me this wasn't healthy. That I needed to just let it go, and move on, but instead, Gio cleared his throat while Kingston rattled the box.

"Your dad is setting up a bonfire outside."

I smiled as Gio stepped in and began gathering boxes.

AN HOUR LATER, I was wrapped in a blanket, outside watching the embers glow against the dark sky. Everyone had pulled up a chair, and at some point, Juan had found a guitar and started singing. It was beautiful and perfect, and as I watched all of Scotty's things burn, it healed something inside me.

The firelight caught on one of the scars over my knuckles, making me inspect the rest of my hands, but a much larger one came into view, covering them.

"One day you'll stop hating him. I promise." My dad held my hand and smiled at me.

I tried to believe him, but I wasn't there yet. My dad had been broken, I was sure, by Scotty's training, but it hadn't quite been the same. Or perhaps it was...my mom once told me that my dad refused to speak or even see Scotty after they had gotten married. Dad even tried to kill him because he had endangered my mother. Ironically, it was her who brought them back together, and with news of being pregnant with me.

How fucking funny life is.

"How did the box even get mixed in with my other gifts?" I tugged at the frayed piece of the blanket in my lap.

"Your mother said it just appeared in the back of the car, along with the other presents she had wrapped. Taylor and Alex had both given their gifts to her because she was going to a local place to have them wrapped while she did her other shopping. When she went back to the car, she didn't notice. She just assumed they'd split up one of the gifts that she'd been given to wrap."

Fucking figured. Of course, Scotty was still watching us like a vulture, waiting for his prey to decay. *I encourage you to release the twins before they take up any more space in that back field.*

"Decker called me yesterday."

I glanced up at my dad, seeing the firelight highlight his green eyes and scruffy jaw, anticipation thrumming through me. This was what I had been waiting for.

"What did he say?"

My dad sipped his drink and shook his head. "Scotty was asking strange bullshit questions as if he were just there to check up on them. But the fact that they hadn't told anyone where they were, set them on edge. We both think it was just a message he was sending to me and you. That he could get to the people who are important to us, even if they haven't told us where they are."

Outrage and disgust had me practically scoffing. "But they're his family, just like we are. Isn't your mother Scotty's sister? That's his flesh and blood. He would never hurt them."

My dad's head shook as his chin fell to his chest. "Honey, I wish that were true, but Scotty made his own family. It consists of exactly three people. I used to think it included your mother, but honestly, I think it's just me and you, kid. He thinks of himself like a god, and we're his creations. He'd never destroy us, but he'd fuck with us if he felt like it made us stronger or served a greater purpose in his eyes."

I stared into the fire, realizing my dad was right. Scotty was made up of nothing but selfish ambition and protecting what mattered to him in his own universe. Did that mean he'd ever hurt my mother? I assumed they were close, but maybe when she attempted to kill him, that broke. Smoke billowed up into the sky as we all laughed and smiled, pretending we hadn't just been infiltrated by Scotty somehow. We all acted as though this night was merely to celebrate me, and I loved them for it even if, deep down, I had my own worry gnawing at my gut.

Scotty was always one to three steps ahead of us. He foresaw every outcome it seemed. How was I supposed to gain the upper hand and fight against him?

Maybe I didn't.

CHAPTER 27

PRESLEY

I spent a week quietly making my plan.

Within that time, I wandered out to the greenhouse early in the morning while the fog still clung to the tips of the trees and the world was cast in shades of gray. The door to the greenhouse gently opened as I pulled it, and my eyes dropped first to the stone where Adrian was laid to rest.

Just like every time, my heart seemed to jolt in my chest at the opportunity to visit him like this. Kingston had automatic watering misters set up for all his plants, which seemed to be thriving. I realized there was something blooming around the headstone where Adrian's name was carved, and under his name was the phrase, "Beloved Fiancé."

I'd hung my engagement ring with a silver chain over the stone, but there, near the soil, were flowers beginning to bloom. Gently touching the small petals with my fingers, they almost looked like night-blooming jasmine. I decided to take a picture of the petal with my phone to see what Kingston had planted. The soil had been covered.

Gladiolus. A flower that represented courage and resilience.

Fresh tears found their way down my face as I began to talk to my dead friend. After my birthday, I felt a strange echo in my soul that I couldn't figure out how to fill. It was a void that brilliant blue eyes and an easy smile used to fill. Hearing him call me *Bellissima*. Hearing his laugh, or the way he touched me at night. I ached for him. Even with the return of the twins, I still longed for my friend.

Each day throughout the week, I'd spend my mornings in that greenhouse. I'd leave a piece of my soul and let my broken heart take refuge in visiting a man who lost his life because of his loyalty to me. By midafternoon, I'd take a different sort of refuge in feeding the cows and tending to the new chickens that had arrived. We also had two new goats that were particularly obstinate when it came to respecting their enclosure. Gio had to repair it at least three times a day just to keep them in.

Every night, the twins would hold me, and we'd fall into a routine where I'd spend time with each one individually. Gio liked to watch movies with me at night, while we relaxed in the living room. He liked to rub my shoulders and play with my hair while my head was in his lap. Kingston didn't mind spending time with us, but our time together was always a little different. It was quiet walks along the property, or me helping him create planter boxes in the backyard. One time, I found him in the greenhouse and decided to show him how grateful I was for the flowers he'd chosen to plant near Adrian.

I dropped to my knees right there, letting the soil stain my knees while I greedily accepted Kingston in my mouth until he finished down my throat. I woke to kisses, being told how loved I was, and I accepted it. I believed it.

There were times we argued too, but I mostly did that with Kingston, and I had a feeling he did it because of the way each argument would end. Typically, me on his bed, with my ass up in the air and his fingers gripping me hard while he fucked me senseless. There were times Gio would sigh and just go to his room and shut the door when King and I would start up, likely because he knew exactly how it would end.

I'd always find my way back into Gio's arms afterward, needing him to put me back together after Kingston would effectively break me apart. While I loved that Kingston never hid his darkness from me, without Gio, it would be too much. I needed his twin's softness and the gentle way he cradled my heart. Gio was protective of me in a way that I felt like no one had ever been, and for that, I found a certain kind of solace in him.

Which is why having him angry with me felt infinitely worse than his brother.

I'd waited long enough to put my plan into action, so I pulled out my phone and dialed. I was in the woods, away from the house and the manor, so I didn't bother lowering my voice when the person on the other end picked up.

"Lánya." Scotty's voice was firm, not curious or surprised at all that I had called.

"I told you to stop calling me that."

He laughed but moved on. "I assume you're either calling to threaten me or to accept the alliance. Knowing you, you've run the scenario through your head enough times that you know I'm right. If you stay with the twins, it'll eventually end with their deaths, which means you need an alliance."

"I know..." I replied, doing my best to keep my true intentions at bay. "I—I can't lose the twins, and I don't want to risk anything happening to them."

He was quiet for a moment before he let out a sigh. "You've let them go once; you can do it again. I'm going to send you an address in New York. I'd like you to meet a new contact...he's young, only twenty-five, but his family is powerful. Up and coming...a connection with them could be all that we need to finally have the edge we've needed."

"I understand," I replied evenly.

"I'll send back up for you, don't take the twins. They'll see it as a threat."

I nodded again. "Okay."

"I'm proud of you, Presley. Even through everything, you're exactly how I always knew you'd turn out."

With that, he hung up.

My chest felt like I'd just rammed it with a two-by-four. I wanted to scream at him, to fight with him, and tell him to fuck off with his pride and all the ways he envisioned me growing up. Instead, I tucked my phone into my pocket and turned to walk back, only to freeze in place.

"You better explain what the fuck I just listened to, right now," Gio snapped with thunder in his eyes and devastation on his face.

"Gio." I stepped closer, but he stepped back.

"You're not going."

"I am," I explained, taking another step closer. "This is the only way to defeat him, Gio. You have to trust me."

"Trust you to be sent into the arms of another man?" His face twisted angrily. "The only other person I will ever share you with is my twin, and I am barely managing that. I know our roots are joined, there's no untangling the three of us, but if there was even the slightest chance you could love me alone, be happy with just me, you have to know I would take it. Sometimes I fucking dream of it, Elvis."

I refused to feel guilty about hurting him. The truth was, there was no way of tearing my heart out of their hands. They each owned a piece. If one returned it, that portion would break, and there was just no way around that.

"Gio, I'm not—" I tried to explain, but he took off walking toward the house, unwilling to hear me out.

I didn't chase him, but I did return to the house where I knew Gio would tell Kingston what he overheard. Taking my time with my shower and getting things prepared, I wasn't surprised when Kingston darkened my doorway with his shadow.

"You're not playing bride to be again," he rumbled.

I glanced up from where I was cleaning one of my guns. "Never said I was."

"Gio overheard—"

Snapping the case for the gun closed, I scoffed before moving to a larger gun. "He overheard shit that wasn't his business."

"You are our business, Presley. Everything you do, every breath you take, and every person who threatens you. That's our business."

I shook my head. "Don't you guys get it? There is no way to get ahead of him. There is no outsmarting him, or outmaneuvering him. He will win at every turn because he has no weaknesses. Except two."

Kingston's amber gaze narrowed on the suitcase behind me while his nose flared. "You're placing yourself back on the sacrificial stone for Scotty's plans. We will not let you do this!" His voice was so loud it made me flinch.

I walked over and immediately wrapped my arms around him. "You have to trust me. I am begging you to trust me."

It took a few seconds for his hands to come around me, but they eventually did. In a rare, tender moment that Kingston and I rarely shared, he hugged me. The seconds passed by, and his hold on me intensified, squeezing me to him while he rasped near my ear.

"I can't lose you again. I refuse to let you slip through my fingers and into the arms of another man. I can't—" He choked back a sob. "I can't go through it again. Pres. Seeing you break over Adrian. Knowing you started a new page with him when Gio and I were supposed to have been your story still kills me."

I pulled back, feeling annoyed. "Well, it literally killed him, so rest easy."

"Pres."

"You either choose to trust me or you don't, but trust has to be a part of what we're doing here, or else it won't work."

He tucked a piece of my hair back before finally heaving a sigh that seemed to weigh a thousand pounds. "We're coming with you on that first initial meet up. Scotty could be setting up a trap."

I nodded, already knowing they would push for that. "Okay, but you have to remain out of sight."

With a kiss to my nose, he agreed. With a glance over his shoulder, I saw Gio's closed door and wondered how long he'd choose to remain upset with me.

I WASN'T sure if the twins had told my father of my plan, but as we drove into the city, the only car I knew of that followed us was Henry's and the twins' extra men.

Our windows were blacked out, so it would be difficult for anyone to see who was with me, but as long as it was only me exiting the car, it wouldn't set anyone off.

Kingston drove, but Gio sat in the back and had still refused to speak to me. Scotty had given me a location near the docks to arrive and then at the last minute changed it to a small eatery near an underpass. I wasn't sure why he changed it, but it didn't matter. El Peligro was all over the city, and when Gio had texted them the new address, they'd already scoped it out. There were five men watching for threats, stationed around the property. No sign of Scotty.

I flipped the vent for the car and changed the temperature, so cooler air blew out.

"Why are you wearing such a thick coat?" Kingston asked. I wore a dress with tights and tall heels under a long, heavy dress coat. The outfit was long sleeved, and the tights were fur- lined, so I didn't need the coat, but they didn't know that.

I glanced out the window. "Just cold."

"Yet, you're blasting the AC; makes perfect sense," Gio mused from behind me.

"What did you find out about this guy?" King directed his question to Gio via the rearview mirror.

Gio shifted in the back. "Fernando Vissimo. He has prostitution charges that never stuck, but a few reports of women who claimed he tried to kill them." His voice became high... "He's a big player for his father's organization...which has recently gained power after aligning with the Mariano fortune."

So, this man was already an ally of Markos then.

"What's your plan, Elvis?" Gio asked while leaning closer.

"I just want to see where this leads. If I manage to convince Fernando that I'd be a good option for marriage, then it would allow me to get closer to Markos again. I need a way to be able to access him again."

Gio began muttering something in the back, but we had arrived. The small restaurant wasn't more than a shack lit up with fluorescent lights. The parking lot, however, was massive, and only one lone light illuminated the dark sky. It made it practically perfect for our first meeting. I was able to see the five men gathered in front of a similar looking SUV to what we were driving.

"I need you both to trust me. I know what I am doing, and I am begging you to stay put."

Kingston glared over at Gio, who had clenched his jaw so tight he looked like he was chewing on glass.

Unbuckling, I clarified before I got out, "Your men are watching the Vissimo crew?"

"They are," Kingston promised.

I gave him a solemn nod. "Trust me."

He nodded while I exited the car. It remained running behind me while I walked toward a group of men. Small pieces of loose gravel echoed under my heels as I walked over.

In the center was a man that was in his twenties, with dark hair, who watched me like a toddler watched a piece of candy being dangled in front of him. The other men were tall, burly, and looked bored.

"Presley James?"

I smiled brightly, showing my freshly shaded lips and white teeth as I approached. "Hi!"

Fernando looked excited and even took a few steps forward when he began muttering to his men in Italian. He was talking about my body, and how he wanted to use it later, and even explained he'd share with one of the men. I'd planned my steps prior to even arriving, but his words only made it easier.

"I'm so excited that we were able to set this up!" Fernando called, getting closer.

When I was within fifty feet or so, I began unbuttoning my coat. He remained oblivious to my intentions until it was too late. From the lining, I pulled up two automatic assault rifles and began shooting.

The men were so caught off guard, they didn't have time to pull out their weapons.

This was a lesson I had learned from Scotty, and how fitting that I was able to put it to use on an alliance he'd set up.

All five of them were down within seconds. Someone in the car began driving away, peeling out of the parking lot, but the twins did the same and cut them off by ramming our car into theirs. Fernando's car flipped, and then Gio was out, walking with his hands wrapped around a hand gun, ensuring whoever was driving wasn't alive any longer.

In my five-inch-high heels, I sauntered over to Fernando and pulled out the note I had written. Grabbing the staple gun I had stolen from Kingston's work table in the barn, I secured the note to his forehead.

Scotty,

Cheers to another great alliance.

- *I'll be in touch.*

CHAPTER 28
GIO

She took a fucking page out of Scotty's book.

For as long as I could remember, he would wear those long, heavy coats, always concealing weapons when we'd go places. The irony that she'd used his classic move while double-crossing him brought a proud smile to my face. But I immediately squashed it because what she did was dangerous as hell.

Once she returned to the car, she tried to resume her position in front, but I stepped out and held the door open for her.

"Funny you think you have a choice, Elvis."

She rolled her eyes before handing me her guns, which I placed in the rear hatch of the car.

Moments later, she was buckled into the back, behind Kingston's seat, with her arms crossed. My brother took off while I turned in the seat and faced her. "The fuck, Elvis?"

She shrugged. "I told you to trust me."

"You didn't tell us shit, which made this entire situation dangerous," Kingston snapped from his place in front.

"If I told you guys what I was planning, you'd stop me."

I laughed sardonically. "No shit. Did you even consider he might

235

have had a sniper set up, or even Scotty himself could have been watching and took you out?"

Her eyes narrowed shrewdly before throwing her hand out. "You guys had your men watching everyone. Of course, I considered it, but I know Scotty. He won't hurt me or take me out. I'm his little personalized Swiss Army knife. He wants me alive because in his mind, he created me. All he'll do is hit back by taking something important to me, which I fucking hope isn't Carter or one of you."

"You're not going to lose one of us, Elvis. Or Carter. Your dad already helped them move to a secure location."

Kingston began traveling to the safe house we'd selected to sleep in for the night. It was some place he hadn't told his men, or even me about, but since it was a few hours back to North Carolina, we needed a place to stop for the night.

"So, what's your plan now? Are you trying to get him to come to the manor or what?"

Presley crossed her leg over her knee, and it made my eyes drop and my cock twitch. She looked so fucking gorgeous tonight, and that was one reason I was so pissed off when we began driving. In my head, she was dressing up for another alliance. Another man who would fall hopelessly in love with her, abandoning his loyalty to his family and his plans, because Presley was impossible not to fall in love with.

I saw how Fernando looked at her. I saw exactly what he'd wanted when she walked toward him. Even covered by her coat, he wanted her for his own nefarious, twisted purpose. I hated this idea that I'd have to share her.

I hated sharing her with my twin, and yet, that I could at least accept. I could stomach it because it meant she was with me at night, and I still had her to myself when I wanted. It was enough for me, but this idea that Scotty was still trying to reach in and toy with her future set me on edge, enough that I was ready to hit something.

Suddenly, Presley slid her hand over mine and gently tugged it over to her lap.

236

"I don't have a plan except that I wanted to kick the beehive hard enough, they'd know I'm a threat."

My brother caught my eye in the mirror, and I wondered if he was thinking the same thing.

By doing all this, she was falling into Scotty's plans. He wanted her to become a weapon. He wanted her to be a tool to be used for his means. Fuck, there wasn't even any evidence that he didn't want Fernando taken out himself, and knew simply by suggesting an alliance, Presley would do it.

I refused to tell her that because she might come to her own conclusion, then be angry with herself for fulfilling it. The only real way to defy Scotty would be by her living her life and forgetting him. Forgetting Markos and leaving this plan for vengeance behind.

"Why are you mad?" she whispered, scooting closer to me.

I glared out the window, doing my best not to lash out at her. That toxic, angry fighting shit was her and Kingston's thing, not hers and mine. I always kept a level head. I always remained calm, and I always remained peaceful with her.

But inside, I felt anything but peace.

Presley kept moving until she was straddling my lap and holding my jaw in her hands.

"Please talk to me."

I grabbed her hand and stopped her from stroking over my face. "I don't want to talk."

Her brows caved inward as her lips pursed.

"Gio, please."

"I'm angry," I snapped, and the way she winced had me instantly feeling like shit.

She was about to slide off my lap, but I felt guilty for being so harsh. I gripped her thighs instead, hoping to stall her. "How come you can fight with Kingston and take his rage and yell back, and you guys end up fucking, but with me, if I raise my voice, you cry?"

Her expression didn't shift; it only worsened as more tears flowed down her face. "I don't like when you're mad at me."

"Well, too fucking bad. I am, and I want to fuck you the way Kingston gets to fuck you when he's mad."

"That's different, bro," my twin replied from the front.

Presley was still trying to get off me, but I continued to hold her firmly when I yelled, "How?"

"Because it is. You never get mad at her...it's like building up a tolerance to something. I'm always an asshole, and I always say shitty things, and Presley says them back. She's a brat, and our dynamic works in some fucked-up way," Kingston explained.

"Well, I want to be that guy tonight."

Kingston shook his head. "You won't like yourself afterwards. That takes the same amount of tolerance being built."

"It's fine," Presley said, swiping at a few of her tears.

"If you think you need that, then fine. Take me rough and be just like Kingston is with me."

"I want to punish you, Presley. I want you to get it through your head that you can't walk up to a group of trained mafia soldiers and just start shooting. You could have been killed or abducted. Fuck, do you have any idea what that felt like to see you walk toward them?"

"No, but you're punishing me right now by being distant and mean. It's like the sun refusing to shine," she cried.

I searched her eyes, wishing it was brighter in the car, so I had a better view of that sparkling blue framed by thick black lashes.

"You promised to be my sky, Gio. To always find me when we got lost. I get that you're upset but—"

"It's not just that..." I shook my head, "It's this need for vengeance you have. It's going to get you killed. You're playing right into Scotty's hand by needing to find him and wanting to kill them. You know the best way to defy Scotty?"

She sat back, still trying to get free, but I held firm, keeping her in my lap. "How?"

"You live. You laugh, and you do exactly what you're doing now. Farm, plant, fuck. Do all those things."

She flung her arms wide. "And never leave the house for fear that

238

we're being hunted? That's not a life either. I don't want to be in hiding anymore. I don't want to train and be ready for a war. I want to smile up at the sun when it shines, and I want to be loved by the both of you. I want to be a mother one day. I want all of those things, but I don't get any of it if he's still alive."

"You know we could protect you. It's why you've been at ease on the farm. Deep down, you know he can't get through our men or what we created. We set all that up, risked everything so you would feel that peace at home. This isn't about not getting to be a mom or being at peace. This is about Adrian."

She shook her head. "It's not."

"Your need to avenge Adrian is so strong that you'll risk losing us," I retorted angrily.

This time, when she tried to crawl off my lap, I let her go.

"Fuck you, Gio."

"Am I wrong?" I gripped her chin so that she was facing me again.

She tried to push at me, but instead I pulled her closer and began kissing down her neck. "Am I wrong, Elvis?"

"I would never risk losing either of you," she replied in a whisper, but she was wrong about that, too.

She had jeopardized us before all to protect her family.

"You risk us every time you engage with Scotty. Every time you need to get back at him, we're in danger. So stop lying."

Our faces were close now, and I felt her tongue begin tracing my jaw. I thought she'd want to start kissing, or making out until she bit down on my bottom lip hard enough to draw blood.

"Fuckkk." I pulled away in pain.

Sounding more determined than ever, she said, "I'm not lying, Gio. I haven't risked you, and I wouldn't."

I glanced at my brother, and he smirked. "See, she's a brat. Now punish her like one."

The gleam in Presley's eye was already there, so I pulled her face in and harshly kissed her. Our tongues moved angrily, and her nails began digging into my arms. I groaned while lifting her, and then we pulled apart. I moved her so that she was on all fours.

Pushing her head down into the seat, I flipped up her dress and yanked down her tights.

"Tell me what to do next," I said to my brother while staring down at Presley's ass. Her pussy gleamed with wetness; even in the darkened car, I could see how soaked she was.

"Push your fingers into her cunt, three of them, and don't be gentle."

I did exactly what he said, which made Presley cry out.

"Pull 'em out and then shove them back in a few times," Kingston ordered.

The sound of her cunt being stretched and played with filled the car, along with her tiny whimpers. "Now what?"

"Slap her pussy."

My hand stalled midair. "Her pussy or her cheek?"

"You're going to slap her pussy. Tilt her up more, make sure her face is against that seat so hard, her fingers should be gripping the leather. I want to be able to hear you slap it."

I'd never slapped her at all, much less her sensitive slit, and since she's the only person I'd ever fucked, it wasn't like I had any other experiences to draw from, but Kingston must do this with her from time to time, so maybe she enjoyed it.

Without thinking more of it, I did what he said and covered her pussy with a harsh slap.

"Ohmygawwwwd," Presley moaned.

"Do it again, Gio," Kingston ordered.

I repeated myself, slapping her pussy three more times. Each time, Presley about lost it.

"You like that, Elvis?"

She began moving her ass back as if searching for friction.

"She fucking loves it, now I want you to push your tongue into that hole you love fucking so much."

I didn't hesitate on that either. I loved Presley's ass and fucking her there was one of my favorite things to do, but I had a feeling this would be used for a different reason.

"Get her nice and soaked. Do not drop down to her pussy no matter how she moves or shifts, keep her in place and just keep your tongue right where it is."

I did as my brother advised and kept my focus on the one spot, even as she writhed and begged under me.

"If she tries to use her hand to get off, I want you to slap her pussy again and then lay a firm slap to her ass cheek. For now, just keep licking between her crack."

My face was buried, my tongue swiping and moving when I felt her hand come up. "Please, Gio. Please, I need to rub against something."

"See how much of a fucking brat she can be. Do what I told you," Kingston said from his spot up front. I caught him moving and shifting a few times, and I had a feeling he'd pulled his dick out.

My hand came down against her pussy again, harder than last time, and she cried out. I followed it up with a slap to her butt, and then I resumed licking through her ass.

"Good. Now fuck her. Hard," my brother rasped, while his wrist lifted and lowered near his lap.

I didn't know how he hadn't pulled the car over yet and demanded a turn back here, but I really fucking appreciated his self-control because I wanted her to myself right now.

"Gio, do not enter her slowly or allow her to adjust. You go in hard and in one thrust. You're punishing her, so make her remember it."

I nodded silently and pulled my cock out, stroking it a few times, and then did exactly as he demanded. My hands went to her hips as I shoved inside her in one deep thrust.

"Fuck," I spat, while Presley moaned loud and agonizing.

I worried for a second that I hurt her, but Kingston stopped me. "She's fucking fine. She loves your cock, even more than mine. Remind her exactly why."

Feeling encouraged, I slid out of her and slammed back in as hard as I could. There was something freeing about letting loose and not worrying if I was careful or if I hurt her. It was still there in the back of my mind, but Kingston just kept assuring me, and from how many times I had heard them fucking in his room, I believed him. She was louder with him, more needy and desperate. She loved fucking me slow, and moaned in different ways, but our sex was always happy. Pleasant. Nothing like this.

Kingston was back to ordering me around. "Slap her ass, Gio. Then grip it hard while you fuck her."

My body complied immediately, copying everything he said. I gripped her with one hand and slapped her ass with the other while I continued to rock in and out of her.

"You can go faster than that, Gio. I've seen you lose control; she should be screaming right now."

He wasn't wrong. I was still holding back, so finally, I just released all my inhibitions and began mercilessly fucking her. She began whimpering against the seat, her fingers curled around the leather as I moved behind her.

"Now start rubbing her clit," Kingston ordered.

"Won't she—" I started on a half a breath when my brother laughed.

"She will, and she'll be pissed about it. Rub her clit."

I did as he said, going as fast as he did the last time he made Presley squirt. She began crying out again.

"Gio. Fuck. Fuck. Fuck," she screamed as a gush of liquid came from her and ran over my hand. The extra lubrication coated my cock as I slid through her cunt, and it felt so fucking good that I exploded inside her, coming so hard I could barely breathe.

"See, told you." Kingston smirked in the mirror.

I slumped over her back, still unable to catch my breath. "Holy shit."

"Holy shit indeed," Presley replied, gasping for her own breath.

I slowly began pulling out of her when the car finally came to a stop. Kingston jumped out and pulled open the door closest to Presley. The inner lights came on, revealing my soaked cock, and the white mess clinging to Presley's pussy. The seat was soaked, and her face was sweaty.

"Come put your lying mouth over me, Pres, and suck my cock."

I thought she'd resist or put up a fight, but she only shifted to her knees before taking him deep into her mouth. I sat there, next to them, while my brother got a blow job, and I watched Presley's head bob back and forth, still trying to catch my breath.

I felt like I'd taken a fucking drug or something. Sex had never felt like that before, not that it had ever been bad, but for the first time ever, I liked the idea of sharing her. I liked that my brother told me what to do to her, and that while I touched her, he wasn't anywhere near us. I liked that even now, as she sucked his cock, she'd had mine shoved inside her first. I made her come and squirt. I did all that before my brother even laid a finger on her.

With her ass still pointed in my direction, I used my finger to swipe through her pussy and smeared my release all over her skin. As if marking her someway. That was all me.

And I fucking loved it.

CHAPTER 29
KINGSTON

I knew Presley's need for vengeance wasn't purely based on Adrian.

Gio was being shortsighted about things and, as usual, leading with that jealous heart of his. This was deeper to her.

I tried to remember that as I watched her walk around what used to be a safe house used by me and Gio. It was back when we were scouting Mayhem Riot, the motorcycle club that we'd tried to infiltrate all those months ago. The memory was still tinged with shame that we'd nearly cost our aunt her boyfriend. Archer's forgiveness was still something that humbled me, but having Presley see this place was like opening my veins in front of her and trying to hide the blood.

"So, this is the place you guys stayed while you were—" she trailed off while dragging her finger over a dusty shelf. Gio had clicked on a lamp to help brighten the room, but it hadn't been cleaned in months since we had no use for it after our attempted takeover. It was something we planned to hand over to El Peligro at some point for them to use or sell.

Presley shrugged out of her long coat and laid it on the back of the couch.

"It's very empty."

Gio's jaw tensed. "Well, we were only here to lay low, didn't exactly set up shop."

"Do you guys smoke anymore?" She picked up a glass pipe before setting it gently back on the shelf.

"I haven't really since all the shit went down here," Gio answered somberly.

Presley inspected him, then swung her head over to me.

"Well, let's go to bed. I'm tired." She slipped out of her high heels and then walked over to Gio, so he'd help with the buttons on her dress. Once he finished, the fabric lowered from her shoulders, revealing bare skin. Her tits were held up by a strapless bra, and the black straps of her thong rose high along her hip bones.

I watched every move she made before admitting. "We only have the two beds, and they're small."

With a smirk, she reached behind her to unclasp her bra. "Better move them together then because I'm not being forced to choose."

My brother and I followed her like lovesick puppies.

Once we pushed our twin beds together, against the wall, Gio stripped and crawled on first. Presley moved next and snuggled in beside him. Her face was buried in his neck, and his hand had wrapped around her waist. For the briefest moment, I felt like an intruder or third wheel, but Gio helped Presley turn so her back was to his chest, and she faced me.

"Come on, King."

Her eyes drew me in just like they always did. The thick black lashes, and the way her freckles splattered over her nose. My heart seemed to ache with a heaviness, a fear of losing this.

Yanking my shirt up and over my head, I tossed it to the floor and dropped my jeans.

Sliding under the covers, I felt her soft skin rub against mine. Her fingers trailed over my neck and jaw until her lips met mine. Once we pulled apart, she said. "Tell me why you both became so determined to hurt everyone after I left."

Gio wrapped a piece of her hair around his finger, but didn't reply.

I heaved a sigh and traced her nose. "It's difficult to explain, but for me it was a form of punishment for myself."

"We'd already lost you, felt like there wasn't much left to lose," Gio added.

Things were quiet while my brother played with her hair, and I drew lines up her hip bone and along her ribs.

"So it was a form of acting out?"

Gio snorted. "What we did was wrong, Elvis. It was unacceptable. We aren't proud of it. Just like we aren't proud of what we did to you. It's not easy for us to talk about, but trust me when I say it was far beyond merely acting out."

Her fingers trailed up behind her, moving to my brother's jaw. Her other hand moved to my chest, over my heart.

"I know it's not easy, but I also think it's important to not lock it away. You're both the most important people to me. I want you to be whole."

Drawing her hand up, I pressed a kiss to the pads of her fingers. "Just don't give up on us. We're trying to get back to who we were and make things right, but it takes time. It's impossible to walk away from all the choices we made...some of them are more permanent."

Presley drew a line over my chest while Gio stroked down her arm. "So walking away from El Peligro is..."

"Not possible," I confirmed softly.

"What happened to the charity your parents were running? All the inner-city things they were doing with the power of that gang...is it all gone?"

Presley had grown up helping in those soup kitchens, alongside us. She had handed out backpacks and went shopping for school supplies just like we had when the inner-city schools would notify my family of various needs.

"Honestly, I'm not sure," Gio answered somberly.

The thick lump in my throat was all the shame I still carried over this topic and the truth that was too painful to confront. "There isn't anyone left to help them. It's all gone now. Whatever is left will run on what money our parents have left to keep it going. There are various donations and things that were made that they'll ensure get stretched as far as possible, but it's all over, and it's because of us."

"You can't put that weight on yourselves." Presley chided, but it didn't matter.

"It's the truth," I explained evenly.

Presley sat up and pressed her back to the wall, bringing her knees up under her chin.

"There must be a way to make the men go back and do what they used to for your father. Can't you just redesign the same nonprofit plan that your parents made?"

Gio shook his head before bringing his thumb and forefinger to the bridge of his nose. "They have a bloodlust for this life. They don't want to help; they want security, power, and money. Moving drugs and weapons gives them that."

Presley forced her lips together before she let out a sigh. "Well, I think all they need is motivation. There must be a way you can do both. Run the drugs but use the money to protect the inner-city kids."

I pulled her ankle, forcing her back down to the bed.

"You have a good heart, *mi reina*."

She smiled up at me. "It's made up of all the best pieces of you..." She glanced over at Gio and finished, "And you."

"Do you want to help us bring El Peligro back to the vision our father had, then?"

Presley nodded. "I do."

"Then we will," I promised her before pressing my mouth to hers once more.

THE FOLLOWING MORNING, I stared down at how Presley was curled into my brother's chest and considered what I had last night. Her need for vengeance wasn't purely based on Adrian, and the number of times she'd asked us to just trust her had something tugging at my conscience. She needed us, and more than just romantically or physically. She needed her best friend's. Just like we needed her to give us hope that we could somehow come back from all that we'd done to ruin our father's legacy.

Gio looked peaceful as his jaw fit over the top of Presley's head, tucking her close. He wouldn't agree with me, and once I talked to her about this, he'd be pissed. Especially after his argument with Presley last night.

I decided to wait until we drove home to say anything. March was warmer than I anticipated, with the sun shining and the warmer air blowing through the open car window. Once we arrived at the farmhouse, Presley went to shower. Gio went to check on all the animals, and I went to find some food. About an hour later, I found her out in the backyard watering our flower beds. She wore a cotton dress with her egg apron tied around her waist, looking relaxed and happier than I'd ever seen her. Her hair was up, revealing her long neck, and I realized she had several of the chickens roaming around the yard with her while she tossed them feed.

"Hey," I called. I walked up behind her, pressing a kiss to her neck.

Turning around with a smile, she leaned into me. "Hey."

"Come sit with me." I tugged her hand and walked over to the porch swing.

She leaned into me while the swing rocked us, and the sun broke through the clouds overhead. A few trees nearby had begun sprouting buds and moss. It brought me immense joy seeing all of this here for Presley to enjoy. Her dream house had been completed, she had farm animals, and now, defeating Scotty might finally be within reach.

"I know last night was not about Adrian, and finding them is not about what Gio mentioned."

She shifted against me while looking down at her nails. "No, it wasn't."

"I know this is about what he took from you. The miles he forced you to run as a nine-year-old. The smell of that ointment that clung to you when your knuckles broke open and healed. The fear he instilled inside you that your whole world would end if you didn't become the perfect weapon."

Her hand came up to dab under her eye. "Fuck, King. Warn me next time you're going to just dig in like that."

I kissed the top of her head. "That's why I'm going to tell you this, and I'm going to respect what you do with it."

Blue, vibrant eyes found mine in an instant, searching for what I'd say next.

"I asked Henry to look into the whereabouts of Scotty and Markos."

She sat forward, pressing her feet to the floor. "And?"

"They're getting on their private jet, bound for North Carolina."

Her eyes searched mine nervously as if she was putting a plan together. "They're coming here."

"Seems that way."

"He'll come for the house, Kingston. He'll torch it to the ground and ensure I have nothing to go back to."

Hauling her back into my arms, I stroked down her arm while we rocked some more.

"He won't get past my men, except for in the places we want him to."

She smiled, tipping her head back. "You're going to force him into a corner."

"The manor, but yes, and when they get there, I want you to have the opportunity to end him."

"And Gio? What does he think of this?"

"He thinks you're fucking crazy if you assume I'd ever go along with this." Gio suddenly appeared behind us, arms folded across his chest, his grim expression set firmly. As twins, we tried to diversify what we wore so we didn't always match, but seemed we fucked that up today by wearing the same blue jeans, navy Henley, and brown boots. Even our hair had gotten to roughly the same length.

Presley let out a sigh. "Gio."

"No, we aren't doing this. You're not risking your life to appease whatever bloodlust is in your heart."

I stood from the swing and faced him. "It's not up to you."

Gio shot back, "And it's up to you?"

"It's up to Presley, but either way, Scotty and Markos are coming. They got the message Presley left when she murdered the son of the Vissimo family, and they are coming to enact their own revenge. They will come for what matters most to her, which right now is us, this house, the animals and the greenhouse. They'll take it all from her and then toss her into another arrangement. So, stop being so fucking stubborn and support her."

My brother's jaw pulsed, but he seemed to get the message as he turned and walked away.

Presley held my hand on her way past me, and I decided it was time to go inform my dad and Kyle about what was about to happen to the manor.

CHAPTER 30

KINGSTON

I wanted to pull my dad aside and tell him Presley's idea about the nonprofit. The more I thought about it, the more excited I became. Just because we'd fucked everything up didn't mean we couldn't put it all back. Gio and I were the leaders; we could simply execute the orders to protect the inner city and give everyone a role. Unfortunately, time was of the essence, so it would have to wait.

I'd explained everything, and now I waited for the room to respond. We were in the manor, near the back terrace, with everyone filling up a spot. The vines over the glass doors looked malnourished, like they were about to die. Some part of me wanted to figure out why and how I could fix it, but I had to stop trying to revive the manor. For all I cared, this place could burn. All I needed was the farmhouse, and the future Presley painted.

"So, you're telling me you allowed my daughter to take a meeting with an ally that Scotty set up, and she killed them?" Kyle asked, tugging on the ends of his hair. He wore a simple black T-shirt with a pair of sweats, and for the first time since I could remember, he wasn't intimidating the shit out of me.

Rylie sat on a lounger, leaning forward with her elbows pressed to her knees. Mom, Dad, and Alex all sat across the room while we tried to explain what was about to take place.

"With all due respect, Kyle, there was no allowing Presley to do anything. Her choices are her own, and we just try to protect her." I explained while Gio scoffed.

"She made us believe she was going to entertain the alliance. We had no idea she'd pull out two assault rifles and begin shooting."

I lowered my hand and agreed. "Right, and that."

Dad pulled out his phone and began texting. I gestured toward his phone and asked, "Who are you messaging?"

Dad's eyes remained on his device. "Archer. I'm seeing if he has any contacts in the area that might be willing to assist us."

Gio furrowed his brow. "We have El Peligro, Dad. It's the whole reason we risked everything."

"I'm not arguing that, but I'd still prefer the extra backup."

Mom glanced up at our sister, who was looking outside toward the farm. "How's Presley holding up?"

Kyle responded to the room. "She's ready to put this all behind her, and we'll do whatever we can to help her do it."

"Well, let's go over the plan then." Gio moved to the large table and rolled out a map.

"THE PERIMETER IS SECURE," Henry said, coming up beside me. Our men had worked around the clock to secure the property. The farmhouse and the barn were insulated and well-guarded.

I doubted that Scotty would be arriving with an army, but I also knew him well enough that he had something up his sleeve that made him feel like he had a chance at winning this disagreement. Especially because he was the one who trained Presley and Kyle.

Gio hadn't said anything more to me or to Presley about his thoughts on her engaging with Scotty and Markos or endangering herself by doing so. I had watched as she watched him, as he moved around in that angry mood of his that seemed to seep into every crevice of the house. He'd shut himself in his room, locked his door, and even when Presley had gently knocked against the wood, he hadn't opened it.

For once, it was me she had turned to for comfort. Her face was buried in my neck, her arms around my waist as she accepted that my brother would remain angry with her over this.

But now, as our hacker had told us the jet had arrived, Presley had exited her room in tactical gear, her hair braided back and a gun strapped to her back. Along her hips, she had ammo and a few more handguns. It took me back to seeing her as the girl who had trained her whole life to become a weapon.

Her shy smile made my belly flip.

Pulling her into my chest, I kissed her. "I love you, *mi reina*."

"I love you, my broody asshole, King." She snickered around the play on words she'd used. Our lips met again in a slow, purposeful wave. Our heads tipped back, and my hands went to her hips to stabilize her.

"Keep one dream with you, *mi reina*. One tucked away inside that broken heart of yours. I want you to think of it and cling to it every moment, and if anything happens, I want you to remember this moment right here and pull the image back up."

She pressed a kiss to my palm in reply. "What will you think of, Kingston?"

"I'll tell you once we're back here, in this spot, and they're all dead."

"Deal." She kissed me once more, and then we walked out of the house.

Gio was with Henry when we emerged from the house. The men were all ready and waiting for us. The afternoon was nearly spent as evening began to crowd the skies.

"It's confirmed, they just landed," Henry said.

Our men were in position to keep a close watch over where

Scotty and Markos went and if the Adesso brothers split up. But we had planned to remain inside the manor until we knew what his plan was.

I had a feeling Presley was right and Scotty would go for her farm first. Beyond just the ranch being guarded by our men, I had other safeguards in place. Bulletproof windows, steel enforced doors, and a few deadly surprises that would shoot if triggered. I had no concern over the farmhouse. The barn, however, might go and my greenhouse. If it did, I'd just rebuild, and replant, and I would kill Scotty before he had the chance to touch Adrian's grave.

Either way, we'd be ready.

With everyone set, roughly half the day later, I headed up to the manor with Presley and my brother.

It was quiet as we walked. The only sound to be heard was the birds chirping through the woods. Things were still tense between Gio and Presley, and while I was inclined to let them work it out, I also wanted things to be okay between us before the shit hit the fan.

"I think we should—" I started, but stopped as my head snapped up. Something must have spooked Presley because she stopped walking. Dread curled inside my gut as I brought my assault rifle up. She searched the woods, and from how many times she had run them, I knew to trust whatever her inclination was.

"Get down," she whispered harshly while bringing her gun up and looking through the scope. "You were given incorrect intel, King. They're already here."

CHAPTER 31

PRESLEY

The air felt still. As if the creatures within the woods were holding their breath and not in anticipation. No, these animals were terrified of the monster that was waiting in hiding, the one that used to train me in that forest. They all bore witness to when I was just a little girl, running through the branches, getting scraped and ruined, while my heart had been traumatized in fear.

I ran in the dark. I ran with no shoes. I ran while carrying heavy artillery.

They knew what danger lurked inside, just like I did.

The scope of my rifle revealed two men hiding in the trees, and I didn't hesitate to pull the trigger while quickly walking backwards. I knew the twins had found shelter and would tell me where to go, but until then, I continued shooting.

"Gio, tell your men—"

His voice was panicked as he interjected, "Already did, Elvis. Get your ass down here. Now."

A shot rang out through the woods toward us, but it wasn't a high caliber bullet.

Anxiety swam through me as I adjusted my scope. I knew Scotty would be a few steps ahead of us, but dammit, I thought with El Peligro, we had a chance of taking him by surprise just once.

Movement to my right caught my eye, but Kingston began shooting in that direction.

"Where are your men?" I yelled at the twins.

This didn't make any sense. I'd watched as they ran through drills and ran through all the spots they'd agreed to patrol.

I heard Kingston screaming something over their coms, but Gio had to cover him while he did. I continued shooting into the woods while the twins covered the other blind spots.

Where were my dad and Juan? They would have been ready for us in the manor, where were they?

"They're closing in," I advised Gio and Kingston while the men from the woods began to draw in closer.

"Kingston, I'm worried about the farm. If you're men are gone—"

"It's just a house, Elvis," Gio muttered as if I were being ridiculous.

Anger and hurt tugged at the remnants of my heart as I took another shot. "It's not just a house, Gio. It'll never just be a house to me."

There was silence among the three of us when Kingston added, "The house will be okay, Pres. I promise you."

I continued to aim while my heart thundered in my ears. "You don't know him like I do. He will come for the house and burn it to the ground. I've lost enough. I will not lose this piece of your heart that you gave to me, Kingston."

"Then I'll go," Gio snapped. Before Kingston could stop him, or I could say anything, he got up and began moving toward the farm. He had his gun up, aimed and ready, but he moved swiftly away from us.

"Gio!" I yelled right as Kingston cursed.

"I can't leave you and go after him."

I kept shooting as I found new enemies popping up. "Then we both go."

I had two flash grenades on me that we could use.

"Where is everyone, King?" My voice wavered as I continued to check my scope.

He continued targeting. "I don't know, but I want to check on my family. I want to keep you safe, and Gio. I don't know how to—"

"Leave me, King. You know I have this, and I know your dad can take care of himself. Go to Gio."

"I'm not leaving you," he replied angrily.

I needed Scotty to show himself, but I had no idea—then it hit me. The woods. His men had been in the woods, where I once trained. I knew he wanted to send me a message, and if burning the house was too obvious, then he'd be somewhere else. Somewhere only significant to us.

"King, go after Gio. We're close to the hatch that leads under the garage. I can get down there and into the house. We have to split up, and you have to trust me."

"Fuck." He cursed before sinking to the ground and pulling me with him. Our mouths connected as he pulled me close. "I love you. Please be careful."

I needed him to give me the freedom to do this on my own. When I faced Scotty, I didn't want him to use anyone as a hostage, and he'd be too eager to grab one of the twins. No, I wanted them to be free of this and to keep my house safe. I remembered what Kingston had told me to do and summoned the image I'd picked out that I was supposed to think of. The hope I was clinging to, and then I moved.

I made my way to the circular hatch in the ground that had a ladder leading down into the garage tunnels. These connected all over the property and led back to the manor, through the armory.

There were motion sensing lights that automatically illuminated the concrete as I climbed down. My gun was slung onto my back as I descended, and as soon as my boots hit the ground, I began running.

I ran as fast as I could back to the manor, and once I made it to the armory, I reloaded my weapons and added clips to my vest. My feet were swift as I made my way up the stairs and into the manor.

Silence greeted me, which again made me nervous about where Juan and the others were. The twins had mentioned going over the plan with our family, but I knew something had gone wrong. I had to stay focused on Scotty and trust Kingston and Gio as much as I was asking them to trust me. I turned the corner, lifting my assault rifle, and entered the gym.

CHAPTER 32

KINGSTON

Gio was holding off five men when I finally got to him.

He was on the porch, kneeling while taking each shot. A few of the men had torches and were indeed attempting to burn the farm to the ground.

Flanking the men, I shot the ones my brother hadn't gotten to yet. After that wave, it seemed there weren't any more. It was silent again as my brother nodded toward me.

"Henry is on." He threw me his cell, and I caught it midair, bringing it to my ear.

"The fuck is going on, Henry? Where is everyone?"

There was an eerie silence in the background. "Half your men were bought off, Kingston. Scotty bribed the men with half a million dollars."

I stopped walking. "And the other half?"

"They're loyal to me."

My stomach dropped out as my eyes bounced up to my brother. He didn't know what was being said, so he still looked hopeful.

"You honestly thought you and your brother would just be handed something as powerful as El Peligro just like that? Men had been loyal to this gang for decades before you were even a thought. They were loyal to your father because he understood the danger of it. He respected El Peligro. You and your bitch brother treated it like an ATM machine."

I spun around and began running toward the manor, already knowing Gio would follow.

"But this war with Markos is beneficial for El Peligro because of the power shift. Aside from us, why wouldn't you want to take him out?" I asked.

Henry yelled at someone in the background while other sorts of commotion took place. "Oh that. You never did piece it together, did you?"

Sweat broke out on my brow as I pushed closer to the manor. My stomach churned painfully. What had I missed? *What the fuck was there to miss?*

Gio was next to me, his brows drawn in tight while he checked the property through his scope.

Henry laughed. "The tattoo you saw in the picture when we invaded the Mariano residence. You looked at it as if you'd seen it before."

Fuck. The image flashed in my head, the hourglass with a knife cutting through it.

It finally hit.

"You work for Markos?"

"Ding, ding, ding. Fuckin' brilliant. There was so much shit you missed because you were distracted by that cunt, Presley. You'll enjoy what her sick fuck of an uncle has planned for her. Markos will be taking your sister as a bride, but Presley, he's giving to Scotty to whore out with some alliance. Word has already spread that she's untrustworthy, so he'll force her to demonstrate she can play well with others."

"You're dead." I seethed while anger surged through me. "Fucking dead."

I heard him laughing again, "So dramatic. You ever ask why

Scotty wears so many layers? Ever consider he might be hiding a similar tattoo?"

He hung up before I could respond.

Gio assumed what had happened. "He double-crossed us?"

"Yeah, they all fucking did. Scotty bought off half the men with a couple million dollars." I had no idea where he'd gotten that kind of money, but hadn't Pres mentioned something about Scotty randomly visiting Carter and asking about her billionaire grandfather?

"We need to go check on Dad and the family. They should have been out here with us."

We were near our family wing, by the back patio, when I noticed Gio was struggling to hold his gun.

"What's wrong with you?"

He twisted his arm around as if to stretch it. "Just a pinched nerve, I'm good."

Brushing it off, we quietly entered the manor through the kitchen doors of our family wing, and the second we were inside, we realized what had gone wrong.

"Taylor, I'm willing to save your children. That's the current offer on the table, but Juan will be killed."

Gio raised his scope, moving silently through the kitchen. Benni and Renzo Adesso stood next to Markos, one had their gun trained on my mother, while the other had one aimed at Alex. Markos sat directly in front of our mother with her between his open knees. Her hands were tied behind her back, and her mouth was covered. She didn't cry though, no. She looked angry. So did my sister.

"Come now. Think of your children, *Aurelia*."

Gio glanced at me, with his brows up high as if he were as confused as I was. I remembered there were things our parents had shared with us, and Dad had said she was once promised to him in marriage. Did Mom have a different name? I knew her father's last name was Varga...

Dad began shaking in his chair and yelling around his mouth gag as Markos stroked a finger down Mom's face.

"Perhaps a more suited fate would be to allow your husband the opportunity to watch me defile you." Markos laughed while he leaned in closer to kiss our mother, but she met him half way and slammed her forehead into his nose, making blood spurt everywhere.

Raising my gun, I focused on my target right as Gio fixated on his, and in unison we shot. A spray of red came from the back of Benni's head, and then Renzo dropped to the ground. Markos lifted his head, trying to gauge what happened, but his nose was busted to shit, so he was disoriented.

"Call all your men off." I pointed my gun at his forehead while Gio helped our dad out of his bindings. The second he was free, he pulled our mother away from where Markos was sitting and undid hers, then he went to Alex.

Markos tried to struggle, but Gio brought his gun up and shot him in the other arm. "Call them off!"

"Fine, give me my phone," Markos spat, but now that our dad was free.

"You touched my fucking wife." His fist flew into Markos's face.

I sat back and watched as Dad's fist came down again and again and again. I realized I might be able to call things off simply by sending a text from his phone. I checked the dead brothers first, using their faces to unlock their phones. Sure enough, they were texting with someone outside who was in charge of bringing all the men. I shot off a text for them to fall back and wait for further command.

I heard a gun being prepared to fire and turned around. My mother stood with her mouth rag around her neck, a smear of blood along her lip, and her hands wrapped around a pistol.

She aimed at Markos.

"Taylor?" Dad said, with his fists still clenched. He wasn't done with him, but he moved out of the way.

Mom didn't seem to care as she pulled the trigger.

I needed to go find Presley. Gio seemed to have the same concern as we left our family and began running through the manor.

"Where are they?" Gio yelled while searching their side of the James family wing.

Empty.

"I don't know, but we have to keep searching." I exited their wing with my rifle raised once more, clearing each space. I didn't think they'd be in Carter's wing, but we checked it regardless.

Then we rushed to the gym as a sinking, nagging feeling relentlessly crept in.

Gio kept his gun trained on the door as I yanked it open, and right as we did, everything seemed to come to a screeching halt.

CHAPTER 33
PRESLEY

I wasn't sure what to make of what had been set up when I walked into the gym, and I was even less sure now that I'd been forced to take a seat.

It was our dining room kitchen table, but it had been moved to the center of the gym. Seated on one side, blindfolded, gagged and zip-tied were my parents. Reaper sat next to Scotty, glancing between where I was walking and where Scotty stood. He emanated a whine like he knew I was in danger.

Scotty had encouraged me to take a seat on the opposite side, with the wave of his gun toward my family. I should have known this would be his play. Deep down, I knew he was capable of truly heinous things, but I still doubted that he'd ever hurt us. I thought we were his chosen family, and yet, here we were.

"We're going to have a family meeting, right here and right now. It seems things have gotten a little out of hand as of late, and I'd like to clear them up," Scotty started while taking the fourth chair and keeping his gun on my parents. He also had a trigger remote in his other hand, which meant he had another weapon somewhere, set up on a remote switch. It would fire if he released it or pressed the button.

I sat stiffly. "Mom, Dad, I'm okay. You're okay. We'll get through this."

Scotty mocked me. "That's the spirit, Presley. Let's have a positive outlook."

"Why are you doing all of this? I thought we were your family."

Scotty scratched his jaw with the barrel of his gun before letting out a sigh. "First of all, you're to blame for it escalating to this level, Presley. You murdered the son of one of the most powerful families in the mafia. The Vissimo family is now after me because of your little temper tantrum."

Good. I hoped they would target him and eventually kill him. Reaper laid on his belly and began slowly inching closer to my legs. I held my hand out for him to smell. If Scotty sicced him on me, I wanted to make a connection with him first.

"As far as you being my family, that never changed, but what *did* change was my need to get back in the game. While everyone was so eager to hide, I had built my entire life around navigating organized crime. I'm good at it. There's not just a legacy to be had here; there's a family name we were supposed to create. Kyle, you fucked that up." He scolded my father by raising his voice, but then, softly his gaze returned to me.

"At first, I had no idea they had a plan in place. I knew about the Adesso's past and my link to them, but I didn't think Markos would be pulling them into that. Regardless, once I found out, I wanted to continue with the alliance because I would have prevented them from ever hurting you. But the twins came and fucked everything up."

I faintly corrected him, "It wasn't the twins who forced me to kill my grandfather."

"That may be true, but you wouldn't have been afraid or even known who Markos was if they hadn't planted the seed."

I knew my mother and father wanted to ask this, so I did it for them. "How could you ever agree to align yourself with him, knowing the vendetta he has toward my family and toward Juan's?"

Scotty glanced at his phone briefly before explaining, "The Mariano family has owned my loyalty for longer than any of you have been alive. Even when Kyle decided to go rogue and kill Ivan Varga, I nearly died myself because I was supposed to owe my allegiance to Markos. He's one person you can't simply walk away from and hope they don't come to collect. Markos asked me to murder Lucian Adesso all those years ago and plant the playing card simply because he knew it would instill the need for vengeance in the three sons left behind. How he planned to utilize that hate was not my business."

"It would have worked," Scotty continued. "If your heart hadn't been broken, you wouldn't have felt the need to have someone try and heal it. You wouldn't have gotten attached to Adrian, and he wouldn't have fallen for you."

I shifted in my seat, irritated all over again at the mention of Adrian. He didn't deserve to be manipulated the way he was, none of them did, but I cared less for his brothers since I was nearly positive they had something to do with killing Adrian.

"So what now? Why are we sitting here?" I asked.

Scotty pulled the hammer to his gun back and leaned forward. "I need everyone on the same page. Presley is to marry into a family of *my* choosing; she will create an alliance for *us*. Kyle, you will come back to the game and reemerge as The Joker. Rylie, I used to like you, but honestly, if you wanted to remain here or fuck off, I couldn't care less. It would actually help if Kyle was single for our debut back into the world of organized crime. I've yanked Decker's father-in-law, Charles Shaw, into this. He invested about half a million dollars into my little come back plan. He wants a cut."

My dad's nose flared in rage.

"Once everyone agrees, and I'm able to leave here safely with Presley, then I'll have someone come in and untie you both and let

266

you go," Scotty explained, right as the gym door opened and Gio walked through.

He aimed his .45 caliber gun at Scotty's head without hesitation. Reaper snapped up with a growl.

"Come join the party, Giovanni," Scotty said happily while waving his gun at my parents and revealing his trigger switch.

If I could get it from him safely, then Gio could shoot him.

"Gio, he has a trigger switch. Wherever the guns are, they're aimed at my parents," I warned as his arm remained raised.

"Lower your gun first, Scotty," Gio warned.

My uncle flicked his gaze quickly to the door where Gio had come through. He was wondering where Kingston was. I had no doubt he was about to order Reaper to attack Gio, so I quickly ordered him first.

"*Sich hinlegen.*" Stay.

"Since you're standing here and not dead, I'm going to assume you killed Markos?"

"You assume wrong," Gio said easily.

Scotty smirked while waving the trigger switch around. "Do you think you're fast enough to save them, Gio?"

I tried to catch his gaze, but his eyes never left Scotty. "I might not be, but she is."

He gestured toward me, but Scotty didn't fall for it by looking over. "She doesn't have a gun."

Gio finally began lowering his weapon as if he were finally agreeing. "Fine, how about we both lower our guns then?"

Scotty watched him shrewdly, but I was still focused on how Gio said I was fast enough. He was telling me something. I didn't have a gun, so the only thing I could be quick enough for would be grabbing the trigger switch. If I grabbed it before Scotty let go, then the automatic firing wouldn't go off. Did that mean Gio planned to shoot him?

Gio was still lowering his weapon when Scotty had set his gun firmly down on the table, with a thud. It was that moment that I caught the slightest movement above me, it was near the attic hatch of the gym. I wanted to follow him with my eyes to see what he was doing, but I was too worried Scotty would see where I was looking.

"How about we toss them," Scotty offered, gesturing toward the firearm.

Gio's jaw clenched tightly, but he didn't react.

Scotty continued, "We're going to count to three."

Kingston was on his belly up on the upper ledge of the ceiling, near the windows of the gym.

"One."

Gio's gaze never wavered as he watched Scotty's movements.

"Two," Scotty drawled, and my heart began to thrash in my chest.

Gio finally lowered his arm, as though he was about to toss his gun to the ground. When Scotty got to three, he tossed his gun off to the side, letting it drop to the mat.

Kingston roared from his position, "Shoot him, Gio! The trigger wire's been severed."

Reaper's ears twitched right as Scotty yelled, "Töten."

Gio still had a hold on his gun, but as he raised it, nothing happened. Meanwhile, Reaper whined while pushing his ears back. "Töten." He ordered once more. Again, Reaper's ears went flat, but he didn't go after Gio. He laid down with another whine.

Scotty faltered. I swung over to figure out what was happening and why Gio wasn't shooting.

"Gio?"

His arm shook, but his trigger finger wouldn't budge. That's when I saw the blood leaking down through his dark sleeve, coating his fingers. The gun slipped, and he stumbled back.

I knew Kingston would take the shot; he'd take Scotty out. Except there was suddenly a new fear cracking open my chest. Henry walked into the room from the side door, where the lockers were, and his gun was aimed directly at Kingston.

No.

"You didn't realize Gio had been shot." Scotty chided, like I had disappointed him, "You also didn't catch on to Henry being one of Markos' men." My eyes grew as my heart tried to catch up with what that meant. I stood from the table, feeling like I was moving in slow motion.

"I've trained you not to miss little details like that. Look what it's done now. Why did you think I was so willing to toss my gun away?"

Because he had Reaper, and I stupidly thought he would assume his dog would attack us. I thought we'd had him. I assumed for once we'd have the upper hand, and I was so tired of losing to him. He'd taken so much from me, and now...Gio. *When was he shot? Why was Henry aiming his gun at Kingston?*

My voice cracked as I called his name again, "Gio?"

I was numb as I dropped to the mats and began to crawl over to him. My mom and dad were trying to talk around their gags, and I saw my dad's wrist was bloodied. The small blade in his palm, that had been cutting through the plastic, was nearly through. Scotty must have forgotten he'd trained my dad first; he had to have known he had extra weapons on him.

My only focus was on the blue-eyed boy who had always been my sky and had brought me the stars. I placed his head in my lap as I stroked over his forehead. A tear slipped down my nose and landed on his face.

"Why didn't you tell me you were hurt?"

He smiled up at me while reaching up to trace the tear. "I'm sorry I was mad. I know you don't like it when I am."

A sob caught in my throat as I held his cold palm to my cheek, but then reality hit me like a train, and I realized he'd been shot.

He was shot. He was dying in my arms while I was sitting there crying as he talked about meaningless things.

My hands began moving as a cry broke from my chest. I tugged at his vest first, ripping off the Velcro and trying to get it over his head. Right as it came free, I noticed another firearm tucked into the waistband of his jeans, along with a few throwing knives.

"Presley, we're leaving. I'm giving you this one kindness before putting a bullet in his head," Scotty yelled, but right as he did, I grabbed the gun from Gio's belt and aimed for him. My finger brushed the trigger when there was suddenly a shot ringing through the room. It was so loud it felt like something burst inside my head. There was so much pain, I dropped the gun and began screaming.

No, Scotty was screaming. He was angry with Henry, who was still aiming at me. Had he shot me? Something wet trickled down my cheek as Scotty continued yelling, and then he aimed his own weapon at the man. Gio held me to his chest protectively as I watched Henry get shot down. Within a blink, Scotty appeared next to us.

"I'm sorry, Presley. Are you okay? Tell me you're okay." He gently touched my ear, and that's when I realized something burned my cheek.

"Just grazed you." He looked relieved, and I realized two things in that moment.

One: I could only hear out of one ear.

Two: Scotty was distracted.

I had begged my father to spare his life when he wanted to kill him last year. I always gave him the benefit of the doubt. Not this time.

This time, I slid the knife from Gio's belt, and I lodged it into Scotty's chest with all the force I could muster.

His face twisted in confusion first, and I hated how I focused on the green tint to his eyes. How they reminded me so much of my father. I hated how familiar they were.

"You just keep trying to break me, and I'm *done*," I whispered while he gaped down at his chest.

His hand gripped the hilt, where he began to pull. The blade clattered to the ground in a bloody mess as Scotty struggled to his feet. Kingston had come down and had a gun trained on my uncle, but so did my father. He'd cut through his ties and found a gun.

Scotty's eyes widened as he took the gun being aimed at him by my father. "You've taken too much this time, Uncle."

I closed my eyes as the shots rang out, and when Reaper's wet nose touched my hand, I sank my fingers into his fur. We'd both lost him. The version of who Scotty once was to us.

Now he was gone.

CHAPTER 34
GIO

Sometimes I dreamt of my childhood.

I'd dream of being on a trampoline, staring up at a sky full of stars while my best friend lay next to me, searching with me. I'd dream of a time when I'd watch my best friend create crowns made of twigs so that my brother and I would be made into little kings while she was the queen to us both.

Those dreams were always something I craved when I was away from Presley, but now that she was next to me every night, I didn't care for them. I wanted the reality so much more than any memory I ever had of her. Yet, when I woke up this morning, I knew there was this strange wall between us as if our reality had been altered and our future threatened.

Now, as I lay here, staring up at her tear-stained face, I wondered if I'd merely go back to the dreams I had of her. Or if I'd get to stay here with her...if I'd ever get the chance to wake up on a random Tuesday and see how the sun highlighted her freckles and soaked into her lashes. I wondered if I'd ever get to see her rock a baby of her own, or if she'd smile at me and ask for me to take a turn.

It used to bother me, this idea that I'd have to share her and all of her future, but now as pain spread through my chest and things became colder, I realized it didn't matter.

None of it did. I'd been so fucking childish about her and her needs. She'd been through so much, a thoroughly broken queen, and instead of the king she'd needed me to be, I chose to be a fool.

My hands reached for hers, but I couldn't make them wrap around her.

"Kingston, why are his lips turning blue?" Her voice shuddered, and I knew she was afraid. I knew she'd lost one love, and I knew she couldn't lose another. There wasn't room in that greenhouse for any more graves, and I didn't want my brother to expand it just to accommodate another broken piece in Presley's life.

So, I dug deep and fought as hard as I could to stay lucid.

"My left arm...did the bullet go through. I think it might still be in there."

I heard my brother curse, and Presley sniffed. "It's okay, Gio. We're going to get you to the hospital."

"We need someone to fly the chopper." My brother pulled out his cell phone, but who was he going to call? El Peligro had abandoned us.

He looked at Presley, who shook her head. "All my dad's men belonged to Scotty. They're gone."

"Gio!" I heard my dad yell as he came into the room. He dropped next to me, then Mom and Alex followed suit.

"We need someone to fly the chopper to get him to the hospital. Scotty's men are gone," Kingston explained.

My mom began tenderly pressing around my wound and trying to inspect it.

"Bullet is still in."

"Where did it hit?" I coughed, which fucking hurt. I felt Presley's fingers in my hair again while she tried to soothe me. Another tear fell from her nose.

"Your right side, under your arm."

I tried to smile, but my mouth felt wet. "That's not so bad."

"We need to get him out of here!" my brother roared.

My dad pulled his phone out. "Where the fuck is your gang?"

A tear slipped from King's dark lashes as he held my hand. "Guess they weren't as loyal to us as we thought. Scotty bought off half of them, and the other half were loyal to Markos."

I didn't see what my dad was doing, but I heard him talking, seconds later.

"I know you're retired, Hector. But, *Primo*, I need you. El Peligro has deserted my sons."

There was some yelling on one end, and then Dad's voice shook. "They took a blood oath, and if they won't show up for my sons, then tell them I'm the one demanding their oath. I am the fucking one calling in their loyalty."

My dad seethed. "Yes, I know they'll demand I step back into that role."

My brother made some sound, worry or anger. "Dad, no. Call Archer's contacts. You were right to reach out to him. You knew the whole time that they wouldn't pull through for us."

He ignored him. "Yes. I am officially taking it back. You tell them that Juan Hernandez, Manny's son, is back. You tell them they will wear their colors and arrive at my home to get my son to safety, and they will stay here, or I will personally hunt them down myself."

My mom held my dad's hand and squeezed it tightly while my father's rage seemed to shake the room.

I didn't know how long it was, but a rush of men came in and placed me on a flat board, which was carried to the chopper we had covered, near the armory. At one point, I felt like I was dreaming again, then I'd blink and see Presley's blue eyes on mine.

"You're going to be okay, Gio." She kissed my knuckles as we took off.

I liked the reality better. Always the reality of her, not the dream.

"The sky is falling," I whispered, and she leaned over me, pressing a kiss to my lips.

"I'll hold it up, my love. I'll hold it. I promise."

I closed my eyes again, and this time I dreamt of her holding the sky at the age of eight, and it crashed all around her.

CHAPTER 35
PRESLEY
SIX WEEKS LATER

Dawn had become an oddly familiar companion lately.

It seemed to gently pull me from a sleepless rest, where I was asleep but not. Then I'd rise and find my way outside.

I had started gathering new flowers for him. To place over his grave, because it had become the only way I knew how to communicate when words didn't seem to come. It seemed I had said everything that needed to be said.

Now, as I checked the greenhouse for weeds and ensured the health of the plants, I knelt on green grass that was lush and full. I wiped off a few pieces of dirt and moss from his headstone and began talking like I always did.

"I think they're going to kill each other." I plucked a petal and inspected it.

"Gio is insufferable when his pain meds wear off, and now that he's starting physical therapy, he truly hates his brother. I suppose it doesn't help that King is the one in charge of getting him back in shape."

My mouth twisted into a smile as I thought over how the

brothers had recently started squabbling more. Gio wanted to be able to hold a gun again, and his brother promised he'd make sure he was able to by four weeks post op. We were at week six, and he still couldn't.

His shoulder was still in a sling, and his doctor had told him to take it easy. Start with small things, but I had a feeling he wouldn't approve of Gio being taken out to the shooting range. But that wasn't the only thing the doctor wouldn't approve of.

"He hasn't even really been cleared for sex, and yet he's been engaging in rather problematic behavior in that regard as well. He really is the worst patient ever."

I thought back to last night and how after his sponge bath, we were in the living room watching a movie, and he'd slid the band of his sweats down revealing how hard he was. He taunted me to crawl on top.

"*Come on, Elvis. You afraid you'll break me? We'll go slow. I swear.*" He'd started slow, but after a few strokes, he lost control. Kingston had walked into the living room and cursed immediately, and not because he was excited or turned on. He knew how dangerous it was for his brother to be ignoring every single piece of medical advice that had been given to him.

"He's sort of come back with this new lust for life," I said to the headstone, while plucking at a few more petals.

He was less jealous than before and more excited about various sexual things he wanted to try. Like being eager to have Kingston tell him how to fuck me again. He went feral when he was being told what to do to me, and I, in turn, loved every second of it. Especially after the back and forth of how little he previously wanted to share me.

This side of him was a welcome reprieve.

"My parents want to leave the manor," I admitted sadly. This was something I hadn't talked about openly with anyone yet. Oddly, it felt good to get it off my chest. Things had been about Gio's recovery and how Juan was dealing with resuming his role as leader of El Peligro. It wasn't going super great, as one of his decisions revolved around what to do with Scotty's dogs.

Most of them were sedated and taken to an animal rehabilitation center. More than likely, they'd be put to work with the police force, but I had to stop asking. It was too painful to say goodbye to that last piece of my past, knowing I'd never see any of the animals again. A deep throbbing emanated throughout my chest as I pictured Reaper's eyes and how I'd never get to see that deep-set brown color again. Aside from his master, he was a good dog. He was kind even when Scotty had tried to make him cruel.

Shifting to my butt, I pulled my knees up under my chin and stared up at the glass ceiling. It was starting to rain, which felt sort of like Adrian was talking to me. I had to move on from the dogs, or I'd cry again.

"Dad feels like he's wasted a lot of his life hiding away. He hates what he put me through and what he robbed Mom of because of our lack of socialization. She hadn't seen her father, and now he was gone. Mom wants to travel. She has old friends she wants to go spend time with, and she's encouraging my dad to go see his mom, too."

Honestly, I wanted them to be happy, but it broke my heart a little that they were leaving. I had the twins and the farm, and a deconstruction process ahead of me, which would require a lot of time and a few crash outs over how I had been raised to be this person, and now I wasn't anything.

"I don't know what will become of us." My voice was quiet, but I should have known a twin would be wandering around and would overhear.

Gio slipped inside, hair soaking from the rain, and soaking his sling too.

"You're not supposed to be outside like this," I scolded, but I wasn't sure that was true. Movement and fresh air were both good for him. With the number of times he took that sling off, I was glad he was at least wearing it.

Gio took a seat next to me and leaned in close. "Well, my hot nurse wasn't in bed when I woke up, so I went looking for her."

"I just needed to vent." I plucked up a flower and gently set it against Adrian's stone.

Gio quietly replied, "You're worried about what will become of us?"

"No," I answered honestly, but added, "I just worry that I wasn't enough... Dad was supposed to escape his enemies, and I somehow was supposed to help set us free from this life, and yet we're still stuck in it."

Gio's head lifted, his blue eyes so gray in this lighting that it made my belly flip. "There is no escaping it, Elvis. You were sold a lie. The grand ideas of men who sought to rule an empire while claiming to run from one. You were a pawn they manipulated into believing you could also become a queen."

"You guys always call me a queen." I nudged his shoulder while his words seemed to expand in my chest.

Instead of nudging me, he carefully held my face until I was looking at him. "You're our queen, yes. Queen of our hearts. Queen of the farm. Queen of the remote."

I tried pulling away as I laughed, but he held me firm. "You were never supposed to be the solution to their problem, Pres. Outrunning your dad's enemies was never going to happen. We're going to have people who want to hurt us and even come after us for the rest of our lives. There will be more complications, and fuck, there might even be more guys who try to be your new husband, by way of an alliance. You didn't fail just because those possibilities are still there. You endured some of the toughest training anyone goes through, much less a child, and you're sitting here as a barely-there adult, thinking you failed?"

When he put it like that, it did sound a little insane.

His lips gently caressed mine. "You did not fail, you *survived*. And I'm so fucking glad that you did. You broke and proved in the face of all that stood against you that you could still be whole. You defied the very gravity under your feet and grew wings. So when you ask what will become of us, I can't help but smile, Elvis."

My eyes felt a little misty as he talked. "Why can't you help but smile?"

"Because you already became it. All of it. You did all that you should do, and now you just get to live. It's not what will become of us; it's what's left to become."

I tilted my head, so we kissed, and when it turned heated, where he pulled me into his lap, we finally broke apart. "Fucking you outside where it's raining and cold is where I draw the line."

He laughed and helped me stand. "Fine. Come inside and let me feed you then. Besides, Kingston has a surprise for you."

I WAS TOLD to shower and eat something warm.

Taking my time with my morning routine, I did exactly that while the boys prepared whatever the surprise was for me. Hours seemed to pass when I finally heard them call from downstairs, "Pres, come down here!"

Elated, I grabbed my phone and jogged down the steps, only to freeze on the bottom one.

He sat there, patiently like the best boy in the whole world, and even began to whine the second he saw me. My eyes instantly filled with tears.

"What's going on?"

Kingston cleared his throat first, brushing his hand over the top of Reaper's head.

"He belongs with you. Always has. If Gio or I can't protect you, we want to know you have an extra pair of eyes on you."

Wetness tracked down my face as I got to my knees in front of Scotty's most favored dog. His brown eyes shifted as he watched me, and then he began licking my face.

"But what about you?" My voice cracked, even as my fingers sank into Reaper's glossy fur. There was no way Kingston would be okay with living with the animal he'd witnessed rip someone's throat out. It had caused him so much trauma.

Kinston knelt down next to me and pressed a kiss to my forehead. "He's a lot like you, Pres. Forced to become a weapon when all he wanted was to be a friend. I think he'd probably love being on the farm, don't you?"

A sob crept up my throat as I leaned in and pressed my head to Reaper's neck. "Thank you for this."

Reaper licked the side of my face before Gio called for him to follow him outside. That's when Kingston wrapped me in his arms, and he let me sob into his neck. I cried for my life, the fractured pieces that still weren't whole. I cried for Scotty, and the person I had grown up thinking he was. I cried for how different things were going to be, and while it was a good thing, it undoubtedly would be hard.

"I love you." I kissed King's throat.

He hummed while brushing my hair aside. "I'll keep finding ways to prove that I love you, too. One day you'll wake up and completely forget that I was a total piece of shit. One day you'll wake up and you'll know you've always been mine."

A laugh tumbled out of me. "You're such an idiot. I already do wake up knowing I've always been yours. I wake up feeling loved and cherished and like this was what you both had been trying to tell me all those years."

"Well, good, that will save us some time."

"Time for what?" I asked, searching his face.

His smile was perfect when he whispered, "Our next surprise."

One Week Later

"This house is so freaking cute, I'm obsessed." Carter gushed over the details of the kitchen while munching on an apple. She'd decided to come visit now that things had somewhat calmed down. I knew her parents had settled in New York, but Carter hadn't decided where she wanted to land just yet.

She'd mentioned wanting to be closer to family, so perhaps we'd be seeing more of her.

Alex walked in, holding a basket of eggs.

"Okay, some of these have actual poop on them, and I'm not sure we'll be able to use them."

Carter's mouth twisted. "Ew, that's disgusting. Farm life could never be for me."

I giggled while I took the basket from her. "We'll just wash it, and it'll be fine."

They both watched me as I filled a bowl with water, and I knew they were going to ask about them.

"So, Pres," Carter started while glancing at Alex, then back at me, "I couldn't help but notice those two new tattoos on your finger."

"Oh, those?" I twisted my left hand, inspecting the ring finger.

"The vines and a cluster of stars?"

Two separate tattoos for two separate brothers. I shrugged. "Reminded me of them."

The twins suddenly came inside, with Reaper happily trotting after them.

Alex spun around first, and I caught how her eyes dropped to Gio's hand. I should have known she'd see past my vague answer.

"I knew it!" She grabbed her brother's hand and inspected the ring finger. There on Gio's ring finger was the same cluster of stars inked into his skin that matched the design on mine.

Carter's eyes went huge as she made some sort of excited squeal. "Let me see yours, Kingston!" She grabbed his hand and inspected it just like Alex had done with Gio.

"He has vines on his finger that match yours!"

"Does this mean?" Alex searched between the three of us.

"There's nothing legal, but yes. Your brothers each asked if I'd promise to be with them for the rest of their lives."

"More importantly." Gio walked over to me ard pulled me against his chest. "She agreed."

"That's so sweet." Carter sighed, emotionally.

Alex moved Gio aside and pulled me into her arms and squeezed. "You're my sister officially now. I couldn't care less about a legal document. They branded you on their skin, you made it permanent, Pres. We're family now."

My chest practically exploded with happiness as happy tears welled in my eyes.

Kingston rumbled somewhere close to my ear. "I'll still call you my wife, though, whenever I want."

If we didn't have company, I'd challenge him and his brother on saying exactly that while they both fucked me.

"But how cute would a ceremony be?" Carter whined. Alex began talking to her about ideas, but I pushed out the noise. I didn't need one; I just needed them, and that would always be enough for me.

CHAPTER 36
PRESLEY
FOUR MONTHS LATER

"Chickens are a great place to start," I told a nervous looking Alex.

She glanced at Gwendolyn, Gretta, and Beverly. "They're staring at me like they know I don't know what I'm doing."

"We talked about this, Alex. You're going to live on the opposite end of the farm and raise horses. You're going to be like the horse whisperer, and once we sell the manor, we're going to demolish it and create the biggest super ranch that there ever was."

"Uh. No. We told you both that was not happening." Gio turned around from his spot near the goat pen and scolded us.

Alex and I both glared back.

"What's the point in keeping the manor?" I asked, handing some feed over to Gio's big sister.

"My parents still live there, for starters."

I waved him off while Alex laughed. "Mom and Dad hate the manor; they're planning to move down to Mexico."

Gio shook his head before loading hay into the pen for Marigold, our pregnant goat. "That's not happening until he figures out how to get El Peligro reconfigured to help the city. So, no planning for any farms or horse ranches. Also, what happens when Pres gets pregnant? You think they're going to miss the opportunity to be grandparents?"

"I'm not even twenty yet, we're not anywhere close to having that discussion yet."

Alex lowered herself to the ground with the chicken feed in her hand and laid it out for the hens.

"Besides, is Alex just supposed to wait to learn how to be a farmer?"

"As she's done for nearly every day for the past six months, my sister is more than welcome to come over and spend as much time as she wants with the animals." Gio sounded so exasperated.

One of the hens pecked at Alex, making her stand briskly. "I'm not sure I'm cut out for farm life, Pres."

"Yes, you are, just give it time." I slightly shoved the meanest chicken out of the way with my foot.

"I think I might just start helping Mom and Dad with the startup of the non-profit and then head to Mexico with them."

My chest squeezed with worry.

"You're giving up awfully fast. Plus, Marigold is about to have her baby. You're going to miss being a goat mom with me." I wanted her to do whatever her heart desired, but I knew she didn't want to live apart from me, or her brothers.

Alex glanced longingly over at our black and white goat, who was just months from giving birth.

Kingston walked into the barn, inspecting all three of us.

"The manor isn't being demolished even if everyone moves to Mexico. There's too much history there. It stays."

I had roughly zero say in any of this. My dad and mom had signed over all their rights, including any financial benefits from selling. The deed was given over to Juan and Taylor. Even my uncle Decker and aunt Mallory had signed over their share of the house.

I heard they were living in New York, all three of them, happy as clams. Our enemies hadn't evaporated, but we'd all decidedly stopped living in fear. The men who betrayed Gio and Kingston from El Peligro were required to bend knee to Juan, and if they didn't, they were hunted down by that motorcycle club, Mayhem Riot. Juan had called in a favor to his now brother-in-law and had every single person found and executed.

"Well, Alex just needs to start small anyway. We have plenty of room for a horse ranch here." I suggested.

"Pres, stop worrying about where everyone is going to go," Kingston rumbled close to my ear. I both hated and loved that he knew me so well.

He added, still whispering, "Alex is still figuring out what she wants to do. She's going to help our parents with El Peligro, and she's still going to see us plenty."

If that were true, then why did it feel like I was losing more people?

"Come on, come with me." Kingston pulled me back with him. I waved at Alex while she moved closer to Gio to talk to him.

Kingston pulled my hand until we were inside the farmhouse. "Come on."

I knew what was coming next; it was what Kingston would do to help me get past my abandonment issues. I wasn't angry that my parents left; in fact, I was happy for them, but I hated the hole I felt in my chest after they'd gone.

Sometimes it just felt like my world was getting too small. But Alex, she helped make it feel bigger. So did game nights over with Juan and Taylor.

I loved being part of their family, and while I would never leave the farm, I didn't want to be here without all of them either.

"I want you to read the letter again," Kingston ordered while he pulled me into his lap and we sank to the floor.

I gently removed the folded note I had tucked away in the front of my overall pocket and began to read.

"My dearest, Presley."

Kingston stroked over my ear and down my arm. "Keep going."

"I need you to understand something..." I trailed off because this part always choked me up. "It wasn't your beauty that stole my breath the moment I laid eyes on you. It wasn't your laugh, although it was memorable. It wasn't your fine taste in beverages."

A laugh scraped up my throat at the memory of how I'd acted as though sprite could be champagne.

"What was it?" Kingston whispered near my ear.

I kept reading. "It was the way you treated the room as if it were merely a moment in your grand, beautiful life. You were queen of the room, and I'll never forget wanting to follow you home just so I could spend a few more seconds watching how you viewed the world. I wanted to be anything in that world. A plant, a star, a piece of fruit. I didn't care as long as it meant you'd pay me some attention."

That was typically as far as I was able to make it when reading this letter but today, I pushed on, needing the rest of it.

"If you're reading this, then it means Markos was successful in removing me from your life. It means Leon was able to mail this to you and ensure you were aware of how deep my love for you truly ran. If you're reading this, then perhaps, you will have found your two kings and are in no way in need of a jester like me, but in case you're ever left wondering how important you are to those around you. Let me be the one to encourage you. Let me be the one to shine a light, break up the darkness, and fear. Let me have a role in your life. My love, even after death."

Sucking in a deep breath, I continued with a small hiccup. "I would give up a thousand lifetimes of having wealth, power, and anything else deemed valuable in this world if it meant I could have you. I would choose you over and over again. I would abandon my roots, tear them out of the soil, and make my own wings if it meant I could be with you again. Enjoy your kings in this life, my love, because in the next, you'll be mine. Forever yours, Adrian."

The letter fluttered to the ground, and Kingston held me to his chest as sobs crept up through my lungs, fracturing my heart.

"Why do you always make me read it?"

Kingston kissed my ear. "Because you fear people leaving you, even when they're right in front of you. You need a reminder of how important you are to people. The ink on your finger means we'll be here with you forever. We won't leave you. I want you to breathe and allow that to sink into your heart. You won't be alone in this life or the next."

I allowed his words to do exactly what he said and let them soak into my heart.

CHAPTER 37
KINGSTON

I t was later that night when I finally had a chance to touch Presley the way I needed to touch her. Emotional days typically ended up with Gio holding Pres and the two of them cuddling. I never cared that much, but it was me who had helped her today. Me who had pulled her heart back together after she worried of it falling apart.

So as she lay between us, I pushed her closer to my brother.

"Presley, I want my brother to fuck you." Her sharp eyes snapped up to mine, heating already with my words as I added, "I want your eyes on me so I can watch every single expression that crosses that beautiful face while he makes you scream."

In the dark, I couldn't completely see her, but there was light from the television that made her easy enough to make out. Her eyes searched mine, but I found a smile lifting her lips. Gio shifted behind her, his hand came over her hip, where he tugged at the thong covering her.

"Pull this off of her," Gio ordered.

I did as he said, gently tugging the thong down her legs. The second my face became level with her pussy, I gently licked through her slick center. Only briefly though, then pulled the underwear completely from her feet.

My brother's fingers moved to her pussy where he spread her lips. "Lick her again, King. Get her nice and wet for me."

Without hesitating, I lowered my face and began licking through her center, around where my brother spread her. She shifted her hips, but I held her in place.

"Are you ready for Gio to fuck you?" I rasped while circling her clit.

She huskily replied, "Yes."

I lifted my head and resumed my place in front of Pres when I said, "Give her your cock, Gio. Stuff her."

My brother shifted and with one hand on Presley's stomach, he slid into her.

"Ohmygod," Presley moaned, while slamming her eyes closed.

"Keep them open, *mi reina*. I want to see you come undone." My erection pressed against my abdomen, making me ache for her touch. I'd wait patiently.

Gio began pumping in and out of Pres, pushing her shoulder forward while he slid in and out of her. The bed began to shift, rattling the headboard. This was a common issue we had, one I needed to fix but kept forgetting about.

"I'm not slowing." Gio rasped, while the two jolted in unison from how hard he was slamming into her.

"Good. Just keep going, she's about to come." I stroked down her face and pressed my fingers to her lips. She began licking and sucking them right as a cry erupted from her.

With the motions from Gio, it had pushed her closer. Her tits slid against my bare torso while my cock continued to weep in my boxers. She was close enough now that every move she made rubbed against me. It felt so good, I lowered the band of my underwear and released my cock so it slid against her stomach.

"Shiiiiit." Presley cried, while glancing down at where my sticky cock slid against her smooth, tan stomach.

"Getting fucked so hard, *mi reina*." I rasped in her ear before slamming my mouth to hers. We made out while Gio fucked her, and my dripping cock slid between us. I heard Gio moaning and his movements beginning to slow. The second he pulled his length out, I pushed mine in.

"You're not done yet." She was slick from my brother's cum, but I pumped my cock in and out of her while sucking her nipple into my mouth.

"Let her straddle you, King," Gio said gruffly before sitting up.

I did exactly that by pulling Presley over my waist, and she began sliding her hips back and forth.

"I'm leaking all over you, King." She muttered on a choppy breath.

My hands were fastened tightly to her middle as I lifted my hips and pushed deeper inside her. "Only for you would I ever drench my cock in my brother's cum. Only ever you, *mi reina*."

Gio moved so he was stroking down Presley's back, kissing her neck, and whispering things in her ear. I couldn't hear it but whatever it was had her moving faster and breathing harder.

"Yes. Yes. Yes." She whined while his tongue dove deep into her mouth, effectively shutting her up. They kissed while I pulled her down against my cock, making her bounce and her tits sway.

"Gio, stick something in her ass. Now," I demanded.

He shifted, likely pulling out a toy from below. I know he must have added lube because he pushed her forward the smallest bit, then began sliding in the dildo. Her movements only slowed briefly before she was moaning again.

"So fucking good," she wheezed.

We moved slowly while her cunt slid over my cock, and in her ass the dildo pushed. I knew she was enjoying the sensations because of how she began to shake.

"Come one last time for me," I begged her, and when her eyes lit up, she moved faster.

Gio was next to her, pulling her tits into his mouth with a loud sucking sound. She came again with a cry that had her practically melting onto my chest.

I came hard with unintelligible curses spilling from my lips while I spilled inside of Presley. She knew what this was about. How I needed to remind her that she wasn't alone, and we could handle her fear of abandonment.

When she brushed her lips over my heart, I knew she understood.

CHAPTER 38

PRESLEY

Alex walked over to the barn early the next morning. She had on a pair of overalls and boots, which made my heart rap against my breast.

"I've made a decision."

She'd already told me. Mexico. I was willing to accept it now, unlike yesterday, when I needed an entire day and night to process another person leaving me.

"I'm willing to visit you in Mexico, I've decided." I rushed ahead, before she could say what she came here to.

With a small laugh, Alex stepped closer. "I want to convert the manor into a sanctuary. El Peligro has always been able to cut through red tape. I want this place to be a refuge for families who are running from the men like Markos. I want this to be a place where kids can learn to ride horses and play with goats. I want there to be gardens and pumpkins."

My expression must have matched my confusion because she stepped closer and shook my shoulders.

"This means I'm staying here. Mom and Dad are going to help

me with the renovations. They'll be around a lot, too, but I'm not leaving. I'm staying."

Tears welled in my eyes, burning my nose. I wanted to play it cool, but I was too far gone. My arms went around her tall shoulders, and I sobbed happily into her shirt.

"I'm so happy you're staying. You have no idea how hard it was to wrap my head around the idea of you leaving."

She hugged me back until we broke apart and laughed. "I've always wanted a sister, Presley James. You're not getting rid of me that easy. Now, let's go check on our goat baby."

"We're going to have to read up on how to deliver her babies. The vet said she's having twins."

Alex laughed. "Of course she is."

THE STARS WERE bright and beautiful as the three of us snuggled on a large couch and watched the meteor shower.

"This is better than the loungers that were up here," I mused, feeling the warmth from Kingston at my side. Reaper lay on my other side, nestling in so I was completely warm and safe.

His breath fanned my hair as he laughed. "The couch was your idea."

I smiled as the warm air seemed to squeeze us. "I know."

Gio looked through his telescope and let out a sound of excitement. "Come here, Elvis."

Kingston opened his arms, so I could escape. I walked over and had Gio's arms around me a second later as he helped me adjust the telescope.

"What do you see?" His warm lips grazed my ear.

Tilting the scope, I squinted. The shape was somewhat difficult to make out at first, but after a few seconds, I saw it. *The twins.*

"You found Castor and Pollux."

"Feels sorta like fate, Elvis." Gio kissed my cheek.

It did feel like destiny like I was exactly where I was supposed to be, and from here, things would only get better.

EPILOGUE
PRESLEY

One Year Later

I stared at the invitation and tried to make it say something different.

"Why do we have to go?" I asked, picking up the beautiful piece of cardstock.

Gio peered over my shoulder. "Dad's hosting it."

Kingston added from across the room, "He also doesn't trust anyone from El Peligro to have his back yet. We're his backup."

That meant we'd have to sneak in weapons, which would be risky. "Fine, but that means you two are going to have to chill out on who talks to me. Let's work on blending into the background."

Both brothers smirked, and it was identical, making my belly flip. "I'm going to get ready. But I'm serious, we can't draw attention to ourselves tonight."

There was no response, which should have been the first red flag of the evening.

THE ROOM WAS DECORATED BEAUTIFULLY.

It reminded me of my engagement party in Italy, with dangling chandeliers and opulent ceilings. People wore their finest clothes and most expensive jewelry. I had on a red, silk dress that spilled over my curves like water.

The twins were in all black, but instead of wearing nice jackets, they'd left theirs at home and rolled their dress shirt sleeves up to their elbows. I hadn't stopped touching them since we arrived, and in turn, their hands had been fastened to my hips, thighs, or arms as if they didn't want to let me out of their sight.

I hadn't bothered with researching who was in attendance. Over the past year, I have truly released the identity that was forced upon me. I had relaxed into the farm life, with a slower routine and lazy Sundays spent with music playing and dancing barefoot around the kitchen. I did what workouts I liked. I ran if I wanted to. I hadn't touched a gun since the day Gio was shot.

I liked this new version of me.

Not on alert, or thinking of anything other than the book on my Kindle and the type of appetizers they were serving. I allowed Gio and Kingston to watch my back, and in turn, worry about what was around us.

There was someone making their way toward our group swiftly. Once a few people parted, I was able to see why they were moving so quickly.

"Presley!" Carter threw her arms around me, drawing me into a tight hug.

I returned her warm greeting until we pulled apart. "What are you doing here?" I asked, looking over her shoulder. I could make out her dad near the corner and her mom. They were talking with Juan and Taylor.

Carter snagged a glass of champagne from the tray that was passing. "So, my grandpa owes Juan a favor. I'm not sure for what.

He got into a deal with Scotty, and it created this huggggge mess with my mom and Aunt Taylor. They were fighting and arguing. I missed literally all of it, but what I did catch was that Grandpa Charlie now came to whatever event Juan asked him to. Since he's paying for most of this party, my mom decided we should go, and that way we'd get to see family."

With a little tip of her drink, she had finished her story.

Gio shifted behind me, and King squeezed my hip. They were trying to encourage me to remain calm. This was all attached to what Scotty had done, how he'd bought off El Peligro and left us stranded with no help. It was the reason Gio had gotten shot. We had been lucky, but if the bullet had been even a millimeter to the right, he wouldn't be here right now.

"Well, I'm glad you're here. We have to catch up," I said, trying to sound happy as I shed the memories tied to such a heavy day.

Carter glared at the twins behind me and pulled me away. "I need to borrow her."

"They aren't my keepers, Carter," I joked as I trailed after her.

She took us to a rather large circular couch. We had it to ourselves, but my cousin still ducked her head close while she asked, "So tell me your decision about having a ceremony."

"I told you last time we talked."

She rolled her eyes, and it made me laugh. Her gold eye shadow was on thick, but it complemented her black dress and red tresses. "You told me you guys were happy. What the hell does that mean? You have wedding bands essentially tattooed to your ring fingers, does that not justify a ceremony of some kind?"

She used air quotes around the word ceremony, which made me laugh.

"I just don't know what good a ceremony would do? We know what we are to each other and that's all that matters."

Setting her glass on the small table next to us, she grew serious. "Listen, I have tried to really respect the sanctity of your relationship, but I'm going to need some details now. When you say you know what you are to each other... Does that mean in the biblical sense?"

"There is nothing holy about what we've been doing, but yes, Carter James, we're fucking."

She smiled devilishly. "But like...individually, right? Each twin takes his turn, or..."

A smile slid along my mouth as I shook my head. "We do that sometimes, but it's typically me between them."

"Hot damn...how does that work with the twins? Do they—"

I moved forward to grab my drink. "Never. They are very careful and are always aware of their body parts when we're..."

She squealed excitedly. "This is so crazy. I can't believe you're with them and like...it works."

We settled in, chatting a bit when there were suddenly a few men who crowded us on the couch. One man in particular, dripping with wealth and radiating power, sank into the seat next to me and sensually held my thigh.

"I wouldn't do that if I were you," I said, pushing at his hand. I made sure I used the one with my tattoos.

He laughed. "You have no idea who I am, do you?"

"I don't think that will matter." I shoved his hand again, but his other hand moved to my neck, where he began pushing my hair out of the way. "You're the most beautiful creature in this room tonight. I want you bouncing on my cock before the night is done."

"Then I guess we'll have to start with your cock." Gio appeared in front of us.

Kingston strolled next to him. "We'll start with the hands since he used those to touch her. If you want the cock when we're through —that's fine by me."

The man next to me shot to his feet while the males around him went to pull out their guns, but stopped. Everyone had been forced to surrender theirs on the way in, and if they didn't and wanted to keep their firearm, it was with the understanding that they'd go to war with the families present if they were to find a reason to fire said weapons.

Except the twins never played by those rules, so I knew they were currently carrying.

"I didn't realize she was spoken for by one of you," the man said.

Gio laughed. "Both of us, actually, which makes this twice as dangerous for you."

"No harm was done," one of the men said, placing their hands up like they didn't want any trouble.

"I guess it depends on perspective, though, doesn't it?" Gio asked while pacing the small area near the coffee table. Carter was between me and the guy, but I caught her nervous expression.

Kingston began picking at his shirt. "From our perspective, you touched her, and we don't allow anyone to touch her."

The powerful man laughed, as if all this were hilarious, and his hands slowly went up. I already knew what was about to happen, so I pulled one of the small couch cushions and covered my face. Carter watched me and did the same thing, moving slowly so no one really noticed.

Sure enough, seconds later, Gio and Kingston had their guns drawn, and two shots were fired. One bullet per hand that touched me.

Blood had sprayed on the cushion when I tossed it away. The man who was shot fell to his knees.

"You're going to regret that," he seethed through clenched teeth.

Movement behind us indicated it was time to move. Security was closing in fast, but we were faster. I lost Carter on the way, but if she was smart, she'd slink out or act like she had no idea what had just happened. On our way out of the room, Juan found us.

"Boys, what the fuck did you do?"

They shrugged as if they'd done nothing wrong at all. "He touched Presley."

"You're aware Presley can take care of herself?" Juan asked while we bypassed valet after snagging our keys.

"Presley is ours to take care of now, so while yes, we know that she can. She won't ever have to again," Kingston replied.

"Well, this is a mess I'll have to try and sort out." Juan let out a heavy sigh.

Gio smirked while getting into the car. "Best of luck, Daddio."

Kingston slapped his chest while telling me to slide into the back seat. Once the three of us were in the car, we shot off into the dark. Gio caught my eye in the rearview mirror and said, "See, told you, Elvis. Our enemies never actually go away, especially because if you're with us, then you'll likely always create new ones. The sky won't fall just because you're not a weapon. You can simply relax and be ours. We'll be the weapons."

I rested on Kingston's shoulder as peace filled me. I was finally starting to accept what he was saying.

My father and Scotty had always wanted a weapon, but the twins merely wanted my heart. Even with new enemies chasing us, I felt safer than I ever had before.

"Let's go home and check on Marigold."

Kingston pressed a kiss to my shoulder.

The whole car ride back, I was held by Kingston, and I thought of all the things that had broken me, and then I remembered all the ways they'd ensured I was whole again.

I wasn't a broken queen any longer.

Now, I was just me. A girl who loved marigolds and highland cows. A girl who loved two boys, one with trapped fire in his eyes and the other with starlight.

I was simply me, and that would forever be enough.

DID you read Wren and Archer's book yet?

Fill in the missing months while the twins and Presley are apart by reading My Darling Mayhem.

· · ·

I'M so glad you finished the duet. If you're not sure what to read next, I highly recommend trying my best-selling motorcycle club romance. Here's a little glimpse of Where We Started.

SNEAK PEEK

1

Callie

I couldn't recall the air feeling so thick or sticky when I was last here, but then again, I had never chosen to stand in the middle of Rose Ridge cemetery in the height of an August heatwave.

Sweat trickled down my back as the humidity curled around me while I watched the spectacle unfolding below. It was pure stubbornness that had me anchored near the tree, along with a healthy dose of resentment.

Neither the heat nor occasion had stopped the crowd around my father's casket from wearing their typical attire of black leather and denim. I was a little surprised they were listening to the preacher droning on about peace and heaven. My daddy didn't know a thing about either, and if he were alive, he'd laugh at the words and roar off into the sunset on his Harley. He probably would have preferred his body burned, tossed into an empty bottle of Jack, and placed on the mantel in his beloved club house.

He'd have wanted a huge party thrown, with naked women, loud music, and all other forms of debauchery. But because I was his only living relative, this funeral wasn't up to him. It was up to me. I chose an outdoor ceremony, with a preacher, a six-foot hole in the ground, and a gaudy headstone that boasted of his accomplishments in the war and the few years he was a husband. I left out the fact that he was a father, because in the end, he wasn't. Not to me, at least.

The only person who knew I was in attendance today was Killian, whom I had messaged regarding the funeral plans. I knew he'd share it with Red and the word would spread. However, he knew better than to look back here or tell anyone else. As it was, I wore a pair of oversized sunglasses to conceal my hazel eyes, which were the mirror image of my father's and a dead giveaway that his only living relative was in attendance. My lips were coated with my favorite shade of pink, which seemed to be the only pop of color among the ocean of black before me. My dark dress was itchy, my heels were too tight on my feet, and all I really wanted to do was walk away from the murmur of mourners, the sea of leather, and the heat.

Goddamn it, I *really* wanted to get out of this fucking heat.

"Amen," the crowd rumbled in front of me, and suddenly heads lifted, and I realized I had skipped another prayer. Being on the edge of the ceremony meant I missed nearly every word the preacher said, but I refused to stand any closer. My father's *family* stood around his casket. The people he put above all else in his life, including his only daughter.

The men and women of the Stone Riders Motorcycle Club.

I knew if I looked closely, tears would cloud nearly every eye and a sorrow would hang around their necks, driving their faces downward. I also knew I'd recognize nearly all of them. My father's club bred loyalty, and the Stone Riders were as steadfast as they came, so the mere notion that the initial members wouldn't be in attendance was unthinkable. Which meant half the men and women responsible for raising me were in that group. I didn't want to pity them, nor did

I want to mourn my father, and most of all, I didn't want to feel sorry for myself.

So, I stood behind the line. Nearby, to oversee that my money was spent properly, and well, to be honest, I wanted one last moment with my father before he was given back to the earth.

The men near the front moved, bent down to grab a handful of dirt, and then tossed it on the casket. I watched as a few women, wearing leather skirts and tight tops, did the same. My eyes locked on Red, Hamish, Killian, and Brooks. My heart was a jagged rock, hammering against my ribs. Once upon a time they were my family, the people who helped teach me to tie my shoes and ride a bike. Red had taught me what to do when I got my period, and how to apply mascara. Hamish taught me how to cheat in poker and the importance of keeping my thumb over my knuckles when throwing a punch. Killian was the closest thing I'd ever had to a sibling, and I knew he was hurting today like I was. All I wanted to do was be with him and mourn the man who'd raised us. He was about as much as my dad as he was Kill's, and yet I was back here, and he was down there.

My lips parted the slightest bit as my toes pressed into the tips of my shoes. The little girl inside of me wanted them today. Seven years had passed since I'd spoken with any of them, including my father. Yet, that brokenhearted little girl wished so badly that they'd look up and turn around. That they'd search for me and pull me into their arms. I gripped the tree behind me just to hold off the overwhelming urge to slip out of my shoes and run down there.

Instead, I watched as more attendees repeated the process of tossing in dirt, over and over, until there was just one person left standing in front of my father's coffin. I imagined what the warm dirt might feel like under their fingers. I pictured the discoloration now under their nails, carrying a tiny piece of my father's resting place with them. It took me back to being ten and camping on the back of the property with my dad, his smile as he took store-bought colored sand and poured it into a jar, telling me it was treasure.

That was before I was old enough to understand that the only treasure he valued was the club.

The group had all departed, gathering near their chrome-laden bikes parked in the grass along the small asphalt path cutting through the cemetery.

The remaining man near my father's casket didn't move. His jeans looked freshly washed, and there weren't any holes in them from what I could tell. His white T-shirt still had the crisp look of a brand-new one pulled from a bundle pack.

The back of his leather cut read *Stone Riders* right above the insignia of their club—a skull with roses blooming from the eye sockets. Below the skull, sewn into the leather, was a name that caught my eye. It shouldn't have made my heart thump as drastically as it did. Still, my eyes narrowed and could have burned a hole in the back of this man's shoulders as I finally processed who he was and what he'd become.

Wes.

President.

Shock had my eyes widening, and my lips parting on a silent breath.

My stomach churned as thoughts flitted through my mind at a rapid pace—questions I had no right asking and confusion all swirled in my chest like a storm cloud. My nose burned, which was usually the only warning I got before the tears started. So, I dropped the rose I had intended to place as an act of peace upon my father's grave, stepped on the petals, crushing them under my heel, and left. With every stride away from the funeral, I felt pieces of my heart tumble around, as frail as the petals crushed beneath my feet.

I wasn't supposed to mourn my father.

I wasn't supposed to be affected at all. And I certainly wasn't supposed to see that Wesley Ryan had decided to stay with the club *and* had succeeded my father as president.

Continue Reading by going to Amazon and finding Where We Started there.

ALSO BY ASHLEY MUÑOZ
READ IN KINDLE UNLIMITED

Stone Riders

Where We Started

Where We Belong

Where We Promise

Where We Ended

A Stone Rider Christmas

Mount Macon

Resisting the Grump

Tempting the Neighbor

Saving the Single Dad

A Macon Christmas

My Darling Mayhem

Rake Forge University

Wild Card

King of Hearts

The Joker

Royals of Rake Forge

The Lost Kings

The Broken Queen

Smalltown Standalones

The Rest of Me

Only Once

Tennessee Truths

Finding Home Duet

Glimmer

Fade

Anthologies/Co-Writes

What Are the Chances

Vicious Vet

ACKNOWLEDGMENTS

This book didn't come together easily.

Truth be told, the second book truthfully wouldn't have really even come together without help from a few specific people.

Melissa McGovern, first and foremost, I can't explain to you what it feels like that you go into such depth with my books, and this one is no exception. Your feedback was so helpful, and I'm so incredibly grateful for you.

Julia Chen – Your excitement for this series and your love for my words pushed me to finish this book. I don't even think you realize how many times I worried no one would want to keep reading, and you would randomly message me something encouraging. I'm so honored to have you on my team, and so grateful that you're willing to help me shape this story.

Kelly Sirak Drudy, As always your perspective has helped me so much with molding the second gen portion of this story and ensuring that the first gen doesn't get left behind. I always appreciate the fact that you make time for my books and that you always, no matter the tropes seem to want to read them.

Thank you to Amanda Anderson, who helped me shape this series even knowing it would be stepping outside of my small-town brand and setting us back a bit on everything we'd built for the past two years. You saw my vision and my heart to write second gen and helped me see that it happened.

A huge thanks to Erica, my PA and proofreader for this book. The number of things you handled for me while I pushed to hit this deadline truly was insane. I wouldn't have met it, that much I know for sure. Thank you for helping me stay on top of everything and ensuring nothing crashed or burned while I ignored the world to complete this book. Thank you for your love and appreciation for this book world, and this industry in general. You're an incredible asset to my team and to me as a person.

Catie Byrd, thank you so much for all you do for my team and how you not just run my reader group but I know you'll answer any time I ever reach out for anything. I can't tell you how much I appreciate having you on my team.

Gel, thank you for keeping up with all of my design demands and ensuring my graphics are always on brand.

Savannah, thank you for being the best agent and always pushing my work and being my cheerleader when the really big things come into your inbox.

Becky, thank you for your incredible editing skills and for helping me get this book exactly where it needs to be.

To my content team, I can't thank you enough. Truly. Your shares, tags and all your gorgeous creations are so incredible, and they mean so much to me. Thank you for being so incredible and sticking with me through it all.

The same goes for all my Book Beauties. Thank you for always loving my books and encouraging me with your posts and interest in literally anything that I do.

Lastly, certainly not least. The biggest thank you to my family:

I know that I'm not easy when I'm stressed, or when I'm anxious about something book-related. You carry me through every season and each scary thing. I love you, and I'm so honored to be yours.

ABOUT THE AUTHOR

Ashley is an Amazon Top 50 bestselling romance author who is best known for her small-town, second-chance romances. She resides in the Pacific Northwest, where she lives with her four children and her husband. She loves coffee, reading fantasy, and writing about people who kiss and cuss.

Follow her at www.ashleymunozbooks.com

www.ingramcontent.com/pod-product-compliance
Lightning Source LLC
Chambersburg PA
CBHW030623110726
47901CB00002B/292